The Grand Anicut

VEENA MUTHURAMAN was born and raised in Thiruvananthapuram, India. She took the long and winding path through Chicago and London to Edinburgh in Scotland where she currently lives. Her debut collection of short stories, *A Place of No Importance*, set in a place reminiscent of where her roots lie in rural Tamil Nadu, was published in 2016. Her stories and reviews have appeared in *Eclectica*, *Wasafiri* and Scroll.in, among other publications. *The Grand Anicut* is her first novel.

The Grand Anicut

VEENA MUTHURAMAN

hachette INDIA

First published in 2021 by Hachette India
(Registered name: Hachette Book Publishing India Pvt. Ltd)
An Hachette UK company
www.hachetteindia.com

1

Maps on pp. vi and vii illustrated by Jit Chowdhury

ISBN 978-93-5195-059-2

Hachette Book Publishing India Pvt. Ltd
4th & 5th Floors, Corporate Centre,
Plot No. 94, Sector 44, Gurugram 122003, India

Typeset in Dante MT Std 11/14.5
by R. Ajith Kumar, New Delhi

Printed and bound in India
by Manipal Technologies Limited, Manipal

MIX
Paper from responsible sources
FSC™ C043100

For Susmit Sarkar.

For the last time: No, darling, this book is not going to be called Pilfering Pearls in Poompuhar.

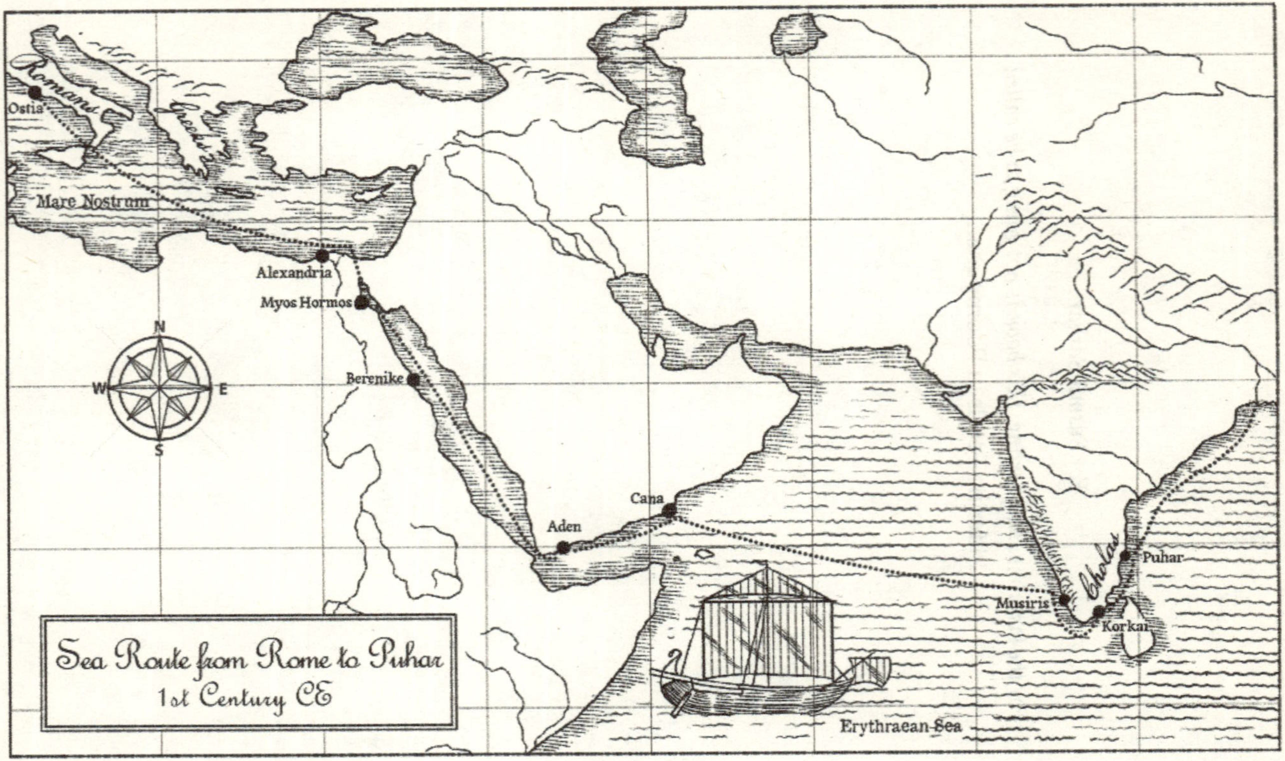
Sea Route from Rome to Puhar
1st Century CE
Romans
Greeks
Ostia
Mare Nostrum
Alexandria
Myos Hormos
Berenike
N
S
W
E
Aden
Cana
Musiris
Cholas
Puhar
Korkai
Erythraean Sea

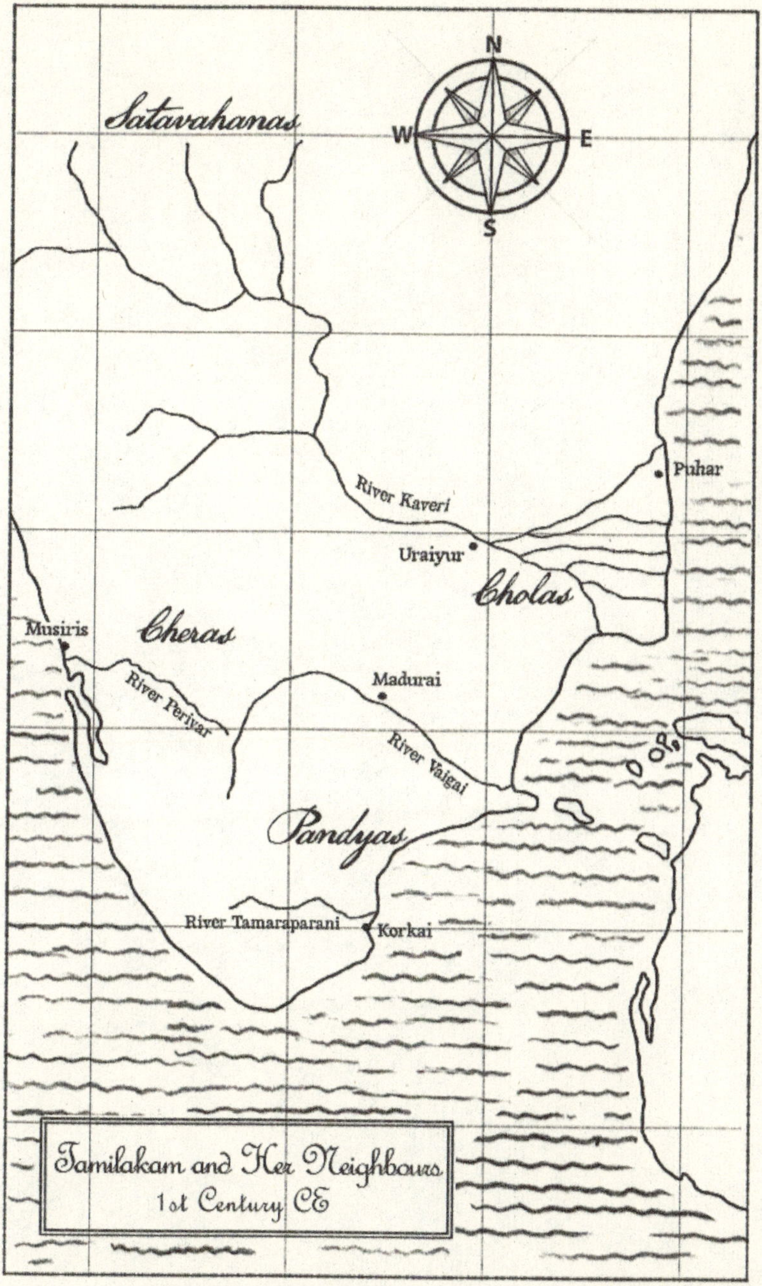

N
W
E
S
Satavahanas
River Kaveri
Puhar
Uraiyur
Cholas
Musiris
Cheras
River Periyar
Madurai
River Vaigai
Pandyas
River Tamaraparani
Korkai
Tamilakam and Her Neighbours
1st Century CE

CAST OF CHARACTERS

The Yavanas

Marcellus	A young merchant of Rome, son of Gaius.
Hippalus	Captain of the *Minerva*, a Roman ship bound for Puhar in Tamilakam.
Aafa	Pilot of the *Minerva*.
Silvius	Gaius's representative in Puhar, formerly of Londonium.
Marcus	A freedman and companion of Marcellus.
Proteus	A Roman citizen in Musiris.

The Easterner

Zhang	A Buddhist monk from Qin/Thinae.

The Cholas

Vallavan	A young merchant of Puhar.
Manaykan	Father of Vallavan, and prominent member of the merchant guild of Puhar.
Kuzhali	Widowed daughter of Manaykan.
Kannaki	Younger sister of Vallavan and Kuzhali.

Malathi Ammal	Wife of Manaykan.
Karikalan	King of the Chola kingdom.
Prime minister	The prime minister of the Chola kingdom.
Magistrate of Maruvum	The King's ranking officer in Maruvum, the harbour quarter of Puhar.
Chief Administrator	Head of the civil service in the Chola kingdom.
Adi	Servant of Silvius and, perhaps, a bit more.
Rajamma	Enterprising appam-seller of Maruvum.
Muthu and Mari	Chola citizens looking to make some quick silver.
Priest(s)	Brahmana priests at shrines in Puhar and the Holy Isle in Uraiyur.
Maran	Overseer of an inn on the high road to the south.
Ponni	The inn-keeper's daughter.
Angavai and company	Bandits from the hills of Chola country.
Physician	A doctor in hill country, part of Angavai's company.

Clerks and soldiers in the Chola service

Pandyas

Maruthappan	A messenger for the pearl traders of Korkai.
Appan	Patriarch of the Appan family.
Veerappan	Appan's younger brother.
Kannamma	A diver in Korkai.
Boy and girl on the boat	Kannamma's children.

PROLOGUE

GULF OF MANNAR

The rain steadied its tempo before slowing down to a halt, and the clouds swiftly made their way north just after dawn. The water glistened under the suddenly cloudless sky as the girl secured the basket around her waist. Her brother checked the knots once more to ensure the rope was tied firmly to the boulder. She looked up at the sky and smiled. When they had left the Korkai shore in the middle of the night, she had told him that the rains would not get in their way; but he had refused to believe her. She now nodded at him and he slowly lowered the rope into the water. She caught the twine and jumped off the boat; her legs found the stone and she carefully manoeuvred herself into position, took a deep breath and went under. In a few moments, she found herself by the seabed and, as she had expected, in the company of oysters. She scooped up as many as she could with her one free hand and transferred them deftly into her basket. Her eyes scanned the bed once again – there were enough oysters here in this secret shoal, away from the pavazha parai, the coral reef, to keep her family fed until the next season. But for now, it was time; she wouldn't be able to hold her breath for much longer. She grabbed one last handful of oysters, dropped them into her basket and tugged at the rope.

Her brother started pulling instantly and, moments later, she was back on the surface. She remained floating on the water, holding on to the edge of their odam.

Breathing in deeply, she turned to look at her brother, her face shining with pride; but his attention was elsewhere. She followed his gaze, and in the distance, perilously close to the isle of Mannar, was a giant ship swiftly cutting through the water. She looked at it curiously – she was familiar with kalams, the three-masted sea ships of Tamil country, but this one was different. It had a massive central sail the colour of cooked lobster and a swan head at the sternpost. Ships as big as this did not pass through the gulf unless one knew where exactly to cross it.

She had heard stories from her grandmother of the time when a vessel like this would turn west towards her town. But since the war Yavana ships had not been allowed into their harbour. The fisheries and emporiums were still there, but traders did not come from the sea any more. The brother and sister watched until the ship disappeared from sight – it was making its way due north to the city of their Chola conquerors. The girl climbed on to the boat and dumped her catch on the bow. Her brother looked at her, pleased. She shrugged and prepared herself for another dive.

PART I

PUHAR: MARUVUM

The billowing sea, her robes. The hills,
her breasts. The broad rivers, her garlands.
The clouds, her shock of hair. This vast
and boundless Earth seemed a woman.
On top of Utaiya Hill the Sun
rose, pulled down the veil of darkness
by splashing his bright rays to light up
this resplendent world. On open terraces,
On treasure houses with ornaments, on mansions
with air holes the eyes of deer, he shone.
Near the harbour, the passer-by was stopped dead
by the homes of Yavanas whose profits never shrunk.
On the edge of the burnished waters lived
and mingled as one traders from distant
lands, come for goods carried
by ships.

The Cilappatikāram: The Tale of an Anklet, Canto 5

1

DESTINATION CAMARA

The *Minerva,* the Roman vessel that had cut so precisely through the narrow gap between the treacherous rocks of the Gulf of Mannar, was a common enough *corbita* in home waters. But here, all the way across the Erythraean Sea, it was a rarity. Not many Roman ships sailed this far eastwards, and the ones that did usually dropped anchor at one of the better-known harbours west of the peninsula. But the *Minerva* happened to be captained by a Greek man – Hippalus, a maverick from the Egyptian Sea port of Bereníke – who dared to sail to those places that made others cower in fear. The sea was calm this side of the gulf, as the brunt of the first monsoon was borne by the Malabar coast, and Hippalus breathed easy as he stood on the deck, surveying the waters below. It was now a short stretch to where the Kaveri met the sea, from where they would be escorted upriver to Camara – their final destination.

Hippalus had made this journey several times before, originally as part of a convoy of Greek and Roman ships from Eudaemon, but, for the past few years, the *Minerva* had attempted the crossing alone. A lesser seaman would have baulked at this idea as the winds often led to catastrophic shipwrecks, but Hippalus had by his side an Arabian pilot by the name of Aafa, who was widely considered the best in this business. As a result, the ship's owner in Rome reaped the benefits of reaching the rich ports of the East several days before the rest of the merchant fleet, and it provided Hippalus with much-needed time to devote to his literary pursuits.

And this, in fact, was at the top of his mind as the *Minerva* approached the eastern shores of Damirica. Hippalus had written in great detail – well, he had dictated while Aafa wrote – of the sea serpents and pirates on the western coast, but how would he introduce Damirica to his hypothetical readers?

It is time, dear reader, now that the storms of the Erythraean Sea are well behind us, and we are safely past the treacherous rocks of the Gulf of Mannar, that we learn more about the world we are in. We find ourselves in a kingdom that is the farthest our ships venture out to – Camara in Damirica as we know it, or Puhar in Tamilakam you'd call it if you were a native of this land. This Camara, on the banks of the river Kaveri, is the capital of the Cholas, who, along with the Cheras (capital: Musiris) and the Pandyas (capital: Madurai) constitute the Tamil kingdoms in the southern part of the continent that the great Alexander, a man with whom I share my lineage, attempted to conquer a few hundred years ago.

A bit of history while we are here. The Chola kingdom is currently ruled by one Karikalan, son of Ilamcetcenni. Following his father's untimely death, Karikalan was exiled and later imprisoned by ministers wishing to hold on to power. The prison he was held in was set on fire, but the prince escaped with the help of a royal elephant and defeated his enemies in the civil war that ensued and laid claim to the throne. Another battle followed, this time against the combined armies of the Chera and Pandya kingdoms, in which Karikalan emerged victorious. A few more conquests came in quick succession – some local and others further afield.

The last few years have been a time of relative peace with the king indulging in civil pursuits, such as commissioning shrines on holy hills, offering prayers to gods, enforcing arcane laws, and building aqueducts and bridges in true Augustan fashion. All this makes it easier for us to conduct our business here in the capital. However, like most hot-blooded kings, Karikalan harbours an intense desire to conquer a few more kingdoms and claim more land masses for himself. And while the Chola king is busy with civil works, the defeated peoples of the Chera and Pandya kingdoms are looking for the right opportunity to strike... And the threat from Satkarni of Amaravati in the north is not to be underestimated.

An aside: I hear you, dear reader. How does a foreign seaman know so much about kingdoms so far from the empire? It is because I consider it my job; I couldn't be a sea captain without knowing what goes on in the ports I dock my ship in. There are many who have tried to come, trade and leave, but let me remind you that they have not lived to tell this tale. I shall continue...

The gubernator looked up, annoyed. He had company on deck – Vallavan, the Chola trader that the little master had picked up at Cana, that Arabian seaport where they smother every traveller with the heady fragrance of frankincense. He was pacing up and down impatiently. The young man had stayed out of Hippalus's way for most of the journey, as was demanded of him, but as they neared their destination, he was up on the deck hoping to catch a glimpse of his homeland. He was about to call out to Vallavan to get out of his sight when the little master stepped gingerly on to the deck. This was the first time in forty days that Marcellus had been seen outside his cabin.

Hippalus scowled and pretended to pay no outward attention to the pair, but his sharp eyes did not fail to observe that Marcellus was dressed for disembarkation. He wore a toga with intricate gold embroidery over a chalk-white tunic and, on his feet, curved leather sandals that could only be from Alexandria – an attire chosen by his discerning mother, no doubt, who would have wanted her son to make quite an entrance in the foreign kingdom. But, despite the adornments, this man was no longer the arrogant young scion who had come to meet him at the Egyptian harbour of Myos Hormos, from where the *Minerva* had started her long journey, bearing a letter from his father, the ship's owner. The prolonged voyage across the ocean had taken its toll on Marcellus. He looked haggard and tired, but even then, Hippalus had to admit that he was a handsome young man, albeit unusual-looking for a Roman citizen of his class. He took after his father, an unusual man himself – the son of a Carthaginian freedman who had struck it rich in trade and ended up marrying a woman of patrician rank. Marcellus had inherited his father's tall frame, burnt countenance and jet-black hair, not to mention the disarming smile that many a rival trader had to come to rue in hindsight. Hippalus was still to see any sign of the little master – a moniker that Aafa had conferred on him after the first night of seasickness that had provided much entertainment for the crew – inheriting anything other than his father's looks, but if the old patriarch had dispatched him all the way to Camara, there was still some hope. On the other hand, it could well be a punitive trip intended to keep the boy away from the races, where it was rumoured he had carelessly gambled away the equivalent of this ship's load of pepper.

'*Mare nostrum!*' Marcellus cried out in amazement.

Hippalus smirked.

This man was as far away as he had ever been from Rome and, yet, these blue-green waters east of the peninsula seemed to him identical to his native sea. *He probably thinks that this is the short run from Messina to the mainland at Ostia, from where he can make it to the Circus for the afternoon races*, Hippalus thought spitefully.

'Our kizhakkadal is not your calm sea, Marcellus.' Vallavan set him right. 'Wait until you survive the first cyclone of the season.'

'*Mare nostrum* is known for wrecking entire fleets; it is not calm,' Marcellus retorted.

Like Hades, it wasn't!

Hippalus was a man of the oceans, and the *mare nostrum*, despite its lofty reputation in the Roman world as the heart of civilization, was no more than an ordinary sea in his view. Only the Romans – a people who didn't know the first thing about water – would compare it to the seas of this peninsula.

Vallavan must have known this too, but he kept quiet. Hippalus surmised that the trader was too diplomatic – he did not want to remind his friend and saviour that he had spent forty of the past forty-one days cooped up in his tiny cabin, not daring to face the ocean.

These young men share a curious relationship, Hippalus mused, *or perhaps it is perfectly natural.* He had met Aafa in Eudaemon back in the day, in that port town where vessels from India did not go to Egypt and those from Egypt did not dare sail to places further east, but came only this far; where seamen and traders from all known lands transit, but no one made it their home. Hence, he was well aware of the kind of friendships forged by young men in foreign lands when confined to close spaces. In any case, the master's son, despite his bravado, was looking for company. This wasn't surprising; any wealthy young Roman with a penchant for the high life, sent away by his family to trade in a remote corner of the world, would be miffed. To make matters worse, the lad's companion, a freedman meant to keep him company, and an eye on him, had abandoned him for more pressing things en route to the harbour at Myos Hormos. Thus, suitably lonely, Marcellus had met another young man, a trader to boot, who happened to be stranded in Cana, waiting for a ship to take him home across the Erythraean Sea. Marcellus had promptly offered the trader safe passage on his ship. Hippalus knew how this particular story would end – in tearful separation – and it was about to end very soon. Amusement was in the offing for the crew.

'Ah, I see that the intrepid merchant-sailor is ready to disembark. It is time. We will be going up the estuary soon,' he remarked dryly. Marcellus nodded.

The *Minerva* slowed down and there was the Kaveri's mouth, as wide as ever, and as always, on either side were two tugs, each manned by thirty or so oarsmen, waiting patiently for the Yavana ship to turn into the river.

'Escorts, similar to what you must have seen in Ostia, so that they can be safely escorted into the empire,' Hippalus explained.

Marcellus turned to Vallavan to ask the obvious question, but his friend had his eyes closed in prayer. Hippalus switched to Greek and answered for him.

'The all-powerful merchant guild, to which your friend here belongs, is so paranoid that every ship has to be escorted up the river to the city. This way they can be sure everything is stamped and taxed.'

Vallavan opened his eyes. If he understood Greek, he didn't show it.

'Manimekalai, the goddess of sea, has to be thanked for the safe journey,' he said. 'Don't you –' He saw the look on his friend's face and stopped. *Good*, thought Hippalus. The little master knew that Roman gods were strictly personae non grata on *this* particular ship. If he had had his way, she would have been called the *Athena*.

'Are they your people?' Marcellus asked Vallavan, pointing to the crowd gathered on the southern bank, watching the advance of the *Minerva*.

'They belong to my country,' said Vallavan. He paused so as to be certain that the distinction was not lost on his listener. 'They are the fisherfolk and they live in Maruvum, the harbour quarter of Puhar. They are an unruly tribe, but under King Karikalan, they are well cared for and have become easier to deal with. They gather on the beach when a Yavana ship arrives and place bets on how much cargo it is carrying.'

Marcellus was only half listening as his gaze went upwards and his jaw dropped.

'Captain!' he shouted. 'The sails!'

'I don't need lessons from you on how to steer my ship,' Hippalus replied coldly.

'You don't need to lower the sails on the Kaveri. Can't you see how wide it is?' He heard Vallavan explaining as he walked slightly away from the pair. 'Welcome to Puhar, my friend!'

Hippalus turned his attention to the harbour as the first sight of market towns was not to be missed under any circumstances. The serpents in the shoals near Barygaza or the pirates lying in wait as they approached Chersonesus were good indicators of what they'd find inland, and Camara, or Puhar as the natives called it, was no different.

Anchored along the northern bank were mostly trade ships. He counted as they sped along: six small tugs – likely from the northern kingdoms or from the island of Taprobane; two galleys with distinctive lateen sails – from Oman or Cana, if he were to guess, plus Aafa would know them and their pilots; three larger ships with rudders mounted on the stern – from Thinae, the land of silk yarn and the one part of the world he still had to make his way to; two brightly coloured ships with curved roof cabins on the deck and carved elephant motifs on the sides – from Kadara, islands of the southeast from where the new king was making overtures to King Karikalan; ten or so catamarans, local, ferrying goods up- and downriver to the ships; two vessels bearing the tiger standard and, hence, belonging to Chola royalty, one probably used for official purposes and the other the king's personal pleasure yacht.

Hippalus concluded that this was a typical year, but then his gaze fell on the southern bank. His eyes widened and he leaned forward to get a better view. There were at least three dozen double-decked, single-masted ships, all flying the tiger standard. But their most distinctive feature was under water – a prolongation of the bow that left no question as to what purpose these ships had been built for. In his previous trips, he had seen a handful of ships fitted with rams, but not so many stationed at the harbour at one time. There was only one plausible explanation: *this kingdom was preparing for war.*

He wasn't the only one to have noticed them.

'Warships,' he heard Vallavan mumble reluctantly to his friend's enquiring glance. 'Similar to your *biremes*, but faster.'

'Yours is a country of peace, you told me.'

'But there are times when a kingdom needs to be ready for war and a navy to defend it. Ours ward off the pirates on the western seas. If your captain had attempted a landing at Musiris, you would have seen what they are capable of first-hand.'

Vallavan must have waxed eloquent about the Chola king, his love for his subjects, his generosity and appreciation for the arts and poetry to Marcellus, but clearly had steered clear of the subject of wars and pirates. The merchants of Camara liked to think of themselves as a peace-loving people, in line with their religious affiliations. The little master would have to find the truth out for himself.

The *Minerva* glided gracefully towards the pier, and a conch sounded announcing her arrival. As soon as the anchor dropped, Hippalus turned away from the two young men and shouted in Tamil at the porters lining the dock, beckoning them to come up to the deck. An eagle-eyed customs official watching the ship gave a barely noticeable nod, and the porters clambered aboard and got to work quickly. The crew had to wait until all the goods were unloaded. Not a single amphora would leave the *Minerva* without being inspected and stamped.

Aafa shuffled up to speak to the captain. 'I don't like it,' he mumbled.

'Warships?'

He shook his head. 'The escorts worry me more.'

'What about them?'

'Why are they still here? They should be heading back to the sea by now.'

'Maybe they take turns.'

'Hmm... What do you think that group of dandies is doing this side of town?'

Hippalus turned to look. Aafa was referring to a small group of onlookers, further away on the pier, who were clearly out of place in the harbour. Four long-haired boys dressed in silk skirts and garlands looked curiously at the ship.

'Your people?' Hippalus snapped at Vallavan.

'My father's men...' the trader trailed off. 'They must have been waiting for me.'

'How do they know you would be on this ship?' Hippalus demanded immediately.

'My family would have been anxious, and I have no doubt they send someone to the harbour every day.'

Vallavan suddenly seemed to be in a hurry to disembark.

'Let's go, the porters are already here,' he said to Marcellus, who started after him.

'Where do *you* think you are going, little master?'

'Am I to be imprisoned here on the *Minerva*?' he snapped. 'Is that what my father pays you for?'

'You can disembark once you supervise the clerks and ratify that you have an account of everything that is offloaded.'

'The clerks are capable of it.'

'If that is the case, there was no reason for your father to send you on this journey and subject you to the indignities of maritime life. Aafa, get the little master the cargo manifest.'

Marcellus appeared aggrieved. Vallavan was disappointed, but he was justifiably impatient to leave.

'My friend, I cannot thank you enough. Remember, this is Puhar; your hospitality will not be forgotten. Farewell!'

Vallavan bowed. Marcellus pulled the young man towards him and embraced him his lips before letting him ago. They watched as he was reunited with his people, and the party walked away from the pier without a backward glance.

Marcellus sighed and walked over to the clerk, who was counting the cargo in the hold. He diligently checked each item on his scroll before the porters were allowed to unload and carry the amphorae towards the port official for inspection.

Once he was satisfied that all was unloaded, Hippalus nodded curtly and Marcellus jumped ashore hastily. Setting foot on solid ground after forty-odd days made him wobbly and he had to take a few steps forward before he could steady himself. He carried a small sack of his prized possessions; the rest of his luggage was unloaded separately. Hippalus joined him and they walked silently towards the gateway leading out of the harbour.

'I'll do the talking,' Hippalus cautioned as they reached the port office, a small building on one side of the arched gate that led to the city. On either side were two fierce statues, wielding a number of weapons, but more pertinent were the two real-life guards donning swords and shields. The visitors walked inside the office where they found two gaunt men, identical enough to be twins, poring over scrolls. The officials glanced up, took a cursory look at Marcellus and turned to Hippalus.

'Is he your master's heir?' one of them demanded in Tamil.

'Yes, I am Gaius Julius Marcellus, son of Gaius Ateilius Euhodus, trader of Rome,' replied Marcellus in the same language. The officials looked at each other, not bothering to hide their surprise, and Hippalus intervened.

'My master here has been taught by the best of our Greek tutors, and he is keen to learn the literary tradition of your divine language. It was fortunate that one of your traders travelled on the *Minerva* –'

Hippalus realized his mistake even before he had finished speaking. He should have seen it; Aafa had warned him. They were waiting for a confession and he had provided one without being asked. On cue, the two soldiers stepped in and stood on either side of Marcellus and Hippalus.

'In the name of Karikalan, our mighty king, conqueror of the world, and the power vested in me by him, I place you both and your crew under arrest for the kidnapping of a Chola subject,' one of the guards said. 'You will be interrogated by the magistrate of Maruvum. Now, if you will follow me –'

'There has been a mistake,' Marcellus cut in, starting to explain. 'Vallavan was not kidnapped!'

'You will get the chance to make your case before the magistrate tomorrow. Until then, I suggest you follow our instructions. I am unable to make judgements.'

Much to Hippalus's surprise, Marcellus did not argue any further. He simply nodded in resignation and followed the official. *The Roman brat must have realized that his entitlement doesn't work everywhere*, concluded Hippalus.

Outside, in the distance, he saw his crew standing in single file next to the *Minerva*. They cried out when they caught sight of him, but were silenced soon enough. Xeno, the slave boy, attempted to flee, but a guard quickly caught hold of him, and, in one quick motion, slashed him and threw his lifeless body into the water. The crew got the message immediately and the clamouring stopped. For once, his crew had been disciplined by a foreign force – the dozen armed Chola soldiers standing on either side, and the escort boats docked next to the *corbita*. Hippalus needed time to think his way out of this particular situation.

'What will happen to my crew?' he asked the official.

'They will be held in your ship until the investigation is complete. You will be housed in the official barracks for the night.'

He glanced one last time in the direction of the *corbita* before turning away. He had not seen Aafa with the rest of the crew, and therein lay his – their – only hope.

2

What He Said

Ayya, I can understand how anxious and distraught you must have been, believing that your only son had been left to die in an infidel corner of this world – or worse, his body lying under the waters of the ocean, serving as fodder for sharks. I sincerely apologize for the anguish I caused you and Amma. I am not a ghost, of that you can be certain; I swear by the Mahaviran and all the gods of our house. I am your only son, the one you sent to Eudaemon, Cana and Alexandria to procure frankincense and glass directly from where it is made. If, as you say, the ship returned with the goods, I may even claim success in that I have fulfilled my duty to you and to the guild.

Amma, I wasn't abandoned, neither have I starved. No one other than myself is to blame for the fact that I was left behind in Cana. I stepped out to the land without informing Ottan, and I thought I'd be back in good time. The winds may have turned just at the time, or the teller may have seen the right omens, and the ship's captain would have left the harbour assuming I was on board. Ayya, no, Ottan did not return once he realized I wasn't on board, but who knows, the direction of the wind may not have been in his favour. Please release him from captivity, Ayya; he may have made a mistake, but we need him for future journeys if we are to trade in equal standing with the Yavana merchants. As for the oarsmen, they didn't deserve the whipping they got; let each man's family be fed and provided with rice to last the season.

Did the ship's teller foretell that I was dead? He is not to be seen? Perhaps he didn't wish to be tortured like Ottan; who is to say?

Your impatience is evident, my akka, but before I indulge you, I'll thank you for not losing hope and for nursing our mother through trying times. I will continue with my story now and you shall see how fortunate I have been. If the teller was here with us, he'd point out that everything happens for a reason. In my case, I was stranded so that I could meet Marcellus – a friend and citizen of mighty Rome – and what's more, he's the son of Gaius Euhodus, the prominent Yavana merchant who has traded with our guild over many seasons. This is how we met.

I took up lodgings at an inn near the warehouses in Cana, far away from the harbour. By then, I had lost hope that Ottan would return, looking for me, and I was resigned to staying there for what could be a long, long time. If it were the case that I had to wait for the next season for a familiar ship to arrive, I had to save whatever little I had of my gold and silver on me, and I prudently stayed away from the expensive lodgings near the port. I didn't attempt boarding a Yavana ship, as I knew they carried no foreign passengers unless they were slaves – and being an oarsman on a Yavana ship did not catch my fancy. I considered my options and decided the best course of action would be to secure passage on an Arabian vessel headed to Oman. There, I would surely be able to find friendly ships returning to the Chola kingdom. It was with this goal in mind that I started frequenting an establishment which served a predominantly Arabian clientele.

Amma, the food was appetizing – bread instead of rice, Amma, but nevertheless as delicious as what we eat here. An Arab ship had come into Cana that morning, and I waited at the tavern to see if anyone important from the vessel would turn up. Three men came in the early hours of the afternoon: two sailors and a slave boy, who ran around fetching them food and drinks from the kitchen. It was then that I noticed the young man to my right. He was dressed in the Yavana style and I surmised that he was a Roman citizen – likely a trader or a bureaucrat from the language in which he spoke to the innkeeper. He was dark for a Roman, almost a native Alexandrian with curly black hair, but otherwise Roman in manner and attitude. I was curious, but I ignored him and was about speak to the sailors when I heard him address the slave boy.

'I will take one of the jugs for this,' he said to the boy in the Roman tongue, holding out a Roman coin. The boy, who was carrying wine to his masters, turned to look at the stranger in surprise. I'd heard the boy speak in Latin earlier with the innkeeper, so I assume had the Roman.

'I said I will take one of those. You can have this in return,' he insisted.

The boy pretended not to understand and continued on his way to his companions. A moment later, they all turned around to laugh at the young man.

'They say you Romans assume everything is for sale,' I said.

The Yavana started at the sound of my voice, and turned around. It must have crossed his mind that the dark-skinned stranger smiling at him from a nearby stool had spoken *his* language and that, in any case, was my intention. He gave me a long, searching look. I don't know what he made of my appearance – I was wearing a long tunic in the Roman style, but unless he was a total ignoramus, there was no mistaking that I was from the East. My forehead had traces of sandalwood paste and my hair, yes, Amma, was well oiled and pulled back in a knot.

'How do they know what Romans think?' he asked me finally. 'Come to think of it, how would *you* know?'

'I know what your people buy and that's all I need to know,' I replied.

This time, he smiled at me and I knew this was no bureaucrat; he had to be a fellow trader. He was about to say something when the three Arabs suddenly got up, a bit unsteady on their feet. We watched them intently. They jeered at him and left the inn, but a few moments later, the boy came back inside. He walked towards the Roman and held out his hand.

'Give him the coin. Looks like your people are right – everything is for sale,' I said.

I had no idea why the boy had come back in. Perhaps he wanted to make some extra money that he could hide from his masters.

The Roman handed over the coin. The boy took it and turned around to leave.

'Hey, boy, my wine!' the Roman shouted after him.

The boy grinned. 'Are you going to cross the water?' he asked in broken Latin.

'Yes. Give me the drink I asked for, or give me my coin back.'

'You don't need the coin if you are crossing the sea. What will the sea goddess do with one of these?'

'What do you mean?'

'You people cannot cross the ocean in such weather – not with your boats. Waiting for the storms to start! Shipwreck guaranteed! You will have no use for this coin, Roman.'

'Give me back my coin, you ass!'

The boy laughed and walked towards the door. My Roman friend lifted the stool next to him and hurled it at the boy. It found its mark. The boy let out a howl and limped out, while I looked at the attacker in shock. He may not have intended it, but it was clear to me what was going to happen now. I didn't need a teller to foretell this particular event.

'You'll need to get out of here before they come back,' I said urgently.

'I am not running –'

'If you have a death wish, the shipwreck is a better way to die.' I grabbed his arm and pointed towards the kitchen. I wasn't taking any chances by using the front door. I could hear a commotion outside on the street. The Roman hesitated, but only until he saw through the window that the boy was bringing a handful of men back with him, their daggers already drawn. This was no even match, even if he had the stomach for it. He followed me out quickly through the back door attached to the kitchen just as our pursuers crashed into the tavern.

No, Amma, I wasn't in any particular danger and you have raised a brave son. And better still, my Roman friend, I found out later, was trained by a real gladiator – you know the men who fight lions and tigers barehanded?

Why, you ask, dear Akka, did I go out of my way to befriend this Yavana when I should have been trying to convince the Arabs to provide me space on their ship? Why did I risk my life to help rescue him when my life wasn't secure in the first place? I felt a kinship with this man that I cannot explain in a way that you'd understand, so I am not going to try. Go on, make fun of me if you wish, but I will not make excuses and, as you'll see, he is the reason I am here in the flesh before you today.

We took a circuitous route to my lodgings – through warehouses and farms that I was familiar with from the previous few days – and managed to give our hunters the slip. We stayed out of sight until sundown, just to be sure that the sailors settled somewhere else for the night. Eventually we made our way to the harbour, where the Yavana ship was anchored. Marcellus, that was his name, laughingly confided in me somewhere along the way that he had not had so much fun since the Reds crushed the Whites at the Circus last winter. They race chariots, Ayya; yes, horses not bulls.

'You should not have provoked them,' I told him. Fun or not, my chances of getting home were now ruined thanks to this man, or so I thought at the time.

'The boy can't get away with cheating a Roman trader!' he declared.

I pointed out that he had indeed gotten away.

'That is because you asked me to run away from them. You… Who are you?'

'My name is Vallavan and I am a merchant on my way back home from Alexandria, and I have been here in Cana for a few days. My ship left without me, and I am looking for passage on a ship back home.'

'But what will you do here until then? If they find you –'

'I will try to stay out of their sight. I can hide,' I said, but I had to admit that he had a point. The Roman would be safe in his ship, but the same could not be said for me.

'Where were you headed?' he asked.

'To the land of the gods and of the valorous King Karikalan, to beautiful Puhar, my home!'

'Isn't that the same as Camara?'

'Yes, the same.'

'This is providence!' he exclaimed. 'My ship is going there!'

No, Amma, I did not ask him; I did not beg for a place on a Yavana ship. *He* offered.

'I can provide you safe passage on the *Minerva.*'

Minerva? This man was obviously Gaius's son. This was fate! Why else should I have run into him?

'I am grateful for the offer, but your captain won't take any passengers. Roman ships don't carry non-Roman passengers other than slaves, and I am no slave.'

'Leave that to me. My captain is Greek and can be convinced,' Marcellus said confidently. 'Do you know when the weather would clear? That boy said that we are waiting for the storms to arrive, which can't be true.'

That's when I realized that Marcellus had never ever made the crossing before.

'It is true. Your captain is waiting for the monsoon to strike so that he can cross. The winds will be bad and there may be storms, but the crossing is quick and we will be home that much sooner.'

'Storms! Then he was right about the shipwreck!'

For ages, the Romans had stopped at Eudaemon and Cana on the southern coast, and it was only in recent years that they had discovered that they could make the crossing quickly at this time of the year. But this young trader seemed blissfully unaware of the ship's route and, yet, he owned the vessel that was waiting for the monsoon winds. I weighed my options and agreed to take him up on the offer.

The captain was a law unto himself, but even he had to take orders from his master's son. So Hippalus took me in and gave me some space in one corner of the bow, but not without emptying what was left of my coins. I wasn't treated as a slave, and for that I am thankful. In any case, my friend needed my help. It turned out that he was seasick and was confined to his room throughout the journey. I introduced him to our blessed land and taught him Tamil as he wanted to learn our language. Who would say no to being paid for eating sugarcane? He told me about himself – Gaius, his father, who was the son of a freed slave; and his mother, the daughter of an important man at the senate. He told me about the household full of slaves, a villa in Rome and another in Pompeii. This was his first trip, and, no, he wasn't sent alone. He had a companion when he started, a freed slave, who had callously abandoned him before they reached the ship.

Why is he in Puhar, you ask? He is here for the same reason I crossed the seas. To trade, of course.

No, I don't believe he hoodwinked me. How would he have known where to find me in Cana? In fact, it is our good fortune that I happened to meet him before he got here. I've told him all about the merchant guild of Puhar, and you can be sure that he will come to us first with matters relating to trade. Who knows what benefits this relationship may bring.

Ayya, why do you look at me like that? You don't believe me! I am not under a spell and I am not possessed by any evil spirit, trust me. Akka, won't you tell him?

Who is there? We have a messenger from Maruvum at this time? What could it possibly be about?

3

THE TRIAL

As the unwitting young master and his illustrious captain spend a restless night in a prison so far away from home, it is time to leave them undisturbed and continue with our account. Now, where were we?

In the Roman empire, the emperor's legions are out west, attacking the Gauls once again, while Rome itself sizzles in turmoil. My prescient master, certain that civil war was imminent, has taken the first available opportunity to send his son to distant lands. The impressionable young man, left to himself and the races at the Circus, would only come to harm if he remained in town at such a treacherous time. The kingdom my master chose for his son was the farthest his ships went – Camara in Damirica – where Silvius, first in command of the eastern trade, made his home. Of the Chola kingdom and its king, we've already heard.

But more about its neighbours and enemies, the Cheras, Pandyas and Satavahanas: their spies roamed the length and breadth of Chola country, seeking to create unrest and disrupt the normal flow of life, especially along the coast where they knew it would hurt the kingdom the most. The fertile plains of the Kaveri delta yielded rice and grains to feed the country, but it was in trade that the real strength of the Cholas lay – in the export of gold, rice, ivory, pearls and a variety of Circus animals, such as monkeys, peacocks and tigers; in the import of silk, wine, glass and metalware; in trade, not just with Arabia and Rome, but also with Kadara and Thinae. Trade was the lifeblood of this kingdom, and the king ensured that ports, shipways and bridges were in place to support it.

The neighbouring Pandyas were primarily an inland empire, with the exception of Korkai, while the Cheras were busy fighting with the pirates for control of the port of Musiris. The Satavahanas, from their base in Amaravati, kept their distance from Chola country, with their king, Satkarni, focusing on consolidating his western empire. The Chola kingdom boasted of a thriving merchant class and a king who maintained a fleet of a hundred warships ready to attack at the least, or at times without any, provocation. Thus, the Cholas reaped the wealth of trade, while their neighbours watched and their envy festered. Because we are in a time of peace, things are calm on the surface, but as you may have deduced from this unwarranted arrest, undercurrents are surging in an entirely different direction.

The common peoples of the Chola kingdom are like the common peoples everywhere else. A hierarchy of caste determined at birth keeps everyone in their place, with priests, royals and the rich merchants at the top of this pyramid. The trade wealth seldom trickles down to the poor; they lose their young men to wars, young women to childbirth and their children to diseases. But there are more than a few ripples swirling in the seemingly still waters...

Hippalus grew tired of dictating to himself. It was of no use. He was an illiterate man who could not record this story without the help of his accomplished pilot. But thanks to the young upstart in the next cell, there was a chance he may never see Aafa again and, worse, he may never finish his manuscript. It was going to be mangled beyond recognition and would likely end up as a lurid guidebook full of half-facts and fabrications to be read out as evening entertainment at a Neapolitan pleasure villa! Hippalus could have throttled Marcellus if he got his hands on him at that moment, but the port officials were wise enough to keep the prisoners in separate cells.

Sometime before dawn, they came to fetch him. Two soldiers led him silently to the river so that he could wash himself. When he returned, Marcellus was already dining. Rice gruel and palm toddy was on offer, which Hippalus partook gladly. As soon as they finished, the harbour official – the same one from the previous day – made his appearance and asked them to follow him. They were led back through the portal towards the docks. The harbour was a ghost town at this time of day. They walked past the *Minerva*, but there was no sign of life aboard.

'Why have they brought us here?' asked Marcellus in a low voice. 'I thought they were taking us to the magistrate.'

'The magistrate of Maruvum conducts his business on the ship over there.' Hippalus jerked his chin in the direction of the ship.

'Oh, I see.'

'No, you don't see at all; it is most convenient. Once the sentence is handed down, execution is simple. Tie a rock and down you go.'

Marcellus did not reply. After a while, he commented, 'There must be separate laws for foreigners.'

'No one cares what happens to Yavanas here, which means that they don't get anywhere close to a magistrate. But they wouldn't want to kill a Yavana merchant prince without showing some semblance of due process, so here we are...'

The magistrate's ship was a narrow and ornate affair with two storeys on deck. To Hippalus, it didn't look as though this vessel ever left the dock. Soldiers were stationed at several locations along its length. The port official nudged them along, and they started up the plank. When they looked back, the official and the soldiers who had escorted them had vanished. They were in the hands of higher authorities now.

'This time, *little master*, do shut up and leave the talking to me,' Hippalus whispered in Greek.

'That's what got us here in the first place!'

The magistrate, a portly middle-aged man, was seated on a low bench with two bodyguards on either side. He wore one item of clothing – a silk wrap – tied around his lower body, and a number of gold necklaces of all lengths and motifs adorned his upper body. He bore no weapons, none that they could see in any case, and he did not give them a second glance. Beside him, on the floor, sat a wiry man practically hidden behind a pile of scrolls. The bodyguards and soldiers around them looked bored. The proceedings did not promise to be very interesting, not at this juncture.

At a slight nod from the magistrate, the deputy addressed them in Latin, 'You are now in the presence of the magistrate of Maruvum, who is the representative of our king, the great Karikalan. You may not speak unless spoken to. For confirmation of identity, state your name and title.'

'I am Marcellus, son of Gaius Ateilius Euhodus of Rome, the owner of the *Minerva*. My father, as Your Highness may be aware, has traded in your land for many years and holds the Chola kingdom in the highest regard.'

'That is sufficient.' The clerk paused before interpreting for the magistrate. The judge looked back at them, expressionless.

Hippalus, meanwhile, was busy mapping out escape routes and working out enemy positions. If all else failed, there was always the knife in his pocket, which could be used to cut the cord while underwater. But first, to see if he could get out of this without theatrics. He turned to the magistrate, his head bowed.

'I am Hippalus, a seaman hired by Gaius to bring goods to your country. I obey my master's command.'

He hoped his message was clear to Marcellus – the son of Gaius deserved a warning of what was to come; he was on his own. Hippalus would not throw away his life, or that of his crew, assuming they were still alive, for that of Marcellus however much of a debt he owed his father.

'The investigation will now begin. The charges are thus: kidnapping and enslaving of a Chola subject and holding him against his will aboard a Yavana ship. These charges carry a sentence of death unless clemency is granted by the king or the prime minister. First, how do you plead? If you plead guilty, it will be considered favourably in the clemency petition.'

'Not guilty,' said Marcellus immediately.

Hippalus took his time and this was not lost on the interrogators. 'Not guilty.'

The deputy turned to Hippalus. 'Could you elaborate the circumstances under which Vallavan, the young merchant of Puhar, happened to travel in your ship?'

This time, Hippalus did not hesitate. He explained how Marcellus brought the young man to him at the harbour when they were anchored at Cana.

'But you don't usually offer passage to foreigners on your ship.'

'It is not *my* ship.'

'Your master here is new to us, but you have been here many times and you come in the *Minerva* –'

'Yes, but it is not my ship. The *Minerva* belongs to my master, whose son is here as his representative. I have been privileged to steer the ship, but it is only on my master's orders. You are a country with loyal servants – you understand my position.'

'Let me rephrase the question. The *Minerva* doesn't usually carry foreigners?'

'She does.'

The interrogator gave a start. He recovered quickly and spoke again. 'Let me rephrase the question once again. The *Minerva* does not usually ferry foreign passengers?'

'That is correct.'

'What do foreigners usually do on the ship?'

'They are slaves.'

'Your master brought the Chola merchant to the ship and asked for him to be taken to Puhar?'

'Yes.'

'Was the merchant harmed?'

'Not that I know of.'

'How do you know he was stranded?'

'My master said so.'

'You took him as a slave. Perhaps as one of the oarsmen?'

Hippalus paused. Again, the pregnant pause was not lost on anyone. 'No, the master asked for him to not be an oarsman.'

'Where did he stay while he was on the ship?'

'In the hold.'

'Was he given food?'

'Same as the crew.'

'And you maintain that he was not treated as a slave?'

'Correct.'

'And that he was not kidnapped?'

'It was not my place to ask how my master came upon him.'

'Did he seem as if he was under the influence of an evil power?'

'Not that I am aware of.'

'Did you abuse him?'

'No.'

'Did your master?'

'You'd have to ask my master.'

The deputy gave him a dismissive nod and spoke to the magistrate for a long time in low whispers. Hippalus concluded that they were done with him for the moment. He wondered how Marcellus would do in the interrogation – any questioning he had been subjected to until this point in his life was likely to have come from his mother. But she, despite her formidable reputation, wasn't looking to sentence him to death.

Hippalus tried to distract himself by thinking of what he would do once he got out of this mess. He would need to concoct a story when he returned to Myos Hormos. He would write a long missive to Gaius about the loss of his son, and it had to be just right. Silvius may prove to be a problem as he would write his own letter, but there were ways around that. Silvius's letter could easily be lost at sea.

'Where did you meet the son of Manaykan?'

All attention was now on Marcellus.

'At an inn in Cana, a seaport on the Arabian coast.'

'We know where Cana is. State your business here in Puhar.'

Hippalus noted the quick change of topic. This was getting interesting.

'I am here at my father's behest to trade with the merchants of your country.'

'What do you trade in?'

'Cotton and indigo, rice and sesame oil, and ivory. We bring plates of silver, topaz, glass, frankincense and' – he paused – 'a little wine.'

Hippalus couldn't hide his smile. If the little twerp managed to get out of this alive, he would be sure to remind him every single day how prescient it was of him to have insisted on Marcellus supervising the unloading of the ship.

'Pearls?'

Hippalus stopped smiling immediately. If Marcellus were to admit that he was here for pearls it was all the Cholas needed to convict them. Pearls came from Korkai and other Pandya towns – the towns the Yavanas were not allowed to trade with directly. Even their ships weren't allowed entry into Pandya ports. Not since Karikalan had won the war.

'Not at this time.'

'Why? We understand that you have been interested in pearls before.'

'Were we? They are not so popular in Rome.'

'Is that so? That's not what we have heard…'

Marcellus shrugged. 'My mother gives them to her slaves.'

Now he is overdoing it, thought Hippalus.

'How about pepper?'

Marcellus hesitated.

'Pepper?' The questioner pressed on.

'We procure pepper in Musiris. On the Malabar coast.'

Hippalus sniggered quietly. If they knew where Cana was, they'd surely know where Musiris was. Especially since their king had taken over the Chera port city briefly during the war.

'You buy them from the Cheras?'

Dangerous question. Marcellus took his time. 'The *Minerva* is not there this year,' he said eventually.

'But another one of your ships may be?'

'I don't know.'

'We do – the *Isis*. Who is on this ship? Is it also carrying another local subject?'

Marcellus tried to evade the question. 'I don't usually travel on my father's ships; I only account for the goods in Rome.'

'Would you care to explain why you chose to travel on this particular one?'

'My father wanted me to see for myself this beautiful land of yours.'

'You have never left your country before?'

'That is true.'

'Yet your father sent you across dangerous oceans to Puhar?'

'Just as my friend Vallavan was sent by his father to Cana.'

'What did he tell you his business was in your lands?'

'Trade. Frankincense in Cana, the town of fragrance.'

'Was he successful?'

'He did not tell me.'

'You claim to be a friend and yet you do not know this?'

'He was preoccupied as his ship had left without him. He wanted to get home quickly.'

'There were other ships from Tamilakam there surely?'

'Are you suggesting that he should have taken a ship back to Musiris? I don't think that would have been a good idea.'

Hippalus looked up at Marcellus with a start. The lad was aware of more than he let on. He knew, for instance, that a Chola trader wouldn't be welcome in Musiris, where the Cheras had regained control of the port. The questioner paused to confer with the magistrate quietly. The latter looked bemused.

'The magistrate would like to know the nature of your relationship with the Cheras.'

'I am not sure…' Marcellus trailed off.

'We hear that in that city there is a temple built for *your* king.'

'I wouldn't know about that!'

Hippalus was starting to get perplexed. If the purpose of the investigation was to get to the bottom of the kidnapping of a Chola subject, this line of questioning did not make much sense. If they wanted to know about Musiris, they were asking the wrong man. He was not going to volunteer that in his possession – rather, in Aafa's possession – existed a drawing of the town of Musiris, which explained in great detail this temple of Augustus they were referring to.

'Did you stop at Musiris on your way here?'

'No.'

'At Tondi?'

Were they really going to ask this boy, who had never travelled this way before, about every little port on the peninsula? It wasn't adding up, and Hippalus was getting more and more concerned with each question. Were they fishing or was this a distraction?

'No. We came straight from Cana to Puhar.'

'You travelled through the gulf and not around it?'

'I believe so, yes.'

'You did not stop at Korkai?'

'No.'

'You knew how dangerous it is to cross the strait?'

'I don't. You'd have to ask my captain that.'

Nicely done. But he wasn't spoken to, so Hippalus kept quiet.

'Do you have dealings with the merchants of Satkarni?'

'No,' Marcellus said, a little too quickly.

This must be why they have warships on the ready. *They worry that someone is going to attack – Cheras, Pandyas or Satkarni – but they aren't sure who is the most dangerous. Or imminent*, Hippalus thought. That explained their line of enquiry.

'Our information suggests that you trade with them.'

'I do not know of all the kingdoms of the peninsula, so please excuse my ignorance.'

'The magistrate is displeased. He wants you to stop lying to us. You pretend to come in friendship, but you trade with all our enemies. The Cheras, Satkarni and now –'

'There are no enemies in trade. Rome does not interfere in the politics of other lands.'

Despite the danger his life was in, Hippalus had to try hard to restrain his snigger. How did Marcellus think that Hippalus, a Greek sailor from Egyptian Berenı́kē, not to mention the speaker himself – the son of a Carthaginian freedman – would become the subjects of the Roman empire? Clearly his all-Roman mother had had too much of an influence on him. Truth and justice, and *non-interference* on top of that!

'I am not lying. This is all a misunderstanding. All you have to do is ask Vallavan and he will explain that he was not held against his will.'

'We have no intention of summoning the poor man, who has been tortured and abused for so many days.'

'Let him say so himself!'

'What makes you think we haven't spoken to him? It is on the basis of his evidence that you are here.'

This time, the shock was evident on Marcellus's face. He hadn't expected to be betrayed by his friend.

'Could you tell me what he has accused me and my men of?'

'He is not right in his head due to the abuse he suffered on your ship. Now, you will refrain from telling us how to run this investigation. In any case, the interrogation is over. You may now await the verdict.'

It didn't take the magistrate long, but his deputy spent some time writing it down neatly on his scroll. Finally he spoke, addressing Marcellus. 'You have been found guilty of kidnapping and enslaving a Chola merchant by the name of Vallavan, son of Manaykan. The crew and the captain are sentenced to death by drowning immediately. You will be imprisoned and granted a clemency petition with the prime minister. This is on account of the high rank your father holds in your kingdom.'

'But my men are entirely free from blame!' cried out Marcellus.

'Listen to him, Your Highness. I am but a poor servant and what choice did I have in this matter? My master told me to take him in, and we did!' implored Hippalus.

'Neither do you have a choice here, seaman. As your master's loyal servant, you'd like to go first, we presume, as would your men. Summon the crew and let's get this done with! The magistrate doesn't have all day.'

A soldier jumped on to the pier almost immediately and ran in the direction of the *Minerva*. Blood was promised, and the soldiers would be entertained. Hippalus knew he desperately needed the soldiers to be distracted if he were to try to escape, but there was none forthcoming.

'At the least, I should be granted a clemency petition. I could be of much use to this country as I can be your eyes and ears in enemy territory!' he asserted.

The deputy laughed. 'We know very well that if you leave Puhar we will not see you here again. Why would we trust Yavana informers?'

'Because your men may not be able to gather the intelligence that I can.'

'We cannot set you and your men free to sail around our waters as you please.'

At this point, there was a shout from the docks and everyone turned around.

A commotion! Exactly what he needed. Hippalus saw a palanquin making its way down the pier towards the ship. The magistrate and his men watched curiously. He took one step backwards, patting his pocket to check if his knife was still there – only one soldier stood between him and the water – but then he recognized the man walking alongside the palanquin. He stayed put; here was a glimmer of hope and Hippalus was a man who believed in timing.

The palanquin-bearers stopped in front of the ship, keeping a respectable distance. One of the soldiers came up the plank with a scroll that the clerk read out to the magistrate. The judge nodded. From the palanquin, a richly dressed man – *the* merchant, Hippalus surmised – alighted along with his equally well-adorned young companion. Hippalus noted that this was not Vallavan. The Yavana who had walked alongside the palanquin stayed where he was, and did not step on board.

The merchant ignored the two foreigners, while the boy who had accompanied him stared at them curiously. The magistrate, Manaykan and the boy went inside the cabin and spoke for a long time. Then the deputy was summoned, and the meeting continued. On the ground, the Yavana's gaze was fixed on the *Minerva* in the far distance. Silvius's expression – a thin smile that left no question about the rage behind it – lifted Hippalus's spirits considerably. Silvius had had to cut a deal, and it wasn't one that he was happy with. This explained his anger. This was more than hope, this was freedom. But for whom?

The deputy stepped forward. He unfurled his scroll, looked directly at the prisoners and read aloud: 'You are hereby released from captivity; you and your men are free to go. There are no charges against you at this time. You are banned henceforth from having any further dealings, trade or otherwise, with the enemies of the king. If it were found that you have disobeyed this order, you and your men will be put to death, and your possessions in Chola country impounded. Dismissed!'

Hippalus was glad he hadn't acted in haste. His gamble had paid off, but he knew that he'd have to deal with Silvius's rage. He supposed he could leave the little master to face the brunt of it, as it was Marcellus, after all, who was going to stay with the crafty old barbarian.

He nodded at Marcellus and jumped ashore.

4

SILVIUS

The harbour's market, the evening angadi, was in full swing when Marcellus and Silvius left the docks and entered town. Smoke billowed out of the stoves as women called out to passers-by, enticing them to try their delicacies. The aroma that pervaded the place was entirely alien to the new arrival. His stomach growled – the rice gruel was too long ago – and he could not look away. There were roasted peanuts with pepper and salt, sugary dough balls, steamed plantains, fried anchovies and piping-hot rice cakes. In time, their names would roll off his tongue effortlessly – paniyaram, appam, kozhukkattai – and his taste buds would develop strong preferences, but for now he had to be content with just gawking.

'My dear boy, would you care for a bite? You must be peckish.'

Marcellus was about to jump at the offer, but Silvius did not give him a chance to respond. 'I must warn you, however, that angadi food is not advisable for your constitution and you could fall fatally ill. But you are fortunate because I happen to have in my service a faithful and dependable cook who is home at the moment, preparing for your arrival. But if you insist...'

'Let's walk on,' mumbled Marcellus.

He had spent many an evening in his childhood, sometimes behind closed doors and at other times in open view, listening to his father talk of this man and their exploits together. Stretching from the lawless streets of Londonium, where they had first met, to the eastern shores of the Erythraean Sea, theirs has been a lucrative relationship. Sometime ago, Silvius had decided to settle down in Puhar and serve as his father's representative in the east. He'd sworn never to return to Rome.

From one backwater to another; that suits him, his father had said. *He remains a barbarian at heart.*

Backwater or not, the years spent here in Puhar must have made him senile. To think that the food served here in this market could make one ill! Had he really forgotten the excuse for food that one had to make do with on board a ship? Or did he think that Marcellus had taken the opportunity to clear out the Falernian wine the *Minerva* was carrying?

But this was no time to ask questions for he was aware that this man had played a significant role in him being alive and free after the ordeal at the harbour. There were more pressing questions Marcellus would have liked to ask but knew he must bide his time. So he walked on, just another Yavana in Puhar town, taking in the sights, sounds and smells of this faraway land.

Behind the food stalls sat grocers, selling rice, grains, sugar and baskets full of cloves, nutmeg, pepper and cinnamon. He stopped at one storefront and gaped at the mountains of spices in wonder. Back home, such an ostentatious display would almost certainly cause a stampede and result in the death of many. Well, mostly slaves, since they'd be out to buy the best for their masters.

'Have you not seen spices before, my boy? After all, your father owns warehouses here in the east and in Ostia filled with every spice known to mankind.'

'I have –'

'Ah, I hear that you are rather keen on the White Shirts at the Circus? Perhaps that is why you may not have had the opportunity to visit your father's warehouses. But don't you worry; you will have ample time here in Puhar to get acquainted with them.'

Marcellus's reputation of whiling away hours at the chariot races had preceded him, and this man had wasted no time in telling him that he knew everything that was to know about his employer's son. No doubt the story of his seasickness, many times magnified, with eyes, ears and a tail, had reached Silvius by now. He glared at the older man.

'We must hurry along, dear fellow, or your food will go cold,' Silvius continued blithely, seemingly oblivious to Marcellus's displeasure.

Marcellus slowed down further on purpose to look at shop displays. The vendors he saw manning the stores were shorter, darker and more sunburnt than he was, but they shared his long black hair. He wondered whether these were Vallavan's people, or whether they were what his friend called the 'people of his country'. He noticed they were muscular; their hands used to working with metal and wood, unlike Vallavan's, whose soft hands had likely never held a real sword.

Swords are not meant for merchant princes. There are others to fight our wars, he had told Marcellus.

Not in Rome, he had responded. And certainly not in Gaius's view. His father was insistent that all his sons should have a full and proper education. And so they spent a number of years not just with Diodorus, the Greek tutor, who gleefully pointed out Roman intellectual inadequacy at every opportunity – Hippalus and Diodorus would make great friends, it struck him now – but also with the sadistic Magnus, the former gladiator trainer extraordinaire, who taught him how to wield a sword and shield.

The spice vendors were followed by a street of goldsmiths and gem setters, who sat in front of their shops, their windows glittering with necklaces and anklets of all sizes, while their assistants were intent on filling, setting and polishing at the back. This may have been a small kingdom, but it was a prosperous one.

'I must tell you, dear lad, that the workmanship here leaves something to be desired. The best goldsmiths are from Chera country; you will be better advised to buy from Musiris. If you'd –'

'I am not buying.'

'But you have to! What will your mother think if you return empty-handed?'

Marcellus ignored Silvius and walked past a side street, strung with silk banners – the textile section – and took note of the location. If he were to be able to afford it, he would certainly be back as the paterfamilias was rather susceptible to silk. Not to mention his brother, who paid a fortune for the dyed red-and-white cotton to wear to feasts and races. But even if he were to make it back to Rome in one piece after everything, his father wouldn't exactly welcome him with open arms. Not after what he'd done. No, it did not warrant thinking about right now.

Soon, they reached the end of the market area and passed under a wooden arch, on which a number of banners were hoisted. In the centre, the tiger flag of the Cholas fluttered, and an eagle standard signifying the Roman empire held a prominent place to the left.

'Which one is that?' he asked, pointing to the one with a golden dragon.

'Thinae. The natives call this the Yavana quarters and the term refers to us, the men of the West. But you'll soon find that there are more Easterners here than us Yavanas.' He spread his hands out wide. 'Welcome home, young master.'

The street they had turned into was lined on both sides by narrow two-storey houses, the most distinctive feature of which were large oval-shaped windows on both levels. Each house had an open, raised platform in front called the thinnai. On some of these verandas sat hawkers selling fresh produce to those who didn't want to go all the way to the angadi. These enterprising shopkeepers paid rent in the form of meat and dairy to the foreign tenants of the houses, who, in turn, paid a much larger amount to the landlords in Pattinam. The verandas which weren't let out to the vendors were filled with sacks full of goods to be imported or exported – the merchants who ran out of warehouse space stored them there. In a few houses, clerks sat on the floor, poring over scrolls of accounts; this was where they conducted their business in the day.

But it was the people he saw in the verandas, and on the street, that left an impression on Marcellus. His kind was easy to recognize and they nodded at Silvius while staring at him curiously, but there were others. Surly Greeks who didn't as much as give them a second glance, friendly Alexandrians, frowning Arabs, slit-eyed Thinaes, stocky men from the southern isles and tonsured northerners in flowing robes. He had not seen such a diverse assortment in Rome – not in the slave bazaars, not in the Circus and certainly not in the house parties at the Palatine – but they were all represented in a single street in this small kingdom.

Silvius stopped in front of the building in the corner, which curved around an alleyway that met the main street. His thinnai was full of cloth sacks and large jars, and Silvius found his way through them to reach the door.

'The warehouse didn't have space for the new cargo, so we had to move these here. All for nothing,' mumbled Silvius. He then turned to him. 'Here is your abode in the East. I'm afraid that it's not quite what you are used to back home, but it'll have to do.'

Marcellus followed Silvius inside. The house consisted of an atrium open to the sky, wooden pillars surrounding it, and a number of small doorways that led away from the courtyard to rooms on either side. On his left was a high, narrow staircase that led to the upper floor. He was used to far worse accommodations, but there was no need for Silvius to know that. In fact, it was essential that Silvius didn't find out, and so Marcellus reacted as would be expected of the son of Gaius.

'It'll do for tonight, but tomorrow I'd like you to find me suitable quarters.'

Silvius beamed. 'Of course, nothing would make me happier than to ensure that you reside in a place appropriate for a man of your rank. It'd be my pleasure.'

Marcellus nodded curtly.

'If I may ask – the landlords will want to know after all – would you be paying for it in gold?'

Marcellus's face expressed surprise, but he remained silent.

'As I am sure you are aware, the firm's travel allowance is capped for boarding and lodging. For a place that's appropriate for you, I'm afraid it will have to be out of *bursa*,' continued Silvius nonchalantly.

'My father owns this outfit and he pays your salary!' Marcellus was indignant.

'Be that as it may, your esteemed father, my dear friend and employer, has not informed me of any changes to the expense policy. I specifically asked Hippalus if there were instructions in this regard, and the response was negative. The firm's policy is to lodge business visitors in the warehouse and, as you can imagine, it is much better than the ship. But, in your case, I made a special exception and I have offered you space in my abode.'

'You expect me to be grateful?' Marcellus was beginning to understand why his father held this man in high regard. *The sly fox!*

Silvius's smile had not left his face. 'Gratitude is overrated. I am but a humble servant of your father's and I am glad to be of service.'

This was not worth fighting for, not when he was so distracted by the aroma of bread and meat wafting in from somewhere in the back of the house. Silvius knew it too and was using it to his advantage.

'You can be sure that I will write to my father tomorrow,' Marcellus said finally.

'As you should. Would you also be kind enough to inform him of the arrest and the loss of his cargo?'

Marcellus looked up, startled.

'What are you referring to? You have my word that nothing has been stolen from the ship's hold since we left Myos Hormos. If Hippalus has been spinning stories about theft and implicating Vallavan in it, you should know it is blatantly false!'

'Hippalus has nothing to do with this. I had to offer half the cargo at minimal prices to Manaykan for taking the trouble of coming to the port this morning and saving your life.'

Marcellus couldn't believe his ears. So that was the price of his freedom? It also explained why Silvius had looked so put out all day. 'We...I...brought his son home to safety! If anyone should be making a payment, it should be him!'

'Well said, my boy! I am sure he will be expecting a bill soon. If you need help in drawing that up, please let me know. But for now, it's time for your meal.'

He clapped his hands and a tray materialized out of nowhere in the hands of a beautiful boy, not much older than Marcellus himself. But he was in no mood to admire this specimen; neither did he feel like eating as his appetite had fled. He ate very little and went upstairs to take stock of the events of the day, but no sooner had his head hit the hard bed than he fell fast asleep.

~

The letter Marcellus had threatened Silvius with remained unwritten as the days rolled by, as did Manaykan's bill. He had no way of knowing whether Silvius had sent a missive to his father pre-empting his own letter, but he was heartened by the fact that no West-borne ships had left Puhar since the *Minerva* made her landing. He attempted to be civil with Silvius and, over the next few days, they settled into a routine. Silvius dragged him out of bed early and they left for the seaside warehouses, where local traders came every morning with their wares. Marcellus spent most of his day counting, measuring, evaluating quality and watching Silvius negotiate with local merchant representatives. He learnt the local weights and measures with great difficulty on his part and a wide range of expletives reserved for his Greek tutor on Silvius's. An amphorae, for instance, meant nothing to these people, and yet, that was the only measure he was used to operating in. Silvius and Marcellus would return to their quarters late in the afternoon for lunch – prepared by the now-familiar Adi, who served as Silvius's own Ganymede. And then Marcellus would get some time for himself before his father's friend reappeared in evening garb and led him a few doors away. Here, a group of Roman merchants and the odd Alexandrian gathered for the evening. Common topics of discussion included the impact of flooding in the Kaveri basin on rice prices, and the labour unrest in the pepper plantations of Chera country, but as the wine flowed, the conversation drifted to more interesting subjects – such as the political strife back home and the qualities of the mixed-breed boys and girls in the brothels of Pattinam. On a few occasions, Marcellus managed to sneak out late in the evening to watch shopkeepers closing for the day and taste foreign delicacies in the evening angadi, but not before listening outside the door to find out exactly what it was that his compatriots thought of him.

~

'This lad of Gaius,' Junius began and everyone turned to Silvius in anticipation.

'What do you make of him?' Silvius snorted derisively.

'Word from Rome says he is hot-headed and, what's worse, a loyalist. Spends an inordinate amount of time at the races and is often seen with girls of all persuasions. Not just girls, in fact... Has he gone for your houseboy yet?'

'Silvius's houseboy is out of bounds. You don't let any of us get near him!' someone chimed in.

'But Marcellus is your master, after all...' Junius said, sipping on his wine.

'He is my employer's son; they are not the same. And I see you have been busy talking to my crew.'

'Since when did it become *your* crew? Has Hippalus abdicated?'

'I can only hope.'

'It is said you could have effected that.'

'That seaman has a thousand lives!'

'And this Marcellus... My source says he is under his mother's influence. Who, as we all know, has an interesting history...'

'Some say Gaius and she aren't actually married!' someone else piped up.

'Oh, they are married. I was there, trust me.' Silvius sighed. 'She'd settle for nothing less. She didn't leave her patrician family to live the life of a harlot with the son of a freedman, however wealthy he may have been.'

'She has political ambitions for the lad, I hear.'

'Ambitions for the son of a freedman from Carthage? Rome is not ready for that!'

'That has never stopped the good lady, now, has it?'

'What is this about her being close to the emperor? Too close, they say. And therefore, her son could be here in the service of Rome?'

'We are all here in the service of Rome. But let's go with this theory of yours. You claim that the emperor sent him to Puhar – a place in which he has no interest whatsoever?'

'Doesn't he?'

'Ah, you can't mean that. Why would he…?'

'In Rome, everyone remembers the young Macedon.'

A guffaw. 'Not the current one in the palace. In any case, you Romans need to get your heroes to do something original.'

Silence reigned for a while.

'Why does he want to go to Musiris?' someone finally asked.

'Who is going where?' Silvius looked up.

'Your lad is looking for someone to take him there. He has quietly been making enquiries at port.'

'So that he can be killed by Karikalan's men? Or the pirates? Whoever gets him first.'

'Silvius, tell us, what game is afoot? What deal did you cut with Manaykan?'

'We all know Karikalan is not to be messed with, and I can bide my time.'

'Well, if the time is ripe, remember, some of us may be interested too.'

'I will. But where did you hear that he wants to go to Musiris?'

'He asked one of the river boatmen. News came back to me immediately.'

'Since you are so well informed, pray tell me, what else has he been up to?'

'Gorging on Rajamma's appams and fish.'

'Now, that is perfectly understandable!'

5

ZHANG, THE BUDDHIST

Rajamma was in her usual spot, wedged between the weavers' street and the waterfront. Fresh toddy had been delivered by the tapper's boy, the fish was frying, and the appams were hot and fluffy. Most of her clientele were local shopkeepers: the weavers, jewellers and spice sellers, who stopped by on their way back home to buy her food. The jewellers were the stingiest of the lot, always complaining about the price, size and texture of her appams, while the naive weavers always took what was on offer without a word. Here was the weaver from the nearby silk workshop buying seer fish for his entire family in return for what was at least an entire ream of silk. And that Yavana boy, who came quietly and asked ever so politely for anchovies and appam, there he was sitting at his usual spot.

But wait!

A couple, looking incongruous in this part of town, walked past the stall. The woman had on a deep blue silk garment draped around her not insignificant figure, and was covered in a sea of bangles, anklets and necklaces, while the man, equally well dressed and bejewelled, carried an urn on his head. Not just Rajamma's, every thieving eye in the market was on them – they would be stripped bare by the time they reached home, poor sods. *Someone should have warned them*, thought Rajamma.

'What a stench! Where have we come, my lord?' She heard the woman address her husband loudly.

'Cover your nostrils; it is someone frying fish. We will be out of here soon.'

'Fish?' the woman asked, suddenly suspicious. 'Have you been here before? Have you been eating fish?'

'Of course not!' the hapless man answered hastily. 'Not since our family took the oath.'

The woman sighed. 'We have prayed to every single god and goddess in this land. I am beginning to think that we aren't meant to have a son.'

'Don't say such things with your black tongue, woman! We are on our way to the beach to make offerings to the goddess, and now is not the time to talk nonsense. God, please forgive this woman!' The man looked up at the sky as he said this.

'You are only half a man, which is why I am sonless,' the woman said after a pause, looking spitefully at her husband. The man raised his hand to slap his wife, but the urn on his head wobbled precariously and his hand swiftly went back up to balance it.

Rajamma couldn't control her laughter. At this point, an apologetic new voice broke into the conversation.

'I am sorry to intrude, but may I please ask if you have any daughters?'

Zhang had materialized out of nowhere as he was prone to do. Rajamma had a soft corner for the Easterner as he paid her so promptly, but this time, he was simply asking for trouble.

'Yes, three daughters,' answered the man stiffly.

'May I ask you, madam' – the Easterner said, turning to the woman – 'the priest who sent you on this journey, is he responsible for your daughters?'

The woman turned pale. The husband removed both his hands from the urn, but was forced to put them back as it nearly toppled forward. The urn, once reinstalled on his head, was not to be put down until they reached the sea. Rajamma had seen variations of this ritual before.

'You abominable foreigner, how dare you insult my wife?' the man cried out in indignation.

'She called you half a man,' the Easterner offered his explanation, calmly.

'She is my wife and she can call me what she wants. Who are you?'

'My name is Zhang, but who I am doesn't matter. Are you heading to the beach to offer prayers?'

The woman opened her mouth to respond, but shut it again quickly, as if struck by the realization that it wasn't a good idea to speak to this foreigner. Who knew what omens he portended.

'What does it look like to you?' the man snarled.

'May I enquire which goddess you'll be propitiating?'

'Manimekalai. The head priest asked us to pour the offerings in the ocean and spend the night here, and the goddess will bless us with a son.'

'Manimekalai cannot give you a son; it is not in her hands,' Zhang said, with great authority.

By now, a small crowd has gathered, curious to see where this was heading. Rajamma did brisk business with one ear tuned to the conversation, and the couple seemed to have forgotten the distasteful stench of fried fish.

'Whose hands is it in, then? Do you know of a special goddess?' the man asked, suddenly sounding interested.

'Well, it is not in anyone's *hands*, if I am perfectly honest with you. How much did you pay this head priest?'

'The priest doesn't take any gifts. Not for himself.'

'Of course not, it is always for the goddess, isn't it? What will she do without all the gold?'

'My lord, this is a madman. Don't encourage him, let's go!' The woman tugged at her husband's arm. Zhang continued as if he hadn't heard her; but this time, he turned around and addressed the crowd.

'You fine citizens of Chola land, don't be taken in by the priests. The rites and offerings are useless; don't believe in them. They will result in nothing!'

'What do you believe in, foreigner?' someone in the crowd yelled.

'The Middle Path. The way of Gautama Buddha!'

The woman let out a startled cry. 'So that is it. You cunning man, follower of a foreign god. You casteless creature! You are like the other one, that insufferable Kavunti woman whom the merchants are in thrall of. Go back to your country; we don't want you here!'

'Where I come from, we follow the way of Laozi, but it is not what I speak. On my way to this country, I learnt the path of the Buddha. Have you seen the edicts of Emperor Asokan of Magadha? If only you had seen them, you would understand –'

A man from the crowd caught hold of Zhang's arm. 'This man is a spy,' he shouted. 'He is from the land of Satkarni, where they have edicts and stupas. They are bent on converting our people to their way of life!'

'I am no harbinger of evil,' Zhang said, his voice tranquil. 'Allow me to explain –'

'If you think your god is better than ours, I suggest –'

'I have no god, madam.'

'Vishnu Perumal!' The husband looked up at the sky again. 'Save this infidel. He knows not what he is saying.'

'On the contrary – I assure you that I know exactly what I am talking about. The prayers you offer on the beach aren't going to help you have a son.' He paused, and added, 'Or a daughter for that matter.'

The woman started hitting Zhang in a frenzy as the crowd watched in anticipation, but no one came forward to stop her. Who was this stranger who had come from the East to claim that there was no god? Zhang took a few steps back.

'Madam, ahimsa is the way of life. You cannot hurt your fellow creatures like this!' he said. The woman's husband shouted at her to follow him as it was getting late and they hadn't even started their prayer. The woman gave Zhang one last thwack before following him. The crowd dispersed once they realized that their evening's entertainment had come to an end.

Zhang walked over to Rajamma's stall.

'Here, take a bite of this and you will feel better.' She handed him a dried banyan leaf filled with appams and fish.

'No food for me. Just the toddy, please,' Zhang said.

'You cannot go picking fights with powerful people like that. They will complain to the priests and you will be in trouble,' Rajamma said quietly. Someone ought to tell him to be careful and she was up to the task.

'It doesn't matter,' he said. 'You believe in the Middle Path, don't you?'

She shrugged. 'As long as it means that the goddess makes my wishes come true, I believe in your path.'

'There is no go– Yes, you can speak to the goddess without any messenger in between. This is what the Buddha fought for.'

'But you said your Buddha believed in ahimsa. Why is he fighting now?'

'He didn't fight with arms; he fought with words and ideas!'

Rajamma shook her head – sometimes, she had no idea what this man went on about. And then, the Yavana boy coughed gently.

Zhang's eyes lit up and he said something to the boy in his language. The boy replied and they exchanged a few heated words before the boy left in a huff.

'What did you say to the poor boy?' Rajamma demanded.

'I didn't say anything. He told me not to belittle his gods and I told him to come back to me once his people have their own gods.'

'What?'

'His people…they borrow their gods from their neighbours.'

'All gods are worth praying to!'

'Or none.' Zhang shrugged and left the scene as quickly as he had appeared. Rajamma turned to her other customers. Time she paid them some attention too, or they would think that she served only Yavanas. She didn't need any more rumours; it wasn't good for business.

6

WAYLAID AND RESCUED

Marcellus walked home, deep in thought. Who was this strange Easterner, who was home here in Puhar but was still as alien as himself? Rome had its own share of foreigners and slaves – from Alexandria, Greece, Judea, Gaul, Londonium, you name it – but he had never seen any of them pick a fight with a native citizen with such impunity. Marcellus had been taught to be careful from his early years, lest he be mistaken for a foreigner himself. He was, more often than not, stopped and searched, and was once assaulted, even though there was no provocation on his part. He'd learnt early on that he had to be careful while dealing with people if there was even the smallest seed of doubt in their heads that you weren't an equal. And he'd never be an equal in their eyes. But this man from Thinae dared to challenge a citizen in his own land!

Marcellus was so lost in his thoughts that he didn't notice the hooded man until he was almost upon him. The Yavana was walking down a narrow, dark alley – a connector between the streets of the Arabs and the Greeks that got him home quicker. His right hand reflexively went to his dagger, but just as he reached it, it flew out of its leather scabbard into the hands of his attacker.

One hand went over his mouth from behind and he bit down on it hard just as his right leg found its mark. The man howled in pain and, just for a moment, Marcellus was free. He ran and turned along the curve of the alley only to find his way blocked by two shadows; the attacker wasn't alone. It was too dark to make out anything about them. Trapped on both sides, he looked for a gap in the walls on either side – there was none. He was in deep trouble. He put his hands up.

'I am not carrying any gold.'

'We don't need gold.' The man behind him laughed. 'Not from you. Tell us what you are doing here.'

'I was on my way to the lodgings of a Roman called Silvius when you attacked me. I am a Yavana merchant –'

'We know who you are. What are you doing here in Puhar?'

'I told you I am a merchant! I buy and sell goods.'

'That's enough. What are you *really* here for?'

'You have the wrong man; I am just a trader! This is all a misunderstanding.'

'Wrong man? Tell us this – aren't you the magnanimous young Roman who offered the merchant boy a lift to Puhar?'

The dagger, *his* dagger, was now poised at his throat.

'Yes, but –'

'Who told you to do that? If it is the pirate who now calls himself the king of Musiris, you'd better admit it right now.'

Everyone in this kingdom assumed he was working for a rival king. This was one paranoid kingdom. But he knew he had only himself to blame for this. Wasn't it he who had made a big deal about asking for transport to Musiris as a distraction?

'I can assure you that my mission has nothing to do with Musiris.'

'Finally! What is this mission, and who sent you?'

'My father in Rome sent me to trade and I need to make a profit. That is my only mission. Please believe me!'

A punch landed on his nose and he reeled in pain. 'Help!' he screamed as the dagger drew blood from his throat.

'No! You can't kill him!' one of the attackers shouted.

'He isn't going to die that easily. Now, are you going to tell us the truth?'

Just then, a trumpet sounded from the far end of the alley.

'Who's there?' one of the attackers yelled, as another gasped. 'Chola soldiers!'

Two of the attackers immediately melted into the shadows, but the third lingered for a moment. 'Don't think you've escaped... I will see you again,' he said, before he sprinted off to join his friends.

Marcellus, too shaken to give pursuit, turned towards his rescuers. He knew by now that Chola soldiers would not take too kindly to his story of being attacked in a dark alleyway. He needed to think of something more convincing.

'Little master!'

'Aafa!'

'I am the ship's pilot, not your bodyguard,' Aafa barked. 'If you'd be more careful next time, I'd be grateful. Are you hurt?'

'I am fine,' replied Marcellus, wiping the trickle of blood from his neck, keeping an eye on the man behind Aafa.

'Who were they?' Aafa asked.

'I have no idea. But who's that with you? Have you befriended Chola soldiers?'

Aafa's gurgle of laughter filled the alley and echoed back, startling all three of them. 'No, that was me. It always helps to learn how to blow your horn like the local soldiers. This trick has never failed me. And this is someone who has come a long way to meet you. He came to the harbour to find you, and I was bringing him over to Silvius's.'

'Does he have a name?'

'You can ask him yourself, but let's get out of here first. Don't want them coming back,' Aafa said and led them out of the alley. 'Any guesses as to your attackers?'

'They were not robbers; they didn't want any gold.'

'What did they want?'

Marcellus shrugged. 'Same as everyone in this place. They all seem convinced that I work for a rival king. They thought you were Chola soldiers, which is why they left in such a hurry.'

'They can't be from here. Chola soldiers don't patrol Yavana residences; they are all stationed at the warehouses. Every local knows this!'

They were back on the main street and Marcellus could see better in the light of the street lanterns. He turned to take a good look at the stranger. He was a swarthy, well-built man with a pockmarked face and a prominent white turban, but what caught Marcellus's attention was his expression. The man was staring at him in open-mouthed astonishment.

'What is it?' asked Aafa, not one to miss much.

'He... He is...so like...his father,' the man said in broken Latin.

'Hmm.' Aafa frowned. 'You are not the first to notice that.' He didn't sound entirely convinced.

'You know my father?'

'This way, please.' Aafa made three quick left turns before jumping over a low wall. Marcellus and the stranger followed him silently. They found themselves next to a well, in the backyard of a small dwelling lit by lanterns – warm light streaming out from its kitchen window. 'We can talk here,' said Aafa, coming to a stop.

'Home of a friend?'

'It's a stretch, but one could say so. Don't step too far behind into the darkness, little master, there's a cobra nest behind you.'

'What?' Marcellus jumped.

'Right. To business. You can speak in Tamil; he understands.'

The stranger took off his turban and bowed.

'Maruthappan, from the house of Appans of Korkai. Yavana lord, on behalf of the clan of Paravans of Korkai, please accept my greetings. I apologize for having come to meet you in the dark of the night, but I hope the day is not far when we will be able to meet under the shining sun.' His language sounded different – faster and thicker – from the version Marcellus was now used to, and it took him a while to decipher what he was hearing.

Marcellus knew of the Appans of Korkai. They belonged to the community of Paravans, the clan of ardent Murugan worshippers, who owned the pearl fisheries on the eastern coast. He knew they employed hundreds of mukuvans and mukuvathisr, who dove deep into the ocean every day to bring up pearl oysters.

'How do I know you are who you say you are?'

'Aafa can confirm who I am.'

'Can you?'

Aafa nodded. 'I was with your father on his trip south.'

This was interesting. Here he was trying to find a way to get to Korkai, and the answer had been in his father's ship all along. When were they planning to tell him that?

'During the war?'

'Yes, the Cholas wouldn't let us past the border and your father had to turn back. However, I managed to get past with a message. I can confirm that Maruthappan here does indeed speak for the Appans.'

Marcellus turned to the man from Korkai. 'Why were you looking for me?'

'Word has reached the Appans that you are looking for us, and so we come to you.'

Now, this was news to him. If anything, he had been careful to enquire only about Musiris, not Korkai, in his time in Puhar. His distraction had clearly not been very successful.

'I come in peace with a message from my masters. Your father was one to bide his time, and the time has now come. We are ready to trade.'

Marcellus frowned. 'But for us, this may not be the time for pearls.'

'You haven't seen our pearls; ours are not the kind you get from Oman. Your father knew the difference and he said he'd be open if we ever wanted to trade.'

'And you didn't until now?'

Maruthappan shook his head. 'The situation has changed.'

'In which case, may I ask why you haven't approached my father's representative here in this kingdom?'

'Silvius cavorts with the Cholas, and we wouldn't want to put that relationship in jeopardy. We don't know where his true loyalties lie. So the Appans would like to talk to you instead. Besides, they prefer to speak to the family directly.'

'I see.' Marcellus paused before continuing. 'But as far as I am aware, you cannot sell us pearls directly. Not since the war. You'd have go through the merchants of Puhar.'

Maruthappan smiled. 'And as per Chola orders, you are not to trade with anyone here in this peninsula other than the Cholas. Yet, we understand that your father's ship, the *Isis*, is currently docked in Musiris.'

'The order is recent, and the *Isis* was on her way already.'

'You are not interested in the pearls?'

'I did not say that.'

'In that case, the Appans hope to meet you in person at the Pillayar shrine in Pattinam on the next full moon night.'

Marcellus frowned. Even the usually unflappable Aafa raised his eyebrows. Pandya traders attempting to cut a deal in the heart of the Chola capital? This was suicide.

'They will never look for us in their midst,' Maruthappan said, reading their expressions correctly.

'The Appans proposed to meet at the temple?'

'We will find a way; it's our problem.'

'This could be dangerous. If we are caught by the soldiers –'

'We'll all be dead. That's the choice you have to make – you don't have to come to the shrine, in which case we will never mention this again. You can tell Gaius-ayya to forget the pearls.'

Maruthappan bowed. 'But if…if you are your father's son, you will come. I take my leave now.'

'I will see you out,' Aafa said. 'One can get lost in this quarter.'

'I will be fine, Aafa. Your duty is to make sure the master gets home.'

'Don't tell me what my job is; Hippalus does enough of that. Little master, jump over that wall over there and you'll find yourself in Silvius's backyard.'

'But what about the snakes?'

Aafa grinned. 'I was just checking to see if you were listening. Good, come with us. I will take you to the front door and we'll be on our way.'

They retraced their steps, and Aafa took them through a couple more turns before Marcellus could make out familiar territory once again. Aafa and Maruthappan watched from the shadows until he reached the door. Marcellus knocked loudly as he had no wish to see Silvius humping his catamite. The door opened immediately, as if Silvius had been waiting for him.

'Marcellus, dear boy, there you are! We were just wondering about you. Did you have a good evening? And what's that on your throat? A *cut*?'

'I was ambushed on my way home.'

'May I take a look?'

'It's nothing serious.'

'You have to be careful in these parts at night. I could perhaps find someone to accompany you? Your father would not forgive me otherwise. May I suggest Adi?'

Marcellus shook his head. 'No,' he said. After a long pause he added, 'The Pandya traders have been in touch.'

The surprise on Silvius's face was real, but it couldn't be because of what he was told; he already knew that but clearly he hadn't expected Marcellus to divulge the information.

'Did they come to the warehouse?'

'They couldn't publicly approach us, so they came to see me in private.'

'Young master, you will not encourage this. The magistrate's orders are clear and it's dangerous to disobey. We cannot negotiate with the Pandyas.'

'How do you know I am going to talk to them?'

'They know you are susceptible and impressionable. Naturally, they came after you. As tempting as the offer might be, I am afraid –'

'I am meeting them in Pattinam.'

'I'd counsel strongly against it.'

'I am going to meet them anyway.'

'I will come with you in that case.'

'No.'

'Young master, how will you get to the shrine by yourself? How will you negotiate?'

Marcellus had not mentioned any shrine. There were snakes in the backyard all right, but they belonged to Silvius. *Adi!*

'I thought you didn't want to negotiate.'

'I owe it to your father that you return safe. I am also keen that you don't gamble away what I have painstakingly built over the years in this kingdom.'

'But my father wants a monopoly on the pearl trade. He has wanted it since the first time he saw the Korkai pearls decades go. He told me so himself.'

'The situation on the ground is different now. He would not trade with the Pandyas if he knew how precarious this is. We risk everything.'

Marcellus considered this for a moment. Silvius was right, but he had to do what he had come this far for.

'We cannot miss this opportunity. I'll meet them.'

'In which case, I'll come with you.'

Marcellus had to admit that Silvius would be useful, given his connections and knowledge. He knew the place well and all the right people.

'On one condition.'

'Yes?'

'Adi stays here. He has spied on me ever since I set foot in this place and it has to stop.'

It wasn't so much the spying that bothered him. The boy surely must have seen him being attacked, and yet he made no attempt to help him. To his surprise, Silvius laughed. 'As you wish, young master. But be careful of pushing away friends – you may come to regret it.'

PUHAR: PATTINAM

What Her Girl Friend Said

to him when he wanted to come by day

O man of the seashore
where old women
dry their wet streaming hair
and look like a flock
of herons in the bay,
when people said,
a chariot comes here often
splattering
the dark neytal lilies
near the bubbling backwaters,

Mother said at once,
'Don't go out.'

Ammūvaṉār, *Aiṅkuṟunūṟu* 186

What He Said

What could my mother be
to yours? What kin is my father
to yours anyway? And how
did you and I meet ever?

But in love
our hearts have mingled
like red earth and pouring rain.

Cempulappeyaṉīrār, *Kuruntokai* 40

7

PATTINAM

Three days later, Marcellus once again made good use of his embroidered toga, which had been carefully restored since the day of his arrest, and set out with Silvius for Pattinam as instructed by the Appans. To his surprise, Silvius had made the effort to look presentable and had worn a white veshti in the local fashion, and put on, for maximum assimilation, a number of arm bands. Adi carefully laid out the offerings for the deity in a basket – coconuts, flowers, sandalwood and frankincense for the god, and corals hidden at the bottom for the priest. He sullenly handed the basket over to the man they had engaged for the day to escort them to the shrine. Adi wasn't happy to have been relieved of his duties.

'Can this man be trusted?' Marcellus asked.

Silvius shrugged helplessly. 'You insisted. I can't vouch for temporary help.'

They set off along the main street, past the angadi, on their way out of Maruvum. Silvius went out of his way to acknowledge, and stop and speak to a number of people, advertising the fact that they were visiting the shrine in Pattinam. Just as they reached the arched gate leading out of town, Zhang materialized out of thin air.

'Going to steal a few more gods, are we?' he jeered.

The Romans ignored him and walked on.

'How do you know *him*?' Silvius asked quietly once they were out of earshot.

'I saw him a few days ago at the angadi. Who is he?' In the excitement of the events that night, he had forgotten to ask about Zhang.

'Zhang, the Buddhist. He has been here for several years – perhaps nearly as long as I've been. The locals have their own gods, and the merchants follow the Mahaviran, but this man tries to convert everyone to follow his god. He has a reputation for picking fights with anyone who isn't willing to listen.' Silvius smiled conspiratorially. 'There was a time when I thought he was a spy, but I know better now. The idiot told me once that silk comes from worms!'

Marcellus burst out laughing at the thought of worms weaving the emperor's toga. But then another thought struck him.

'Pearls come from oysters,' he murmured. Silvius didn't deign to reply.

As they walked further away from Maruvum, the smell of salt receded and it was perceptibly less humid. The late afternoon sun traversed west over the hills, lighting up the horizon. The town that Marcellus had come to know over the past several weeks was all about the sea, the fish, the warehouses and the *angadi*, and there was hardly a tree to be seen other than the mangroves and palms by the waters. In contrast, the wide avenue they were now travelling along was lined with enormous banyan and peepul trees. Beyond the foliage, on either side, he could see mango and cashew groves and, further still, what looked like tilled farmland.

About two *stadia* later, a statue made of wood and straw came into view: a menacing figure – tall and broad-chested – sitting on an equally fierce-looking bull that was sticking out its tongue. On one arm, he wielded a billhook.

'Aiyanar. Natives stop and pray to him before they come to our part of town.'

'Why, are they afraid of us?'

'Not us, they are scared of the fisherfolk and gypsies. The shop owners stop here every morning.'

'The fisherfolk seem friendly.'

'Say that to Kalachari, the jeweller whose throat was slit open last year. How naive you are, my dear boy.'

'Did they find out who did it?'

'One of your friendly fishermen, as it turned out.'

'Did they find any evidence?' It was fair to say that after his own trial, Marcellus didn't possess much faith in the Chola justice system. Not that he possessed much faith in the Roman justice system either, but, thanks to his father, he was kept away from facing the brunt of its injustices.

'As much as was needed to drown him and send his family into exile. Which admittedly is not much, but trust me, men get executed for much less where I come from. You cannot trust any of them.'

You never know when they will turn and stab you while you are asleep; you can never be too careful. It was a common enough refrain in Rome when speaking about slaves. He had often wondered how his father had felt about this, given his ancestry – but did he care? And even if Gaius did have an opinion about this, he had never mentioned it to Marcellus. They didn't share confidences of this kind. Theirs wasn't that kind of relationship. In his childhood, he'd barely spoken to his father, though they lived under the same roof. But he knew that Gaius took an interest in his education. And when he had come of age and started working in the warehouses, it was all about work and trade. His brother, on the other hand, shared a more filial relationship with their father, but not him. Never him.

'And who do the fishermen pray to on their way to Pattinam?'

'They don't have a reason to go there. They will be driven out of town if they are seen there.'

Soon, they reached a three-way crossing that served as the border of Pattinam. They turned left and a few hundred paces later, Marcellus saw a sight that filled him with a longing for Rome – a large reservoir with steps going down to the water on all four sides.

Baths! Oh, how he missed them!

On the side closest to the path, women of all ages were bathing, splashing each other and laughing. On the opposite side, he saw men engaged in similar activities. There were a few women on the steps, drying out their garments and changing into dry clothes. Their clothing consisted of a single long yard of muslin wrapped around their lower bodies and, in some cases, draped over their shoulders as well. Most of the younger women adorned themselves with flower garlands over their clothes.

'Their doe-eyes will make you melt, the fragrance of turmeric and jasmine will assault you from a pagam away; they are like apsaras, shy and gentle. They are coy and hardly speak; they hide behind doors and windows waiting for you to speak and pretend not to listen.'

If Marcellus needed any further proof of his friend's inexperience with the women of his own country, here it was laid bare before him. He did catch a whiff of turmeric and jasmine, but that was where the description ended. Their eyes were large and round, like that of a fish. None of them were hiding behind anything as far as he could see; they were changing their clothes as if in the privacy of their chambers and chattering away while doing so. Vallavan clearly needed to get out more.

'Do you think they smear sandalwood paste all over themselves?' he overheard a girl asking another. It was then he realized that the women were all staring at Silvius with undisguised curiosity, which was making the old man rather uncomfortable. A flesh-and-blood fair-skinned Yavana, however much he had gone native, may be passé in the portside of town, but not here in Pattinam. Marcellus was not too much of an anomaly thanks to his relatively darker skin and, for once, he was glad of his ancestry.

'The younger one looks almost human. He is not as pale as the other one, but why hasn't he covered his legs?'

Marcellus now wished he had followed Silvius's example and dressed in the native garb; he could have easily blended in. He looked down at his legs nervously.

'Pretend that you don't understand what they say. They don't expect you to anyway.'

'Are we allowed in these baths?' he asked hopefully.

'Let me draw your attention, young master, to those two soldiers in the corner there... The ones with the lances. They will pounce on you the moment your foot touches the water. Now, walk straight on!'

They continued in silence until they reached another intersection. On their right was an avenue with large gardens and groves on either side. He could make out a few two-storey mansions hidden between the trees.

'The street of merchants,' said Silvius, gesturing at the stretch before them. 'They may lack the columns of your father's villa in the Aventine, but don't be deceived. They more than make up for it inside.'

Marcellus remembered that Vallavan had spoken eloquently of his town's mansions and gardens, of the street of elephants and the king's way, of boulevards that reverberated with the sounds of the flute and the lute. His villa must be somewhere close by.

'Vallavan, my friend from –'

'Are you referring to the stowaway?'

'He wasn't a stowaway. He paid Hippalus many times –'

'Did he now? I am not aware of any payment being made and, if it was, I can assure you it did not make it to my accounts. As I have brought to your attention already, I am only aware of the payment made from our side. In any case, no real merchant gets lost. Young master, I am sorry to say this, but you have been the victim of deception.'

Marcellus did not see the point in replying and Silvius continued with his geography lesson as if he had never been interrupted.

'Now, look left – this is the street of Brahmanas and it leads to the king's palace. I'd caution you to stop staring. They will have to make special offerings to cleanse the pollution if our eyes fall on them.'

'We are pollutants?'

'But nowhere near the bottom; in fact, you'll be glad to know that we are rather close to the top. The fisherfolk, for instance, shouldn't be seen within *mille passus* of this place. This is not an egalitarian paradise, I am afraid. Not like Rome, where even slaves are allowed inside temples.'

'Only to work hard and carry sacrificial offerings.'

'Ah, yes, that is there.' Silvius sighed. 'Here in Puhar, you won't see temples of the kind you are used to.'

Marcellus was taken aback. He'd never heard of a town without temples.

'People go to priests and astrologers to make their offerings and prayers. The gods are usually found in hillside and wayside shrines, while urban centres celebrate them during festivals. But the mercantile Jainas have built a number of statue houses in the city over the past few decades and the Brahmana priests don't want to be left behind. Most merchants follow the Mahaviran and the priests feel it is only a matter of time before their gods are entirely abandoned. So, in retaliation, they have built a shrine in town – the temple of Pillayar, the elephant-headed god, funded by royal patronage.' He lowered his voice. 'Now this is where we are supposedly meeting your new-found friends.'

The temple was not far from where they were. They passed a series of lotus ponds beyond which the shrine came into view. It was small by Roman standards and was a rather simple affair. The sanctum was a square structure made of granite, surrounded by a shaded courtyard with a row of cylindrical pillars made of carved wood. It was too dark to see the idol from where they stood. As they entered the courtyard, two docents were diligently lighting the lamps that hung from the ceiling. The temple was slowly beginning to fill up with men. On a raised platform sat two of the priest's helpers, one of whom ran into the sanctum as soon as he saw the foreign visitors. The man who had carried their basket put it down gently in front of the platform and withdrew discreetly.

A moment later, the priest came out of the sanctum, smiling from ear to ear. He was a fat man of indeterminate age, and he wore a single piece of cloth folded through his legs and covering his upper body – not very different from what the women wore in the baths. A well-oiled tuft of hair spouted from his otherwise bald head.

'Welcome,' he said. 'I am glad you have finally decided to pay Ganesha a visit.'

Silvius smiled and rushed to explain. 'We were waiting for the most auspicious of days to pay our respects to the god. The Navallur astrologer suggested that we wait until today. Otherwise, you can be certain that I would have brought my young master here on his first evening.'

Marcellus had heard enough to know that the priests and merchant princes were the real powers behind the Chola throne, and if this man was the chief priest in the first Brahmana temple to grace this town, he must be a powerful man indeed. It wouldn't hurt to be respectful to him and Silvius knew it too. But an astrologer being consulted in the matter of their temple visit? In his opinion, Silvius was being unnecessarily obsequious.

'As you say, Silvius-ayya.' The priest continued smiling, but it was difficult to decipher whether he believed them or not. 'I hear he can speak Tamil?' He turned to look at Marcellus.

News travelled fast here.

'Just a few words, swamy. It is not an easy language for us foreigners to learn.'

'And yet Silvius-ayya speaks it like a native!' The priest laughed and addressed Marcellus once again. 'What brings you to our humble Chola country?'

'I came to see for myself the beauty of your blessed kingdom, and to trade with your countrymen. May you and your god ensure that our lands continue to trade with each other in the ages to come.'

When in doubt, flatter. Thank you, Diodorus, Marcellus thought.

'Why, young lord, has anything led you to believe that the relationship between our lands will not be what it is today?' the priest asked, his eyes narrowing.

Silvius cut in before Marcellus could speak. 'Why do you say that, swamy? There is no question about that, but we need Ganesha's blessings so that it continues to be so.'

'Yes, indeed. What do I, a simple priest, know of matters of trade other than to pass on your message to him?' the priest said. 'He will hear your prayers and I will be your dutiful messenger. You have a god of beginnings too, I gather?'

'Janus, the only –' Marcellus began, but Silvius interrupted again.

He was taking no chances. 'We don't have a temple for Janus here and who knows whether his power holds in your country. We dare to hope that Ganesha and Janus can conspire for our well-being.'

The priest roared with laughter. 'You are a clever man, Silvius. Your people and us, we understand each other – and our gods do too. I am sure you will agree with me that it is the sanctimonious followers of the Buddha and those of Mahaviran who pose a real danger to our culture and to this kingdom. I suspect they'll come over to yours too if we let them continue in this manner.'

Marcellus thought of Zhang and wondered what his people had done to incur this priest's wrath. Silvius, meanwhile, agreed wholeheartedly. 'Any peoples who don't believe in the power of trade and industry, and that of the gods who enable them, are a danger to our world, swamy.'

The priest frowned. 'Hmm, you'd think the merchants would think so too, but they seem to be taken in by these new-age gods. Ah well, they will see the truth in the end. We'll see to it.'

A docent approached and signalled, at which the priest took his leave. He walked back quickly into the sanctum and closed the thick wooden door behind him.

'Do we get to see the god?'

'We now wait for the sanctum to open. The priest will perform the rituals and will be granted a special audience with the god first. Once he opens it to the world, the devotees can pray. Look at the people filling up behind us – they are hoping for a first look as soon as the door opens.'

'There are a lot of people. Looks like the entire town will be here.'

Silvius shook his head. 'Only Brahmanas are allowed on that side of the line,' he said, pointing to a rope tied from one pillar to another across the path. 'Where we stand now is reserved for the merchant families, and we are being granted a special favour today. It is not every day that Yavanas are allowed to see Ganesha. Other than for Brahmanas, royals and merchants, no one is allowed inside this temple. Death by elephant.'

Marcellus winced. 'Not a great tactic to win the hearts of the masses if you ask me. Especially if they are worried about people moving away from their gods.'

'My dear fellow, you need to learn so much more about this world. It's not the huddled masses the priests want; they have the royals by their privates, and now they want the merchants too. Once they have them, it's as good as having the rest.'

'How will the Appans – ?'

'*Hush!*'

Just at that moment, there was a sudden ringing of bells from outside the temple, and the Yavanas turned to see a palanquin being set down in front of the lotus pond. A dour woman wrapped in a parrot-green garment stepped out and a young girl followed her out gingerly. Every eye in the temple was on them. The girl was fair, with flowers in her hair and adorning her upper body. An indigo-blue garment was wound around her lithe frame. She held on to the older woman's hand, but looked curiously to the left and right until she was admonished by the older woman to keep her gaze lowered.

'Your lucky day, young master. That palanquin has gold encrusted on its roof and that doesn't come cheap in this town. As a matter of fact, I recognize that insignia rather well. What a coincidence that your friend's family is here,' Silvius whispered.

The older woman led the young girl down the courtyard, and they came to a stop across Silvius and him.

The girl looked straight at Marcellus before springing back, surprised. She hadn't expected to see foreigners. Marcellus realized that this must be Vallavan's younger sister, Kannaki, the little one in the family whom he was so fond of. He had talked about his thankai with much affection so often during their journey. Not like his akka, he had said.

As he stared at the girl, a thousand bells started ringing as the door to the sanctum opened. The elephant-headed god wore a blood-red robe that shone with the light of a hundred lamps, and his most distinctive feature was his elephant trunk, sheathed in a silver ribbon. The priest circled a flame in front of the god, while chanting in a language that sounded entirely alien to Marcellus. Around him, devotees were engaged in their own intense, private conversation with the god. But the girl across him had no time for all this; she was staring at him – she seemed to have got over her initial shock. Silvius, who had his eyes tightly shut and palms folded, gave him a hard nudge with his elbow. Marcellus immediately brought his hands together and looked down. His eyes fell on her small, soft feet and ankles, adorned with gold anklets, and her toes covered with silver toe rings.

The priest stepped out of the sanctum with the lamp in his hand. The crowd gathered around, cupped their palms over the flame and brought their hands to their eyes. A sudden strong gust of wind blew from nowhere and the flame went out, as did a number of lamps in the courtyard. The temple was suddenly plunged into near darkness.

A moment later, a girl's scream rent the air.

'My necklace! Someone snatched my necklace!'

Kannaki!

Marcellus saw a figure darting out of the crowd and without a moment's hesitation, he gave pursuit. He could make out the man heading for the wall at the far end of the compound, and he picked up pace to catch up with him. Behind him a crowd of men followed, but they were still too far away. The man scaled the wall and vanished. Marcellus did not hesitate, not with the girl watching him from behind. He scaled the wall easily and, without a second thought, jumped down to the other side.

'*Ouch!*' he screamed as he landed on a bed of prickles. Before he could scramble to his feet, he felt himself being picked up.

'Who are you? I am following a thief!' he shouted.

But it was to no avail – he was blindfolded, bound and gagged, and bundled into a sack. By the time the first of the men from the temple had climbed the wall, Marcellus's abductors were well past the first clump of trees, hidden from view.

8

WHAT SHE SAID

Woe befall the Navallur astrologer on whose advice I went to the Pillayar temple with my daughter. I should have listened to Kavunti Adikal, who warned me not to follow false gods. We are indeed very fortunate to follow the path of the austere Mahaviran, she had said, but I did not heed her then. Just mark my words, my lord and husband, from now on I have no need for other gods, and certainly not those of the Brahmanas – an elephant head, can you believe it? The valorous Aiyanar of the lower castes is at least useful in warding off ghosts and robbers, but what is this god good for? You don't believe me? Once you hear the ordeal we have been through, you'll agree with me, my lord.

Taking the advice of the wretched man, whom I shall never consult again, I took my daughter, our little one, to the temple of Pillayar. You don't have to tell me that our girls don't leave their homes until they depart for their marital home; let it be said that Malathi Ammal was possessed by a yakshi on this occasion. I ordered the palanquin-bearers to take us there.

Ask not what happened, my son, ask what did not happen! From the time we alighted, strangers – common folk, lecherous shopkeepers, greedy priests – stared at us. There were tens, no, hundreds of them. They gawked at us like they leer at the girls on the balconies of the street of the courtesans. Oh my daughter, how many hundreds of evil stares were you subjected to in that place! A place of god, they say, but it is a den of iniquity, I tell you. Why else would there be Yavanas in a place of worship? Yes, there were Yavanas standing across us in the courtyard.

Don't you have any shame, my lord? How would I know who they were or what they looked like? Do you think I spend my time staring at strange men? What do you take me for? Listen to me, Manaykan, listen to my vow – when my children and you have no need of me, I will starve myself to death. Only then you'll understand the virtue of Malathi Ammal.

My son, in the hope that you understand me, I'll tell *you* what happened next. The place was thrown into pitch darkness as all the lamps suddenly went out – what more omens do I need? It is indeed a cursed place. Taking advantage of the darkness, a thief snatched Kannaki's maanga malai. No, son, I am not okay; these tears haven't stopped flowing since I left that wretched place. If that josier from Navallur comes through this door ever again, I will hit him with the ulakkai, so that he does not subject anyone else to the ignominy my poor girl had to go through. Our daughter screamed; what else was she to do? Just when I realized this was all a big mistake and we should turn back as quickly as possible, Kannaki ran after the thief!

What do you mean why didn't I stop her? Who do you think brought her home? I ran after her and pulled her down from the wall she was trying to climb, and I dragged her back to the palanquin all by myself. Your honour, my lord, my son, the honour of this house is in ruins. Not only has a necklace been stolen – where is the king, if I may ask? Where is that man who is supposed to guarantee our safety when burglars run wild? – but the whole of Puhar watched me drag your daughter through the temple and push her into the palanquin. Who'll marry her now?

Why, you ask? You think I didn't enquire? It is the Yavana, she says. The Yavana ran after the thief and she ran after him. He is Vallavan's friend, the man who brought him home in his ship and she thought she'd follow him – that's what the elephant god had ordered her to do. Now do you understand why I will not go after these gods any more? Ganesha possessed our daughter and told her to run after the *Yavana*!

You, unfortunate older daughter of mine! Did you have anything to do with this? I knew the moment we set our eyes on you before we left for the temple that it was a bad omen. Have you done anything to possess your sister? May your ill luck not befall her!

How do I know what happened to the Yavana, my son? Didn't I have enough to do, getting my daughter home, or did you expect me to run after Yavanas too? Look at her now, the runaway, standing in the corner, with no contrition on her face. Oh, what has happened to my little one? Are you... *Kannaki!* Why are you standing in a pool of blood? What have you done now?

9

THE DEAL

Marcellus may have acted instinctively in following the chain-snatcher, but his actions weren't entirely bereft of logic. Pearls or not, he needed to get to Korkai and the Appans were his best bet. Since they had started on their journey from Maruvum to Pattinam, he had been waiting for a sign. The robbery at the temple was either a diversion or they had expected him to follow the thief, and he chose the latter. He didn't, however, consider the possibility of being abducted and that this particular robbery may have had nothing to do with the Appans. Now that he was being carried in a rice sack among the groves, he had ample time to consider such possibilities.

Were his abductors petty chain-snatchers and, if so, why kidnap him? Obviously, they had the wrong man; he didn't know anyone in Pattinam. Alternatively, it was possible that they knew who he was, and they were planning to hold him to ransom. It wasn't uncommon in Rome and he had heard that it happened frequently to merchants in foreign lands as well. Little did they know that it was of no use in his case. He wondered whether his father would come to hear of it at all. What would he make of his able-bodied son, tutored in the art of battle by a *magistri*, defenceless against two common thieves in this little kingdom? He'd probably be glad that it was Marcellus who was kidnapped, and not his brother. As for Hippalus and his crew, they'd have a good laugh over the little master being kidnapped in his attempt to catch a common thief. He'd have to find a way out of this predicament himself; no help would be forthcoming.

He wiggled his legs to check the knots. They were tied professionally, but clearly his kidnappers hadn't accounted for the possibility of the victim being well trained. If they stopped even for a moment, he would be able to untie the knots. They couldn't possibly carry him for very long without stopping; he could wait.

'What do these Yavanas eat that make them so heavy?' one of his attackers grunted.

'Hush!'

'He is a Yavana, he knows no Tamil, and all I said was that he is heavy! He must know that already,' said the first voice indignantly.

'Be quiet, Muthu, and don't draw any more attention.'

'But his long legs weigh so much that even our Kesavan elephant won't be able to lift him.'

'I am sick of your whining, cousin. Let us stop for a while, but just a vinadi as we are expected at the mandapam soon.'

The men stopped and plonked Marcellus down on the hard ground, and he heard them gasping for breath. They must be exhausted, and this was his chance – he felt his way around the knot and untied his hands quickly.

These are things that every slave knows, gladiator or not. You should too, as who knows when the tide will turn?

Thank you, Magnus, for the foresight. And thank you, Father, for insisting on the training, Marcellus thought as he wiggled around in the sack.

'What do they want from him?' Muthu asked, his voice fading as he drew large gasps of air.

'His father is a rich merchant in Yavana country. They are hoping he will give them gold to free his son,' the second replied.

'Whatever they get, they would have to spend more than that in feeding him!'

A moment later, he heard the men relieving themselves, and used the opportunity to get his hands out, pull off the blindfold and the gag. He peered out of the sack. Both men had their backs to him. The brand which they had used to light the way was kept close to him on the ground.

'Why don't we take the gold ourselves? Why should we take him to them?' Muthu asked. He was the tall, stocky one, Marcellus understood.

'You will get us both killed. Those men are dangerous; they aren't to be messed with!'

'They are cowards! If they were so brave, why couldn't they kidnap him themselves?'

'Muthu, stop saying these things now. They pay us well and we should treat them like gods.'

'Which god sends you to kidnap a Yavana who weighs as much as an elephant?'

Marcellus stayed where he was and weighed his options. Listening to them, there was some merit in letting them reach their destination; these were only hired goons and he would be able to find out who had ordered the kidnapping in the first place.

Muthu turned around, but he was too excited to notice that the sack's mouth was open and that his victim's blindfold was off. 'He should have coins in his clothes. At least let us get those.'

'What if they find out?' The second man sounded hesitant.

'They won't believe him and anyway he doesn't speak Tamil!'

'That's true. Is he wearing any jewellery?'

'Let me see…' Muthu walked towards him, but Marcellus was

ready. His hand came out from behind and punched Muthu on his face.

'*Ahhh!*' Muthu screamed, and before he could react, Marcellus punched him again. The Yavana went straight for the brand and swung it around, threatening the second man. The two men recovered quickly, but they didn't dare come too close to the fire.

'Who are you? Who sent you?' Marcellus shouted.

'Mari! The Yavana speaks Tamil!' exclaimed Muthu in disbelief.

'It is time to run. This won't end well,' shouted his accomplice. They managed to reach the nearest clump of trees before a man emerged and caught them by their ears, and dragged them back into the clearing. Marcellus, too focused on them, started in surprise as his weapon was suddenly wrested out of his hand by two men behind him.

Maruthappan.

'You Chola oafs!' Maruthappan said. 'We should have known not to trust you with this. You nearly bungled the whole thing. You wanted to make off with him, did you now?'

'No, ayya,' Mari said in a plaintive voice. 'Muthu sometimes doesn't know what he is saying. We weren't –'

'Enough! Tie them up and bring them along with us. Don't let them out of sight,' Maruthappan ordered his men before turning to Marcellus. 'Nothing to be afraid of, Yavana lord. I apologize for the inconvenience. I promise you that you will be returned home safe and sound, and very much in one piece.'

Marcellus played the part that was expected of him. He asked, incredulously, 'Does Silvius know of this kidnapping?'

'You are too dramatic, young lord. We are singers, not koothu performers. Silvius knows only what he needs to know. Come with us. They are waiting for you.'

Marcellus walked alongside Maruthappan in indignant silence and they went single file down a small path by the side of the woods.

'Who am I meeting?' he asked finally.

'Be patient, we are nearly there,' Maruthappan told him and turned around to his men. 'What are those two making that racket for? Ask them if they want their tongues cut off!'

After a while, they reached a clearing with a mandapam – a raised stone structure with pillars on all four sides, the kind frequented by weary travellers on long journeys to rest, quench their thirst and pray for a safe onward journey. Firelight lit up one side of the mandapam, where he could make out a few shadows.

'Here we are,' Maruthappan shouted as they walked up the steps. 'The Yavana lord is here, and we also have the Kavilur rascals – they nearly lost our man.'

Marcellus could now see four men in the dark on the other side of the mandapam. Three of them rose when they saw the visitors, came forward and stared curiously at him. Two appeared to be bodyguards or soldiers, from the spears and swords at their sides. The third man turned to Maruthappan.

'Are you sure this is him? He doesn't look like a Yavana...'

'It is him, I swear. If you had met his father, you wouldn't doubt it.'

'Yavana, greetings from the Kadalamman, the guardian goddess of Korkai... We are glad to meet you... Welcome,' the man addressed Marcellus in broken Latin.

'I was brought here forcefully. Since when did a Yavana merchant get kidnapped in this kingdom? If Rome comes to know of this, there will be repercussions,' Marcellus warned, speaking in Tamil.

The man smiled and replied, 'Rome is far away from here. And I am told they have other things to worry about in these times.'

'Perhaps. But this is no way to treat a man of trade. I was informed of your hospitality, but I would never have guessed that it involved tricking and kidnapping. A cowardly act such as this doesn't reflect well on you, sir!'

'There is nothing cowardly about your abduction. Let me assure you that stealing you away from the heart of the Chola capital is one of the bravest acts this city of cowards has ever seen. I'd go to the extent of saying that these men here are the bravest Cholas I have ever encountered.'

As if on cue, the guards guffawed. The two kidnappers were being held at the ground level below the mandapam, but they could still hear what was being said, and Marcellus saw them look up expectantly. As the key protagonists in the brave act, they could still receive some remuneration.

'Take them away from here,' Maruthappan shouted. His men led the two abductors away.

'But we got him here!' Muthu wailed and was promptly rewarded with a slap.

The fourth man, who had been seated in the dark until now, moved forward towards him. He was a wrinkled old man with a scratchy, barely audible voice.

'Veerappan,' he addressed the man who had spoken to Marcellus. 'You will not disparage the Cholas in their own land without reason. We have come here like common thieves, and this young man is right – this is not a welcome fit for a Yavana merchant.'

'But, ayya, you realize the danger we are under in Puhar! We could not possibly have done anything else.'

So Maruthappan wasn't lying; these were the Appan brothers themselves and this was indeed the meeting he was supposed to be in.

'You could have shown us some respect by letting us know in advance how we were supposed to meet,' he said. 'This kidnapping will sow more suspicion in the minds of the Chola authorities, who are already on high alert. We've been warned to stay away from you.'

Veerappan glared at him and retorted, 'What choice do we have under the tiger flag? We are reduced to common thieves; our wares taxed at punitive rates. The Chola merchants live in luxury here in this golden city, while we languish in poverty and our people starve.'

'Thambi! We didn't come all the way so that you can give a speech on the nature of Chola rule to a young Yavana, who neither knows nor cares about our country. We came here to speak to him about pearls and that is what we will do,' the senior Appan admonished Veerappan.

There was an uncomfortable silence. Marcellus waited for the men to sort things out among themselves. The more time they took, the more time he had to plan his strategy.

'All right.' Veerappan's voice softened and he turned to Marcellus. 'I am under the impression that you will need the entire crop this season. Is that true?'

'That depends on the price.'

Marcellus did not have the faintest idea how much the entire crop would entail, but there was no point in displaying his ignorance here.

'How will you pay us?'

'My father has traded in your kingdom for decades. Everyone knows that he is an honourable man.'

'But you are not your father. And even then, he has traded only under Chola or Pandya law. What we are about to do here has no precedence. This trade will be under the laws of my family, but it will also be in contravention of existing Chola laws. Your ship will have to come to Korkai because we will not be able to deliver to your warehouse here in Puhar. We will need half the payment before loading.'

That the *Minerva* would have to dock near Korkai was good news in one sense; it was his only way to get there, and get there he must. That much he had promised his father. But he also knew by now that the *Minerva* couldn't simply glide into the Pandya port town without raising suspicion. What they were suggesting was dangerous, if not downright suicidal.

'How much can you supply?' he asked.

'Three-quarters of your ship's cargo.'

Marcellus tried to hide his surprise as he quickly calculated what this meant. On a regular journey, the *Minerva* took about 30,000 *modii* of goods – a significant portion of which consisted of cloves, cardamom, pepper, cotton and silk. If the Appans were able to supply three-quarters of that in pearls, his father would have enough to sell across the empire and then some. Lucrative as it would be, Marcellus could not ignore their regular cargo. He would not only have to smuggle the pearls out of Korkai, but also find a way for the spices in the warehouse to make their way to Rome on some other vessel. They would not last until the following year.

'How do we know you will deliver the shipment? I can't let my ship leave Puhar empty, without any assurances.'

'We do what we say and your father trusted us. As for getting out of Puhar, all of us know that your captain can be very resourceful. You claim to have conquered half the world, but you are now frightened to leave a small seaport?' Veerappan sniggered, but stopped abruptly as the old man's steely eyes fell on him.

'How much?' Marcellus came to the point. That was what this was all about anyway. These men wouldn't have been here and executed such an elaborate plan to abduct him if they hadn't been serious. They knew he wanted the pearls, but they didn't know how much he was willing to pay for them.

'Same as you pay for silk. An oyster for a yarn.'

Marcellus drew in a sharp breath.

'And we mean the silk that you get from Thinae... Not the inferior material that traders sell here in Chola country.'

'They cannot be worth that much.'

'You decide how much it is worth to you. Please remember that we may have brought you to this mandapam, but we didn't approach you to trade. We only came to you because we were told that you were looking for us. We don't have a shortage of buyers. The northern kingdoms will take the pearls off our hands gladly if you do not wish to proceed.'

By now he was in familiar territory.

'You may not have a shortage of buyers, but you have no way of reaching them,' he said, smiling. 'Which northern kingdom is brave enough to send ships to Korkai, bypassing the Cholas? Will Satkarni of Amaravati dare to cross the Chola navy and send his ships to Korkai?'

Everyone stayed silent for a few moments. Maruthappan, who had been quiet all along, spoke up.

'Yavana, your father wanted to negotiate and trade with us. If you don't want to, we will leave it at that.'

'But there can't be a negotiation while I am being held hostage!' Marcellus protested.

The old man muttered something under his breath and then said aloud abruptly, 'You are free to go, young Yavana. No one will stop you. We should not have come, or brought you here for that matter. We cannot negotiate with you as we are not selling commodities like the spices you trade in – pearls aren't things that grow on trees. I lose men and women to the Kadalamman regularly in this business. For every person I lose, I hold myself responsible. Their children become my children. I cannot, and will not, gamble away their future.'

Marcellus considered his position. He felt an affinity to this old man who talked of a world that was alien to him, and yet felt so familiar. But this was trade and he was, first and foremost, his father's son. He could stall and leave, but he doubted whether this door would ever open again. He knew what he had to do. For the first time since the *Minerva* had left the harbour at Myos Hormos, he was glad that it was not his brother who was here in this situation. His brother would have absolutely no idea what to offer.

'Pepper. I will pay the same price as for pepper.'

'You think our pearls are comparable to that contemptible black seed from the Chera hill dwellers?' Veerappan yelled. But Marcellus noticed that the old man had sat back down on the floor and relief had flooded Maruthappan's face. This discussion was over – the deal was done. These people were desperate if all they had hoped for was the price of pepper. He should have negotiated the price further down.

'A quarter of the gold upfront, here in Puhar. The rest at Korkai, once the loading is complete.' He drove in his advantage as it slowly dawned on the Appans that they may have been too transparent. But despite Veerappan's bluster, there was no going back now.

A few moments later, Maruthappan lit a lamp using camphor and brought it to the old man, who looked at Marcellus straight in the eye as he put his hand firmly over the flame and extinguished it. 'I promise to fill your ship with the best of pearls from my sea,' he said. Before Marcellus could process what was happening, he found himself in front of another lit lamp and all attention was on him. He thought of his brother, his father and the request he had made; trade was a bonus. He pressed down on the flame with his palm until it went out. His palm stung as he pulled it back.

The meeting concluded, Maruthappan walked with him to the road, while the rest of them stayed at the mandapam. When he came out of what he thought was the forest, he discovered to his surprise that they were almost at Maruvum, and he could see the port gate from his vantage point. The two abductors, he was informed, would be taken by Maruthappan's men back to Pattinam, but it wasn't clear to Marcellus what would happen to them.

'Local thugs,' Maruthappan explained when he enquired.

'Will they talk?'

'My men will put the fear of Kali into them, and by morning, they would have forgotten everything about the night. They both have families in Pandya lands; they know better than to talk.'

Maruthappan took leave of him just before they reached the entrance to the harbour.

'Young lord, I will await you in Korkai, where you'll feel at home,' he said gently. 'But be careful in this kingdom; it is not safe.'

'Then I look forward to seeing you at home.' Marcellus smiled and said goodbye.

He took his time on the way back as he wanted old Silvius to sweat a while. There was no reason for him to think this had been easy. When he finally reached his house, he found Silvius pacing the length of the corridor.

'There you are! I can't believe that the double-crossing bastards took you and left me alone. I was supposed to go with you. Your father would have had me tortured –'

'I am fine, Silvius.'

'I know that, young master. The question is this: what is the price you agreed to?'

He should have known that the old man didn't care what happened to him as long as he got the pearls at bargain price. He hesitated before saying, 'Pepper,' and before Silvius could react, there was a knock on the door. He signalled Marcellus to hide behind a pillar, while he made his way to the door. Marcellus couldn't make out what was being said, and Silvius returned alone sometime later, a palm leaf in hand.

'An invitation addressed to you – your first in Puhar,' he told Marcellus. 'To the Manaykan residence. Vallavan, the young merchant of Puhar, requests the pleasure of your company on the occasion of the victory day, to mark our king's triumph over all Tamil lands, and to celebrate the maiden of the household's blooming womanhood. And that is not all. The messenger wanted to confirm that you reached home safe and sound.'

Silvius looked at the young man thoughtfully, as if seeing him for the first time. Marcellus didn't miss it. He'd have to be very careful from now. It was only a question of time before Silvius would be on to him.

10

THE PRIME MINISTER AND THE SPY

In the courtyard of the royal quarters, the prime minster was about to step into his palanquin when he caught sight of an old woman gesticulating wildly to the guards outside the Hearing Hall.

'Find out what she wants,' he said to his aide, who motioned quickly to the guards.

'Let it not worry you, Your Highness,' one of the guards said. 'The hag is dumb and no one can understand what she is trying to say. We told her that the administrator is not here today, but she refuses to leave.'

'I'll see her,' the prime minister said, and started walking back to his quarters.

'But, Your Highness,' the aide whispered, 'you wished to leave early –'

'I can't drive a poor dumb woman away without hearing her petition. The king will not tolerate it.'

A few minutes later, the woman was ushered into his office. The prime minister waited for the aide to leave before he turned to her and said dryly, 'Next time, I suggest you do away with the theatrics and use the signet ring I've given you. They'll let you in without any trouble.'

'But they will know, Your Highness. *I* cannot trust anyone!' replied the woman who wasn't at all what she appeared to be.

'Well, I am late, and I need to leave for Manaykan's feast. What news from the city?'

'I am informed that tortoise meat is being procured from down the coast especially for the occasion. You do not want to miss it, Your Highness.'

'Do you have any information other than the dinner menu?' asked the prime minister, his impatience showing in his voice.

'The town is peaceful and people go about their business, but they miss their king. The angadi is rife with rumours of his absence.'

'What are they saying?'

'That he cares more about Uraiyur and the peasants of the delta than those of us in Puhar; he spends his time with his elephants hunting for sport. That he is enamoured of the girls of the country –'

'Nonsense!'

'– and that he is a puppet of the priests in the holy island, who want the place for themselves.'

'Surely the king can give his land to whoever he chooses?'

'I am the messenger here, Your Highness. I am only conveying what I've heard. There is also talk of bandits attacking Puhar while the king is away.'

'These infernal dacoits are everywhere! And the number of crimes have gone up here in town. But I can assure you that this city continues to be well guarded. Have you actually seen any of the bandits here in Puhar?'

'No.'

'Then they know how to disguise themselves. Keep your ears and eyes open. They are emboldened and are attacking villages on the outskirts.'

'There is some talk of them recruiting inland to establish a militia...'

'It would be a terrible blow to us if they set up and ran this sort of a parallel administration. We cannot let it happen. I'd like to find out more about these bandits in the kingdom. Who is their leader and what are their plans? Make this your priority.'

'Yes, Your Highness,' said the spy dutifully.

'Who else have you seen?'

'Pandya spies are about – nothing new there. I haven't seen much of the Cheras the past few weeks, but this is to be expected as the pirate menace in the western sea seems to require all their attention now. But we have our friends from the north to worry about –'

'Your friends, you mean?'

'I ran into a man recently at an inn, who I believe is a spy, an important one... One of Satkarni's men.'

'Satkarni is busy with unfinished business in the west. We have established that. In fact, if I remember it right, it was *you* who confirmed it for us.'

'But that was some time ago. His men are active and they may be heading inland... I suspect they are going towards where the dam is being built.'

'To Uraiyur?' The prime minister started and shook his head. 'Must be routine work. Why would they want to go there?'

'The king is there; the action is all there!'

'Is it? In any case, I am heading to the anicut site myself soon.'

'There is a rumour that the Chola capital will be shifted to Uraiyur.'

The prime minister laughed. 'I see. So people haven't caught on to the fact that this kingdom runs because of this port.'

'But the royal entourage has not been here for a while. You run the city and are the ruler while the king is not in town.'

'He may not be here himself, but Karikalan is here in spirit. Don't forget that he has eyes everywhere. He will be back here once the Kallanai, his grand anicut, the dam to channel the Kaveri, is completed. That's why I am going there too – for the opening.'

'When is a dam just a dam?'

'Is that a question?'

'It is meant to be rhetorical.'

'Keep your rhetoric and speculations to yourself.'

'But you pay me for them!'

'I pay you for facts.'

The spy grinned. 'I am glad you can tell the difference.'

'You forget who you are speaking to,' the prime minister warned. 'Anything else?'

'The merchants are restless. They are anxious about the Pandya trade.'

'Hmm...'

'A Yavana merchant and his captain were arrested some time ago –'

'Based on a kidnapping charge from one of our traders.'

'So they say, but the prisoners were released rather abruptly. I'd heard that the same merchant was himself kidnapped recently.'

'Ransom?'

'We don't know. It wasn't *our* people. Rumour has it that Pandya traders have approached the Yavanas directly.'

'*That* is against the law. The Pandyas know this, as do the Yavanas. They have been warned. They are not allowed to land in Pandya ports. Our navy takes care of that.'

'With the ban on Pandya ports and all the trouble with the pirates near Musiris, Yavana ships now come to Puhar. But this doesn't mean there aren't ways for them to trade with Pandyas and Cheras.'

'How do you mean?'

'I don't know, but I mean to find out. Speaking of merchants, I am told of a secret conclave of our traders today at Manaykan's residence.'

'That cannot be true… Not when I am there.'

'That's what my information says.'

'Well, your information isn't always accurate.'

'Yet, you find it useful.'

'Yes, I do indeed.' The prime minister rose to leave. 'The king needs me in Uraiyur and I'll be there until the pujai. The administrator here in Puhar cannot be trusted. If you have any urgent information, see my aide and he'll get a messenger through to me.'

'I am usually my own messenger, Your Highness.'

'I am aware of that, but the Chola kingdom is not just this city. The countryside may prove to be too much for you. And now, you may leave. I have to be in Manaykan's house soon. The tortoise beckons.'

'Not just the tortoise. There is a lady there who I am told –'

'Enough! You will desist from unnecessary speculation and slander!'

The spy withdrew hastily.

11

SISTERS AT HOME

The sun was yet to slide into Maraya Hill, but the boulevard of the merchants was already lit up with a thousand lamps. Every household on the street was invited to the feast at the Manaykan residence, an imposing two-storeyed mansion spread out over the northwest corner of the merchants' quarter. The grounds in front of the house consisted of a well-tended flower garden with jasmine, hibiscus and sunflower blooming in abundance. The mango and jackfruit groves were behind the house. On the eastern corner of the garden was a small alcove, with idols of Mahaviran and Murugan, both facing the entrance of the sprawling mansion. A raised platform went all the way around the house, dotted with wooden pillars that held up the tiled roof. The entrance was secured by enormous rosewood doors, with two identical carved yakshis on either side staring down at visitors menacingly. Inside, the house was essentially a series of courtyards, the middle one being the most ornate, with teak pillars and polished floors. There was a bustle of activity in the front courtyards as the evening's guests started trickling in. The first floor had low and sloping ceilings, but to make up for it, it boasted of a number of small oval windows through which the evening light came streaming in.

Perched on one of these windowsills, Kannaki spied on the guests making their way in. She had an unobstructed view of the main gate and the front garden. The maids were still plucking the last of the mallikai and nandiyavattom, which would soon be threaded into long strings to be offered to the visitors – garlands for the men and bangles for the women. Behind her, in the back courtyards, the feast was being cooked – bubbling away in large vats to feed the scores of guests who were expected. But the object of the day's festivities was not feeling particularly joyous. She hadn't been allowed outside the house since that evening at the Pillayar temple. Her life had changed in a flash, and it wasn't for the better. She blamed the young Yavana for her current predicament, as there was nothing else that had happened differently on that fateful day. He was the reason she was now in chains; forbidden to leave her room, even to pluck flowers from the garden, climb the mango trees in the backyard or accompany her father outside the house. She would not be allowed out of the house until her wedding day.

She was the first to run after him, the Yavana, as others stood around, confused. She was trying to scramble up the wall behind him, to help him catch the thief who had stolen her necklace, hitching up her pavadai, when her mother had grabbed her from behind, roughly and forcefully, and pulled her down. Back at home, she hadn't quite recovered from the adventure when her mother noticed it – a thin trail of blood running through the house and stopping just where she stood – and fainted immediately. The girl had become a woman. It was time for the ceremony that many on the boulevard had been eagerly anticipating. The Navallur josier was summoned immediately, despite her mother's protestations, to set an auspicious date, and the invitations were sent out that very night.

The trade guild had used the opportunity to convene a conference in the north wing later that night – for all the merchant princes and everyone who mattered in Puhar would be in attendance. And most were, at the moment, greeting each other in the courtyards downstairs and congratulating her father on the happy occasion. Many of the guests had sons who would be eligible to marry her, and there was no doubt in anyone's mind that her father would give her a mouth-watering dowry. A marriage with the Manaykan family would also result in an exceedingly lucrative trading partnership for both families involved. There were rumours that her marriage had already been arranged, but many still held out hope.

'You will see, akka, I'll soon escape this prison and be able to do everything like before. I wonder who it is that I will marry. What do you think?' asked Kannaki.

Kuzhali looked at her younger sister and wondered if she should be the one to burst her bubble. She was too young to understand that marriage was a prison in itself, much worse than the one she was in at the moment.

'Marriage is not what you think, kutti,' she said gently. 'You will have much less freedom than you have now; you'll be under the control of your husband and his family.'

'Do you really believe that, akka?' Kannaki's eyes widened.

'I don't believe it; I know it. Enjoy your time here at home while you can.'

'But… Isn't it ... Aren't you sad that your husband is dead?'

'I suppose so, but it's not the end of the world. I still have many other things to keep me occupied.'

'Do you wish for him to come back?'

Kuzhali shrugged. 'The dead don't come back. But this is not the time to talk about me. This day, my kutti, is yours.'

Kannaki nodded absently and turned her attention back to the window. Oh, there he was, the culprit, the reason she was shut in this room – the Yavana was making his way towards the house.

'Akka, he is here, the Yavana!'

Kuzhali ran to the window and the sisters gave Marcellus a thorough once-over. Dark as far as Yavanas went, his long, curly hair untied, no moustache, and, to top it all, he was wearing just a tunic and a shawl. No veshti! There was no way he was going to be able sit down cross-legged without harming his modesty. They looked at each other and burst out laughing.

~

Vallavan seemed overjoyed to see him, and Marcellus shared the feeling.

'We have been hearing many stories. I was anxious for your safety. Who were the kidnappers? How did you escape their clutches?' Words tripped over themselves as they escaped Vallavan's mouth.

'Some hooligans who thought I'd be carrying Roman gold. I told them that I didn't have any, but they didn't believe me. And I had to fight them to escape.' Marcellus shrugged.

'Like how we fought in Cana?'

'Not at all! This time I attacked them and they ran away from me, instead of the other way around. Your Chola men aren't quite the Arabs!'

'You haven't met any of our warriors yet. But enough of this talk – how are you, my friend? How is Puhar treating you?'

'Very well – so much so that I don't feel like a stranger in your country.'

Vallavan made no mention of Marcellus's arrest and trial, and the part his family played in it. Surely he would know; in fact, as per the magistrate, he had supplied the evidence claiming he had been kidnapped. But Marcellus did not bring it up. Instead, he wondered how Vallavan might react if he were to tell him about the deal he had struck with the Pandyas, but he swept away that temptation quickly. Friend or not, he had no intention of spending the rest of his life in the dungeons of Puhar.

'How is business?' he asked instead.

'We have had some recent successes with merchants in the West but…' Vallavan looked around and whispered, 'I am afraid our borders aren't safe any more, and we cannot guarantee the delivery of shipments.'

'Why is that?' Marcellus asked.

'There is news of rogue Pandya incursions in all main routes into the kingdom. The guild is getting restless and they want the king to act, but, unfortunately, he is inland in "Uraiyur", building the dam.'

'What do they expect him to do?'

'Maintain law and order, and bring the troublemakers to justice. We have the prime minister with us today. The guild impressed upon him the need for action.'

That explained the elaborate elephant procession Marcellus had seen on his way in.

'How is your brother?' he asked. He was curious about the boy who had accompanied his father on the day of his trial and, yet, he had never heard Vallavan mention a brother to him.

'My brother? I don't have a brother. You already know this!'

'But I saw on the day of the tr –'

'Oh, you mean Kuzhali, my akka. She likes to dress up as a man and go everywhere with my father – she has always been like that; even before she got married. She thinks she runs this place. You won't meet her today, I'm afraid. She is not allowed to take part in the festivities. But you have seen my little sister, Kannaki, haven't you?'

'Have I?' Marcellus feigned surprise, and pretended as if their encounter was slowly dawning on him. 'Oh, was she at the temple? Was it her necklace that was stolen?'

'Yes, that's her. You will see her as soon as it is time for the ritual bath.'

A bath? Clearly he had a lot left to learn about Chola feasts if they involved parading their daughters in a bathhouse in front of the assembled guests. Vallavan must have noticed his expression and he rushed in to explain.

'Not quite a bath. The women of the house pour turmeric water on her, and she receives all her gifts. It is a special occasion, but I must say I feel sad, as she will soon leave us to get married. I will miss her.'

This wasn't so different from patrician Rome, after all. The girls had to be found suitable alliances as soon as they reached a certain age.

'Are there many suitors?' he asked.

'Too many for comfort, if you ask me! Come, have a drink, and I will take you to meet my father. He is looking forward to meeting you. He says he has not thanked you enough.'

Marcellus forced a smile and wondered what Silvius would have to say to that. Before they reached Manaykan, he was introduced to a number of local merchants, most of whom Silvius had briefed him about. Marcellus soon realized that he wasn't the only foreigner in the party. A couple of Silvius's pals were on the list too – the Alexandrian and the Greek, who had spent a long time in the city and traded regularly with the family, were there too. Silvius had very much wanted to come, but he wasn't extended an invitation. He was livid, however, there was nothing he could do about it. Marcellus was welcomed warmly by the members of the guild he met. He had dispatched a vat of Falernian wine to the residence before the feast and this was widely alluded to – he surmised that this singular act endeared him to the merchant populace for the moment. Even Sudar, the leader of the merchant guild, was not immune to the effects of Falernian grapes. Silvius had given Marcellus the low-down on this character – the canniest of them all, the leader of the guild. He bore no heirs and was determined to run his business until the day he died. A dangerous man to cross. But, for the moment, Marcellus had no worries on that account.

'Welcome to Puhar, son of Gaius,' he heard Sudar say. 'If you need anything at all in this kingdom, please bring it to my attention and I will see it is done.'

So far, so good.

When he was finally introduced, Vallavan's father was courteous but seemed preoccupied. Manaykan showed no outward sign of having seen Marcellus at the trial. Vallavan said he had to see off the prime minister, who was leaving, and Marcellus was left to wander around by himself. He followed the crowd into a large hall, where the gifts for the lady of the occasion were laid out on a long, low table: clothes of green, saffron red and indigo hues, gold necklaces, armbands and rings, gemstones on gold-inlaid bowls, a collection of sandalwood idols and dolls, and, at the far end, a mirror that reflected the assortment and made it all seem twice as grand.

It wasn't so much the mirror that caught Marcellus's attention – the *Minerva* carried many on its way in – it was the figurine that held it high on her head. He cut through the throng to take a better look: an ivory statue of a voluptuous female figure, adorned with armbands, anklets, dangling earrings, and long necklaces squeezed between her breasts; her legs were turned to the side, one crossed in front of the other, and on either side were two attendants holding up containers, one with turmeric and the other with sandalwood paste. Marcellus was mesmerized by the craftsmanship of the piece.

The blaring of conches broke through to him and he looked up. He had been so engrossed in the statue that he didn't realize that the crowd behind him had thinned significantly.

'You are missing all the action. Pots of turmeric water are being thrown on the poor girl in the courtyard over there. Would you care to take a look?'

Zhang! What in Jupiter's name was this infernal man doing in this household?

'Ah, you seem rather taken in by the native Venus here. A gift for the young maiden, and, if I am not mistaken, it comes from the north. Satavahana handiwork, that one. And, if I may say so, you surprise me, young Roman, with your good taste. I must admit it is not something I am used to seeing in your kind.'

Marcellus had heard enough. He turned around without a word and left through the first door he saw, straight into the hall where food was being served. A long stream of guests was sitting cross-legged on the floor, large banana leaves placed before them on which the steaming hot food was served. The chef in charge beamed and found a spot for the Yavana, who attempted to sit down, alongside the native guests, and immediately became the object of amusement as his toga didn't leave much to the imagination. But Marcellus was made of sterner stuff and he turned his attention to the food.

The main course consisted of appams and toddy, thala and crab curry, and steamed tortoise, followed by rice and buffalo curd. Dessert was three kinds of fruit payasams. Marcellus took his time – this was the best food he had tasted in a long time. His annoyance with Zhang was almost forgotten as he ate his fill. Once he finished, he was about to make his way back to the main courtyard when he stopped short.

Two men were sitting in a corner, on either side of a large snake gourd, and were chopping vegetables with swift precision. He had recognized them instantly. Marcellus collected himself and walked purposefully towards them. One of them looked up and his face contorted when he caught sight of him. He looked back down quickly and continued chopping.

'Why are you so slow? I am nearly halfway –' Muthu looked up at his cousin and caught sight of Marcellus. Unlike Mari, he did not flinch; he smiled instead.

'Yavana, have you come to see how our delicacies are made?' he asked, and held up his sharp knife, which glinted in the lamplight. Marcellus took a step back involuntarily.

'What are you doing here?'

'We work here; we are part of the chef's team.'

'Since when did you start cooking?'

'That's our profession, Yavana; our master is the best chef in all three kingdoms. Haven't you heard of him? Are you here with your master?'

'Don't pretend you don't know who I am.'

'Who are you?' Muthu asked. 'I apologize if we are supposed to know you and your master. We meet many Yavanas in our line of work.'

'Let's see about that. I will let my friend Vallavan, the man of this house, know of your true colours.' Marcellus whirled around and started walking away.

'One day, not long ago, my cousin and I happened to be in the grove between Maruvum and Pattinam, to make offerings to the Aiyanar. It was a dark and stormy night, and we had to take shelter in a mandapam...' Muthu's voice floated behind him.

Marcellus stopped dead in his tracks. 'Why are you here?' he asked again.

'To cook. Please believe us. We have to make a living and we have nothing to do with anyone else, not any more. We don't do that.' This time it was Mari who spoke.

'So you kidnapped me on orders from the Appans?'

'My sister and her family live in Madurai; we did it so that they would be safe.'

That wasn't quite what Maruthappan had told him, but Marcellus let it go. He couldn't possibly do anything else without giving away his part in the tale.

12

AT THE FEAST

A conch sounded just as he walked back to the main courtyard. 'The evening's debate is about to commence. Please be seated,' a man called out, guiding everyone who was in the courtyard to their seats.

Marcellus wasn't aware of any debate taking place that night. This was not the senate as far as he knew.

'Who is debating whom?' he asked the man.

'Zhang is here to make his case for the Buddha. The head priest of the Ganesha temple is here to speak for his gods. Kavunti Adikal was supposed to be here representing the Mahaviran, but the word is she has decided not to come.'

'But why not? This house is, from what I gather, a Jaina household.'

'Yes, we follow the Mahaviran's teachings where it works for us, but we are not averse to following all gods. You must understand that we have our traditions from before Adikal came here and we can't just give them up. She wants us to give up eating meat, can you believe it?'

Marcellus couldn't. That seemed a step too far. Marcellus sat down on a step that gave him a good view of the raised platform on which Zhang and the priest sat across from each other. So Zhang not only preached to the fisherfolk of Maruvum; here he was, in one of the most illustrious merchant houses of Puhar, engaged in debate with a venerable priest. There was something about this man, decided Marcellus. He had to be careful of him.

'Greetings to the king! Before we begin,' the priest started, looking around, 'let me remind you all to take a bath before you enter your homes tonight. Please pour water three times over your heads. This house, this lovely mansion, is now besmirched with this Shakya's presence and will have to be thoroughly cleansed. I will personally come here tomorrow to perform special rituals to purify the house. But for now, foreigner, let us hear of your Gautama.'

Zhang didn't bat an eyelid and spoke as if he was a native. 'Let's leave aside for a moment your motives for offering to purify a Jaina household. This mansion needs no cleansing; certainly not from you. But tell us this, how much does the lord of this house pay you for your special rituals, Brahmana? Perhaps the audience would like to know that too before we begin.'

The priest smiled. 'Everyone here knows that I am but a poor priest, and I don't ask for gifts. It is you and your mendicant friends who keep asking for alms endlessly.'

'Unlike you, priest, we don't have the patronage of the king and the merchants, who shower you with gifts because they think they need the rituals you perform. We don't claim to cleanse anything. The Buddha doesn't peddle meaningless rituals that serve no purpose.'

A collective gasp went up in the audience.

However unconventional his childhood may have been, Marcellus had grown up in a Roman household and rituals were an intrinsic part of it. But then again, he had heard Zhang before. The man clearly lived to anger all the gods but his own.

'That is because your Buddha is powerless; he can't change anything. Tell me, Shakya, what will the Buddha do against our mighty Vishnu? Just one of his avatars, the lion, can come out of a pillar and devour your Buddha!'

Someone at the back sniggered and, taking the cue, the crowd roared with laughter. Zhang remained unperturbed.

'Ignorant priest, the Buddha is beyond the reach of your god! While you will be stuck forever in the endless cycle of rebirth.'

'You think Vishnu will deign to come down to defeat as lowly a being as you, Shakya? He has already dealt the right blow to your master. Who knows what creature your master has been reborn as!'

'Ignorant priest, the Buddha is beyond the reach of your god! While you will be stuck forever in the endless cycle of rebirth.'

The priest laughed. 'You fool, I will be in heaven drinking toddy and goat leg rasam with the Devas.'

'What is this heaven of yours, priest? Have you seen it? Has anyone else here seen this place you refer to?'

'What do you know of heaven, you who will be born as a worm in your next birth?'

'Ha, then I will be the worm in your rasam – the one you drink with the Devas.'

Laughter filled the courtyard. Zhang had scored.

'You will be a worm all right. You who hang around Shudras and outcastes all day, what else will you be?'

'The Buddha makes no distinction – you are an arahant not by birth but by what you are and what you do. The folks whose company I keep are arahants by that definition.'

'Sacrilege! You dare to say that there is no difference between the fisherman of Maruvum and the gentiles of this house?' the priest sputtered.

A stunned silence fell over the courtyard as the audience pondered over this and looked expectantly at Zhang, waiting for him to speak. It was a trap and Zhang had walked into it.

'The Shakya is mad,' someone suddenly shouted, breaking the silence. *Zhang couldn't win this – the debate is over*, Marcellus thought. But he had underestimated the Buddhist.

'What the fisherman harvests from the sea is served in this house. The food you eat, the rice from the fields, has been touched many times over by the very people you call outcastes, and yet I see you enjoying your food with gusto. I not only mean to say that there is no difference between the fisherman, the peasant and the people gathered here, I proclaim that there is no difference between you and the fisherman, or you and the people here. They don't, they shouldn't, need you to speak to the gods they believe in.'

At this rather crucial juncture, Marcellus's sharp eyes noticed a figure at the top of a flight of stairs leading into the courtyard vanish into a room. He had had his eyes on her for a while; she had been sitting surreptitiously at the top of the stairs listening to the debate. Marcellus didn't hesitate. He could listen to Zhang pontificate any other time, but the opportunity to speak to Vallavan's sister – the older one, the one who dressed up as a man and travelled with her father – would not come his way again. Every pair of eyes was fixed on Zhang and the priest. Marcellus slipped away quietly and walked up the stairs.

'Let them speak for themselves, Shakya!' he heard the priest say as he reached the landing.

'Like a thief he enters, as the world watches the play of words.' A mellifluous voice, trained in singing and speech.

He walked towards the room from where the voice reached his ears and pushed open the screen.

'She who pretends to be a man cannot complain when a man pretending to be a thief enters her abode,' he said, flashing her a disarming smile.

'Why are you here?' Kuzhali asked. 'I don't want company in my confinement.'

'I'd definitely like company if I was confined. I'd find it lonely otherwise.'

Kuzhali scoffed. 'Are you afraid of being alone, Yavana? My brother was right; he had to hold your hand throughout the sea voyage.'

'Is that what he said? I don't remember it that way at all.'

'Yes, perhaps you were not as afraid then as you were during your trial.'

'I am pleased to discover that there is at least one person in this household with a good memory. Your brother has no recollection of this trial you speak of.'

'My brother blocks out anything he doesn't want to see or hear. Forty days' – she paused – 'and nights have not been sufficient for you to learn that about him.'

'And your father?'

'What would he gain from acknowledging the trial?'

'What do *you* gain? Why did you dress up as a boy and come to the harbour?'

Kuzhali's eyes flashed. 'How else would you suggest I come to Maruvum? Imagine the horror if the daughter of Manaykan was seen alongside the stevedores at the port! Not to mention the unlucky daughter… The omen that brings ill luck to anyone and everyone.'

'Why so unlucky?'

'You don't want to know. I was at the trial because I wanted to see you for myself. My brother sang such praises of you that I wanted to make my own judgement. My brother's opinion cannot always be trusted.'

Marcellus bowed. 'And?'

'You are still alive, aren't you?'

'Are you suggesting that I should be grateful to you for sparing my life?'

Kuzhali smiled coolly. 'My father was ready to let the law take its course.'

'What made him change his mind?'

'Not what. Who, rather. And the answer is me. What would we gain from your life, Yavana, other than the sworn enmity of your family and every Roman ship that comes to trade in Puhar? How does that serve *our* purpose?'

'So, instead, you cut a deal with Silvius, who came asking for help. Is that the price I pay for offering your brother a safe passage? Half of my cargo?'

'We are all very grateful to you for getting my brother back home. We wish you no harm, but you should understand that we wouldn't want to get in the way of the magistrate when he believes he has a case. Especially in these times, when danger is afoot.'

'I will have to remember that next time I am in a position to help a man stranded far away from home.'

'He was not abandoned; he was stupid enough to leave the ship without telling anyone. In any case, Sudar-mama's ship was not far behind. He would have reached home eventually.'

'Is that his view as well?'

Kuzhali looked away. 'My thambi is very dear to me, but as I have indicated, I have never placed much weight on his judgement.'

Marcellus laughed and stated the obvious. 'You are jealous.'

To his surprise, she immediately acknowledged it. 'Why wouldn't I be, Yavana? I am a better trader than he is, and look at me! Confined within these four walls! I don't want to be shut out from anything of importance, but that's what happens to me. For instance, they are about to begin their conference, supposedly about my sister's wedding, but no one is fooled. Kannaki's marriage is a foregone conclusion – it's the wrong match but there is not much I can do about it. They are there to talk about far more important things, and here I am, a mere woman, and hence not allowed to attend it. What could be more insulting?'

He was no stranger to being shut out and insulted, but there was no reason for him to share that with this girl.

'I am certain that no insult is intended. A woman's place is –'

'You will see where my place is when you and your ilk will have to bow down to my orders.'

'But why in the future? Let me bow to your orders now. I am at your command, my lady.'

'Do not patronize me, Yavana. I will one day run this country –'

'While the king...?'

'Builds his dams and fights his wars. Someone needs to fund his projects, keep the country prosperous and trade flourishing. That is what I intend to do.'

Marcellus was starting to understand that she was serious about this. 'How exactly do you plan to accomplish this? What do *you* know of trade?'

'Mark my words, Yavana: one day, a hundred ships will sail from here for Rome, every season, carrying the harvests of this country. My family and the guild wish this, but they don't know how to make it happen. They travel, yet they do not learn anything from the places they travel to. You Romans rule your world by conquering sea and land, not just by sending ships to trade.'

Marcellus was impressed. His experience of a certain class of woman was severely lacking; however, he'd seen enough of the woman who was married to his father. The same ambitious streak ran in this girl, and he wondered what they would make of each other. They'd get along famously, he concluded.

'I hope you can come to Rome in one of your ships one day,' he said.

'You don't want me in your kingdom.'

'Rome is not a mere kingdom, my lady. We have foreign merchants in Rome who truly –' Marcellus froze mid-sentence as he heard footsteps on the stairs.

'Quick, hide, this way. You can jump off the balcony,' Kuzhali whispered, pointing to a screen on the other side. Marcellus ran behind the screen just as a girl entered the room.

'I brought you dinner,' he heard the newcomer speak.

'Thank you. Obviously, I cannot be seen downstairs today. The sky will come crashing down if I were spotted there.'

Marcellus stuck his leg out of the window and squeezed himself into the small balcony. All the rooms facing the front courtyard had their own balconies, and he realized he could jump from one to the next to get to the end of the building. And from there, he should be able to jump down to the soft grass of a side courtyard without being seen. It was too dark for anyone below to notice him unless they were looking up directly at him. He began his trek and two balconies down, he heard voices from inside the room. He paused.

'Manaykan, it is time to discuss your daughter's future. Everyone here is of the same opinion.'

'Yes, but she is still a child. I don't want to lose her.'

Marcellus recognized the voice of Vallavan's father. So this was the meeting Kuzhali had referred to. He wanted to see who else was in the room, and for a moment, he considered making himself known. But he decided against it. Propriety had not stopped him from eavesdropping before. Besides, he had no way of explaining what he was doing in the balcony without telling them that he was visiting a daughter of the house.

'You are not losing her. She will always be your daughter; you will, instead, gain a new family.'

Manaykan sighed.

'She'll be the queen of our house. We'll take good care of her,' said the first voice again.

Just then, to his surprise, Marcellus saw Kuzhali climb out of her balcony and nimbly jump into the adjacent one. She edged towards him. Pointing to the end of the building, she signalled him to jump down from there. But Marcellus stayed put. If she didn't want him to overhear the conversation, she'd have to expose both of them in public and admit to eavesdropping herself. Somehow he didn't think she would do that. He could afford the gamble. He moved in and made space for her. She glared at him but remained silent and settled down next to him. Marcellus smiled. He was starting to enjoy this.

'You didn't give me the opportunity with your oldest. Look what happened.'

'Nothing is enough for Kuzhali,' Manaykan said quietly. 'She wants a navy to conquer worlds and establish trade.'

A third voice entered the conversation. 'It is a pity that our king doesn't care about our trade and now our women – in this case, our widowed girls – have to.' Beside Marcellus, the girl in question squirmed. Widowed? Well, that explained it.

'The king only cares about peasants and dams. One wouldn't have thought the mighty Chola kingdom would come to this.'

It was Sudar.

'Sudar-ayya, you cannot speak ill of our king; especially not when we have his representative here,' cautioned Manaykan.

'I am not afraid to speak the truth, and the king himself would have to agree with me.'

'I am here to listen, not to speak. Speak your mind, ayya.' It was a calm and measured voice, one that Marcellus did not recognize.

'The king cares deeply about our welfare, and the welfare of all his subjects.'

There was Vallavan. He remembered that his friend was loyal to Karikalan and regarded him as a god – not unlike how the emperor was treated by many in Rome.

'How did you come to that conclusion?' Sudar asked. 'He is meeting with the Pandya merchants as we speak, and, as far as we know, he has already promised to return their trade and freedom. That is no way to care for the welfare of merchants of Puhar, thambi.'

Marcellus could no longer restrain himself. He peered through the side of the screen – in his line of sight, he saw seven men. Vallavan, Manaykan, Sudar, three other merchants he had met earlier, and a figure in the shadows he could not make out. The merchant princes of the city of Puhar were in attendance.

'How do you know this, Sudar-anna?' Vallavan's father enquired respectfully. 'We have no reason to think that the king has granted the Pandya traders an audience. In fact, we have confirmation that he is not in Pandya country right now. He is in Uraiyur, supervising the build of the dam.'

'I don't doubt that. But there is no question that the Pandya guilds have sent numerous missives to him. My source tells me that they waited until he was safely out of Puhar, and have met him at Uraiyur. What he had agreed to is yet to be confirmed, but the word is that he will be looking to remove restrictions and reduce taxes. The pearl and the gem traders would not have to go through us any more, and there would be no punitive taxes or restrictions against them. Anyone – the northern kingdoms and even the Yavanas – would be free to trade with them. Do you realize what this means for us?'

'This cannot be true!' Manaykan looked enquiringly at the man in the shadows.

'I'd caution against coming to any conclusions until you know the truth. Don't be hasty.' The man spoke so softly that Marcellus could barely hear him.

'If you could give us your advice –'

'No, it's for you to consider and decide what is best for your guild. I promised to listen, and I cannot advise you on this matter.'

'The king is weak; he does not –'

'He isn't weak,' Vallavan interjected. 'A weak person cannot have escaped the fire, and conquered his enemies as he has proven again and again.'

'Bravery in battle doesn't count for much in times of peace. He is a man of great valour in the battlefield, but he doesn't understand trade – which is why he entertains the traders of Pandya country. He thinks it is fair and just, and wants to keep them happy to fund his next conquest; justice plays no part in trade, and the king doesn't know it is folly. He is a man who is great at fighting battles, but not a king who knows how to run his kingdom in a time of peace.'

'Enough, Sudar-mama, I can't stand by silently while you disparage him,' Vallavan cried out.

'Vallava!' his father warned, but the young man paid no heed and continued. 'Why do we covet Pandya trade wealth when we have our own? We don't need a restrictive tax regime to show our dominance; we will overpower them fair and square. We are wealthier because we are better traders, not because we have a better navy.'

There was silence in the room for a few moments as the group pondered over his words. The young did not challenge the old – not in Marcellus's native Rome, and not here in Puhar.

Sudar spoke slowly and quietly. 'Perhaps you should listen to your sister more.'

A collective gasp went around the room. Marcellus couldn't see her, but he sensed her reaction. Kuzhali smiled. *She* was certainly enjoying this.

'Manaykan, the boy was always given to emotion and ideals, but I am afraid you are right; we should never have sent him to the West. It has had an adverse effect on him.'

Vallavan ignored the insult and continued. 'You want to know what I learnt there? Free trade is the way forward, and it is the way of the world. The Romans know this and understand this, which is why they are so successful now.'

Sudar laughed. 'Is that what they told you in that ship where they held you hostage?'

'They did not hold me hostage.'

'They were arrested –'

'For no fault of theirs and were made to pay a hefty price.'

'Manaykan, your boy has truly lost his head! He thinks the Yavanas believe in friendship and free trade! Is that why they conquer every piece of land they see? Is that why they maintain the greatest army in the world? Free trade is a fallacy. No two people, no two *sides*, are equal. We do what we have to do to maintain our dominance, and I for one am not going to let the king stand in our way.'

Vallavan's father spoke up, his voice cautious. 'Sudar-anna, I don't disagree with you, but we first have to find out what the king has agreed to, if he has agreed to anything at all.'

'But –' Vallavan began.

'Quiet, boy!' Sudar interjected. 'Manaykan, there is a way to achieve the end we all want, but it requires unconventional means.'

'Such as?'

'Such as trying to work better with the kingdoms around us.'

'Is it something the king would support?'

'We have all the support and blessings we need...from his representative here. The administration will be with us.'

The room remained silent for a long time. 'I see,' said Manaykan at last. 'And the priests? They are with us?'

'There could be a problem there, but we can –'

'Thief! Thief in the display hall!' A cry rang out from downstairs, followed by the frantic sound of running feet.

The men rushed downstairs to where the commotion was, but one of them moved in the opposite direction. Marcellus saw him step out from the room through the other window into the next balcony, making for the wall on the side. The man was close by, but he did not notice Marcellus and Kuzhali.

'Get out, Yavana. And forget everything you heard,' Kuzhali whispered as she moved swiftly towards her balcony and melted into her room. Marcellus could have jumped down to the ground, but the memory of being kidnapped was still fresh in his mind. He followed Kuzhali into her room.

'I may forget everything I heard out there, but I am not going to forget you. Farewell,' he said and left the room. When he came downstairs, he noticed no one had missed him as they were all talking about the robbery.

'The king is not in Puhar and look, there are burglaries everywhere.'

'What are the king's men doing? Every day, one of us is robbed in Puhar!'

'The king is building a dam to keep the peasants happy while we have to deal with this.'

'A robbery in Manaykan's house! His daughter's dowry of all things! Who would have thought!'

Marcellus gathered that, despite appearances, the king wasn't very popular in this part of town, and his friend Vallavan was a rare loyalist. He looked for the chef's helpers but did not see them – he had no doubt that they had made off with whatever they could get their hands on. But he couldn't let Vallavan on to the fact that he knew the robbers without going into the details of his Pandya sojourn, which was best left unexplained, especially after what he had just heard. He needed to stay out of this business. He looked around for familiar faces for it was time to take his leave. Zhang tapped his shoulder from behind.

'Young Roman, may I have the pleasure of your company on the way back to Maruvum? The moon will provide all the light we need.'

Marcellus had no intention of leaving with Zhang, but then again, it was dark and he wasn't sure if he could remember the way back.

'I promise you that I won't let you get lost in the forest along the way,' Zhang continued. 'If you do, you may have to spend the night in a mandapam, which I am told isn't particularly comfortable.'

Marcellus was startled by Zhang's allusion, but he was too tired to pursue it further. They left together for the seaside without taking leave of their hosts, who were otherwise engaged.

13

FAMILIAR GHOSTS

The two unlikely companions walked out of town, towards the avenue that led to Maruvum – each immersed in his own thoughts. It was dark but the street lanterns provided enough light, and they passed the merchant quarters and the baths in silence. As they neared the road by the groves, Zhang spoke. 'They say that Manaykan's daughter is the sharp one in the family.'

'She is a child!' Marcellus was quick, but not quick enough.

'You know which one I mean,' said Zhang. 'She was not a child even before her marriage. She should be Sudar's true heir but that is not to be. But it won't stop her from trying to establish a monopoly over trade with you Romans.'

Marcellus looked up. Here was this interfering Buddhist monk, barging into his thoughts uninvited and seemed to know exactly what he was thinking. He was fully aware that he was no neutral foreign trader in Puhar, playing a waiting game with the kingdoms. By forging a deal with the Pandyas secretly, he – and his father's business – was now fully implicated in going against the law of the land. He had a vested interest in the political relationship and trade between the two kingdoms, and whatever action he was to take in relation to Korkai, he would have to take this factor into account. Just a few days ago, he had considered asking for Vallavan's help in getting to Korkai, but clearly he could not do that. And then his thoughts went to Kuzhali, that fish-eyed girl who seemed to know so much, whose body exuded the fragrance of jasmine, turmeric and sandalwood, and whose words were sharp as daggers. What to make of her and her ambitions?

'Who won the debate?' he asked Zhang, ignoring the question.

'I could have sworn that you were watching.'

'My friend called me away before the end, so I did not have the pleasure of seeing them fling you into a vat of boiling oil,' Marcellus replied.

'Nobody throws me anywhere; I am too fat for that, haven't you noticed?' Zhang laughed. 'But tell me, Roman, were you not invited to the secret conference upstairs?'

Who exactly was this man who seemed to know everything that went on behind closed doors? Was his Buddha really so powerful that he had a few more eyes than normal humans? Talking to him about anything was dangerous.

'I am not aware of any conference, secret or otherwise. Even if there was one, why would they invite a Yavana trader?'

'A good question, and one I am sure you have considered. But if you were not in the meeting and your friend must have been, where exactly were you?'

'You aren't accusing me of being the thief now, are you?' Marcellus asked, shaking his head.

'You did have an eye on the Venus of the East.'

'She is gone?'

'That, and a number of gemstones and necklaces from the display.'

'The nerve!'

'You know the thief?'

'No. Why would I? Are there any suspects?'

'We will find out soon enough. Foreigners and servants are usually first on the list; so if you have soldiers at your door tomorrow, you know why. Who knows, we may become cell mates!' Zhang said cheerfully.

'Are burglaries common here?'

'From the house of a merchant prince? No, I am afraid it is not common at all; so this is a really big deal. Let me ask you this, this mirror and this lady – the Eastern Venus – she still interests you?'

'What do you mean?' Marcellus asked, although he had a fair idea where this was going.

'A piece like that doesn't come up often. It's an inspired creation – a Gandhara design I'd say, but it betrays the intricate workmanship of the sculptors of Bhokardan. The blending of a local fertility goddess with what they had seen of Aphrodite in the temples of Gandhara, she is a stroke of genius. The gemstones and necklaces could be pared down and sold easily, but the thief would have to be careful with this lady. If you are interested, I could discreetly put the word out that there is a prospective buyer in the market.'

If only Zhang knew the real state of his finances, he would never have approached him. But Marcellus did not enlighten him.

'So that's your real profession? A black market art dealer masquerading as a man of god? Does your Buddha approve of this?'

'The Buddha doesn't involve himself in my mundane everyday activities.'

'Of course he doesn't,' Marcellus said drily. 'Tell me, Zhang, are there many followers of the Buddha where you come from? Do you adorn your god with the best of your silk?'

That seemed to do the trick and Zhang launched into his

favourite topic. 'He is no god! He is an enlightened man who understood suffering and the human condition.'

Marcellus had no idea that the Buddha was one of *that* crowd. Gods and godmen, he understood, but philosophers belonged to a different league altogether.

'What is the use of understanding the human condition? Isn't it self-evident?' The hundreds of hours that he had been subjected to under Diodorus ensured that he could hold his ground on Platonism, Stoicism and Scepticism, but that didn't mean he found any of them particularly useful to *his* life. They were not meant for people like him. His brother may one day find them of use, if he ever were to make it to the senate. Not him. Never him. He continued, 'What real use is this man you follow and why do your people worship him?'

'My people don't worship him, if by my people you mean the people of the country I was born in. They have gods such as your own and the emperor rules by a heavenly mandate. I was introduced to the Buddha in the course of my travels. Gautama Buddha was a prince, but he renounced everything. Wars and trade did not matter to him; he saw our world in a different light.'

'That doesn't sound like a sensible man. We progress because we conquer, we trade, we create new things. This is why you and I are here, and that's why Rome is the greatest –'

'There he goes again!' Zhang laughed out loud. 'What does all this matter once you are dead, Roman? All these empires and riches can't save you from dying, can they?'

'Neither can this Buddha of yours. What is your real story, man of the East? You are a man who knows many things, and I am sure there is an explanation.'

'As the Buddha once said, not –' Zhang stopped abruptly.

Marcellus was about to speak, but the monk put a finger on his lips. 'Hush! Listen!'

Marcellus heard the faint clinking of bells. Zhang pulled him back behind a tree. As they waited, the sound became louder and, this time, there was no mistaking it – it was the tinkling of anklets. A woman at this hour near the forest between Maruvum and Pattinam? This was turning out to be his day for meeting strange women.

A few moments later, the owner of the anklets came into view. She walked past them, oblivious to their presence. She wasn't a merchant girl or a fisherwoman, as far as Marcellus could tell. She was dark as the night sky, and her attire was unlike anything he had seen Chola women wear. She wore a veshti tied around her long legs, like a man, and, on her upper body, instead of flower garlands and gold, she wore two beaded necklaces. Over her right shoulder hung a bow, but there was no sign of arrows. Her right hand never left the bow, while she held a large cloth bundle in her left hand. Just before she reached the fork in the road, she stopped and looked around cautiously. She bent down and gingerly removed her anklets. She opened her bundle, put the anklets inside and carefully tied it again, but not before Marcellus caught the shiny glint of metal from within. The girl turned towards the main street and soundlessly continued on her journey.

'That's our thief! A bandit in Puhar town!' whispered Zhang, once he was sure she was out of earshot. 'Shall we see what she is up to?'

'She was not in the house.'

'How do you know? There were hundreds of people at the feast.'

'But someone dressed like that would have been noticed!'

'She must have been in disguise.'

'And now she changed out of it? It doesn't make sense.'

'You saw the stolen goods as well as I did. I am going after her; I'd like to see where she is heading.'

'All right, but I don't think she stole them. The thieves could have been her accomplices,' Marcellus said reluctantly.

'You seem to be sure there was more than one.'

'Listen, Zhang, I know who they are. In fact, I've seen them before…' He sighed before continuing. 'If I head the way she came, I may be able to catch them red-handed.' Marcellus had no intention of interrogating them and implicating himself in front of Zhang, but if he could get them alone, he would be able to find out what they were up to. This girl was a distraction and the sooner he sent Zhang after her, the better.

'You say you know the thieves? I've changed my mind… I'll come with you.'

'But she has the evidence with her. Why don't you go after her, and I'll find the accomplices?'

'No, she was heading towards town. The soldiers will catch her soon enough. Besides, I feel responsible for your safety.'

'I am more than capable of getting home by myself.'

Zhang smiled. 'But who knows who will kidnap you this time.'

He started walking briskly in the direction the girl had come from, this time hugging the forest along the eastern border, and Marcellus had no choice but to follow him.

'Do you know this girl?' he asked Zhang. It struck him that she could be one of his art suppliers. In which case, Zhang could be an accomplice to the crime.

'I know *of* her.'

'Who is she?'

'A girl of the hills. And unless I am mistaken, she is well acquainted with your friend. If you wish, I'm sure your friend would be happy to make the introductions.'

'Vallavan's friend?' This did not make much sense, but Zhang wasn't saying more.

Now, they were inside the forest; however, instead of making their way swiftly to the Maruvum gate, Zhang stopped at various points, listened carefully and took a few detours leading them deeper inside the woods. Soon, it started to annoy Marcellus.

'I don't think we are likely to find them. I am going home.'

'I thought you were determined to find the thieves!'

Marcellus tried to turn back, but Zhang put his hand on his shoulder and beckoned the Roman to follow him. Zhang walked slowly away from the moonlit path into the pitch darkness of the forest, and Marcellus could hear incoherent voices in the distance. They could not yet see anyone, but the voices became clearer.

'Sivane! How did we end up like this, Muthu? Tied up by a ghost who took away our jewels. I should never have listened to you!'

Marcellus recognized the now-familiar voice of Muthu's partner-in-crime, Mari. Just as he had suspected initially, the two were behind the theft at Vallavan's house. But what was this ghost they were referring to?

'Stop talking to the gods and figure out how we are going to escape from this forest,' said Muthu curtly.

'The ghost has tied knots that only the ghost can undo! I don't see how we are going to get out of this. We should just wait for someone to come and rescue us.'

'Are you crazy, Mari? The only people who come this way are those who don't belong to the kingdom! Better to be caught by the soldiers of Puhar than by those who will cut our balls and throw us into the sea.'

'Maybe the ghost will come back and set us free,' Mari said hopefully, sounding more than a little frightened. Zhang seized the moment and made a slow rumbling sound. Everything went quiet for a few moments.

'What was that?' asked Muthu.

'The ghost heard us. It may be coming back!' Mari gasped.

Zhang cupped his mouth and spoke loudly. 'I am no mere ghost, you imbeciles. I am the king of ghosts!'

Mari screamed and a soft thump indicated that he had fainted. Muthu mustered all the courage he could before he spoke. 'O, king of ghosts, what do you want? We can get you all the jewels of Chola country if you so wish.'

'You humans are fools. What will a ghost do with jewels?'

'But a ghost just took some from us! What would you like then? Your wish is our command.' Muthu sounded encouraged.

'Blood! Human blood, and I smell it right here.'

'*Ayyo!* Please spare us. We have not done anything to deserve this fate.'

'Have you not stolen jewellery from the merchant's house?'

'Yes, but –'.

Zhang pressed on. 'Did you not kidnap a young man from a distant land who had done you no harm?'

'But he escaped from us! Otherwise we would have gladly offered you Yavana blood.'

Marcellus had not missed it: how did Zhang know *who* his kidnappers were?

'He is not here, is he? For now, I want human blood and I will not be –'

'Please tell us what else we can do,' Muthu pleaded, his voice quivering. 'I have a large family that depends on me.'

Zhang spoke after a long pause. 'There is one way to save your life. Tell me who put you up to spying on the merchant's house, and I will drink his blood instead of yours.'

'Yes, release us and we will lead you there.' Mari had awoken and had caught the last part of the conversation.

'If you try to deceive me, I will be back for you.'

'Mari, no! O king of ghosts, it wasn't a man. A ghost threatened us and asked us to spy on the merchant's house.'

'I know all the ghosts of this kingdom and I am their ruler. I know that no ghost asked you to do such a thing.'

'But it was a ghost! And now its accomplice has stolen everything we had.'

'Muthu! You told me –'

'Shut up. I have had enough of this. I just want to go home and be left in peace.'

'I don't have time to listen to your banter, you fools!' rumbled Zhang. 'Tell me where you met this ghost and what it looked like.'

'It looked like a ghost! It came looking for us in our home, and it knew about us already. It said that the Pandyas sent it, and it was a messenger of the Pandya prince.'

'Tell –'

The forest suddenly started to light up and they heard a number of voices coming their way. Zhang hesitated for a moment.

'I will spare you for now. There are people here to see you,' he said, and started walking away quickly with Marcellus trailing behind him.

'No! King of ghosts, please untie us!' shouted Mari, but his voice was drowned in the chatter of the group of men walking towards them.

Zhang and Marcellus walked together silently until they were almost at Maruvum. Finally Marcellus asked, 'Who were the men?'

'I suspect they are soldiers looking for our jewel thieves. Let those two enjoy Chola hospitality for a while. If the soldiers had seen two foreigners with them, we'd have been arrested too. We've had a lucky escape.'

But Marcellus wasn't feeling particularly relieved. Who knew what the duo would confess to. If they let the Chola soldiers know of the deal he had made with the Appans, he'd never get out of Puhar alive.

'But who sent them to spy on the house? Who is this ghost and what is the girl's involvement in this?'

'We will have to make our own guesses. I doubt we would have gathered any more information from those dunces.' Zhang paused as they reached the Maruvum gate. 'And now, the time has come for us to part again. Thank you for being a faithful companion on my journey tonight. My advice to you, young Roman, is to not spend time thinking about internecine dealings of this kingdom, and instead focus on what you came here to do. Goodnight.'

Zhang vanished quickly, as he was prone to do, leaving an open-mouthed Marcellus to interpret his parting words.

What exactly did Zhang think his mission was?

14

ATOP A MANGO TREE

Perched atop a branch of her favourite mango tree, Kuzhali watched the sun disappear behind the western hills. This had been her hiding place when she was a child and it remained so once she returned home after the death of her husband. She wondered how long it would be before her mother realized that she was missing and sent the servants out to find her. The question was, would her mother get to her before the red ants on the tree did? The ants had stayed away until then, thanks to the limestone paste she had smeared generously on the branch, but nothing kept them away for long. They would be emboldened soon enough and be back to reclaim the branch. *The only person I know who has been kept out of her rightful inheritance is me*, Kuzhali thought bitterly. She riled at the unfairness of it all.

As if this wasn't enough, they were now going to do the same to her little sister, Kannaki. They were going to marry her off to that good for-nothing playboy. Everyone knew that Kovalan was only interested in the songs and dances of the town's courtesans, and, hence, the only thing he was competent at was squandering away his family's wealth. Kannaki was too much of a child to know better, and even if she did, she couldn't refuse their father. The poor girl!

To top it all, the merchant guild was in total disarray. There was no real leadership among the members and there were too many factions operating within it. The Pandya traders were being kept at bay for the moment, but it wasn't clear how long this would last. There was unrest in the northern border, which had to be addressed immediately, but the king was away on a civil mission – to build a dam to pacify a few peasants in the delta. In their last meeting, the guild, after much discussion, ratified the decision to send a missive to the king: an ultimatum of sorts crouched in deeply respectful language. They requested him not to mollify the Pandya traders, risking Puhar's interests, and to assign military escorts to safeguard goods across all borders. The king did not need to be reminded that it wasn't that long ago when the guild had maintained its own militia. Whose idea was it to send the message? Hers. But who was taking this message to Uraiyur? Her brother, Vallavan. As much as she loved him, she knew he was so taken in with the king that he would be unnecessarily subservient and would not be able to convey the import of the message.

She saw a lone red ant crawling up the branch, having found a way around the limestone barrier. It was time she left, and she was about to scamper down when she heard a noise behind her. Two dark shapes, entwined, squeezed through the hedge from the pleasure gardens next door to the mango grove. This was unusual, to say the least. Other than on festival days, the gardens weren't used in this season – in the summer, a stage would be erected for kuruvai koothu that would be performed over many evenings. She could not see clearly in the dark, but they were coming towards the tree she was perched on. She held her breath as the couple stopped directly beneath her.

'Wait for me near Kavunti's grove tomorrow and we'll travel together.'

Vallavan! She had a good idea who he was speaking to. He had been told by their father to stay away from *that* girl, but he'd paid no heed to the warning.

'I am not travelling with you. I have other things to do!' The girl spoke a strange dialect that wasn't easy to understand.

'Why do you torment me so much? You don't need to work for them; I will give you everything you need.'

'They are my people.'

'No, they make you do things that... Let's not talk about them. I'll take you away.'

'Where will you take me?'

'I will find a house –'

'Where? You forget that I don't know how to sing, dance or recite poetry like the pretty girls hanging out of the balconies in the street of the courtesans. I am utterly useless in that respect.'

'You have other talents. You got back the stolen jewellery. I haven't told anyone how they magically reappeared in the courtyard.'

Her brother was an idiot! He hadn't realized that she must have stolen them in the first place.

'Yes, I suppose I could make a living as a private investigator. Or maybe a debt collector. Would you like that?' The mockery in her tone was unmistakable.

'Angavai –'

'You cannot find a place for me in your town, so I suggest you leave me with my people.'

'But you travel alone and I worry –'

'My lord, you should know by now that I can take care of myself. I don't get kidnapped since *I* do the kidnapping –'

'Hush, don't say that. You are not a bandit; they have somehow managed to make you work for them. How and why I have no idea!'

Angavai laughed. 'Think what you will, but promise me you'll be careful this time. Let me remind you of what happened when you took a shortcut away from the high road last time…'

'If I were to be kidnapped and left to die only so that you can bring me back to life, I am happy to be kidnapped a hundred times over.'

'Oh, it's not exclusive. It is the same service I provide the firstborn sons of all rich merchants, didn't you know?'

'Enough.' Vallavan pulled her close and kissed her, but she pulled back quickly.

'If anyone needs protection here between the two of us, it's you.'

'If I agree, will you come with me to Uraiyur?' he asked. 'You can be my protector!'

Vallavan is entirely unsuitable for this mission, Kuzhali fumed. He was treating this as a pleasure trip with his woman friend and had no idea of the importance of the task. He wasn't in the right state of mind for the job.

'I have work here in Puhar. I'll follow you once I am done, and I promise you that I will catch up with you. Tell me, why are you meeting Karikalan?'

'A message from the guild…an urgent one. There is one other thing too, but…' He paused.

'Will you not tell me?'

'No, not yet. Not until I can talk to my father… Listen, if you come, I'll make sure you meet the king. He is as just as he is brave.'

'Have you met him?'

'No, but everyone in Puhar knows of his magnanimity –'

'I don't need to meet your king to know the havoc he wreaked in my people's lives.'

'You don't understand, Angavai.' He shook his head. 'The pain your people are going through is not because of the king. If you petition him and your needs are just, he will provide what you want. He is a generous ruler.'

'I don't need your king to give me what is my birthright. Did your father petition him for this mansion? Who is he to give me anything? We'll take it ourselves!'

Kuzhali was getting increasingly enraged at the turn in the conversation. *This* was the girl her brother had been secretly meeting all this time?

'Angavai, I know how you talk, but I also know you don't really mean it. You have been influenced by them. But you have to be careful. You know you could be beheaded for –'

'No, I came here to tell *you* to be careful. There seems to be an unusually large number of spies and foreigners along the high road at the moment, and it's not safe.'

'Let us not worry about the future. You are here now and that is all that matters.' He pulled her into an embrace again and this time she didn't resist. Kuzhali decided it was time she showed herself when she heard her mother.

'Where is that girl now? She has vanished. Mythili, go to the grove and see if your cousin's hiding there.'

The couple separated in a hurry.

'Mythili? Is that the girl you are going to marry?' Angavai asked.

'Don't be ridiculous,' Vallavan said. 'But it's best if you –'

'Be careful,' Angavai said one last time and vanished into the darkness before he could complete his sentence. Vallavan turned towards the house to check if they had been seen.

'Don't worry about Mythili. She is too frightened to leave the house after sunset. You have bigger things to worry about, thambi,' said Kuzhali, as she landed on the grass next to her brother.

And so Vallavan spent the evening beseeching his angry sister to let him undertake the mission to Uraiyur while, unbenownst to them, the Yavanas were busy planning to hoodwink the merchant guild in the most audacious manner possible – by smuggling away an entire shipload of pearls from under their very noses.

15

LOGISTICS

Hippalus had made his stand known and it was a great one as far as tantrums went, but Marcellus knew the intrepid captain would come around sooner or later. There was no love lost between them; however, he knew Hippalus wouldn't be able to resist a good dare. It was Silvius whom he did not trust. With each passing day, it was becoming clearer to him that the old man was waiting for something to happen. Adi had vanished for a few days, which did not augur well for him. Marcellus knew it wouldn't take much to expose his deception, if only Silvius knew what to look for. The convoy of ships from the West had come in the previous day, but there were no missives addressed to Silvius. The question remained: how long did Marcellus have before he was found out? And when – of course, it was a question of *when* – he was found out, what choices did he have?

'This is all one big adventure for you, little master, a once-in-a-lifetime journey to prove yourself to the pater before you go back to the chariot races and pleasure villas, where you can boast about all this!'

Hippalus exploded. 'For me and my men, it is our lives that you are dangling in front of me. What do you think is going to happen? They warned us not to trade with anyone else – under pain of death – what part of this instruction wasn't clear to you?' He whirled around to face Silvius, pointing his index finger at the older man's chest. 'What about your friends, Silvius, your partners in trade, the Chola merchants? What if they find out what you are up to? Above all, they would like to control the Pandya trade, and they financed the king's war for that reason and that reason only. They will ask the king to put pressure on the Pandyas, and what happens then? A full-scale navy awaits orders across from where the *Minerva* is anchored. Are they going to wave us goodbye as we leave the port loaded with far less than what we normally take? How exactly do you plan to hoodwink the port authorities?'

'Leave the port officials to me. I have a way of working with them,' Silvius said quietly.

'The same ones who arrested and nearly drowned us? Our little master here may have forgotten, but I happen to remember that we weren't exactly saved by the port officials you had bribed so handsomely.'

Silvius immediately went on the defensive. 'You and your man aided this deal, and now you think I am to blame? We all know that the young fellow here is playing a dangerous game. Despite my advice, he has gone ahead and cut a deal with people we should not even be seen with. But here is the thing: *it is a good deal*, and it promises us a monopoly, at least in the short run. So, no, I will not take any responsibility – that's up to the boy here – but I will make sure you have a clear run with the port officials.'

'And what part is the little master going to play in the game?'

'Well, his friendship with the local traders is not of insignificance. There will be no suspicion attached to us as long as that relationship is kept intact. Hippalus, even you have to admit that his friendship with Manaykan's boy will continue to serve us well in the coming days.'

But Hippalus was not so easily convinced. He smirked as he said, 'I would not underestimate the Cholas if I were you. My sources tell me that his kidnapping and subsequent escape has not gone without notice in certain circles. Manaykan's boy may be in love with ours, but that is not going to blind the traders to our illicit involvement in the Pandya pearl trade. Who knows what our boy here has blabbed in the throes of passion.'

Silvius laughed. Aafa cleared his throat. Marcellus's face remained impassive. He could have gone straight for the sailor's throat, but he needed this man to steer the *Minerva* with her load of pearls all the way to Myos Hormos.

Hippalus continued, 'Silvius, I know how you think. You think you are going to get away with this by blaming the rogue captain and his crew. We take the blame whatever happens, and everything continues as per usual in Puhar. But it won't work that way – not this time. The Cholas aren't fools; they aren't going to fall for this little charade. Your trade with this kingdom will be over after this incident, one way or another. Have you considered that?'

'The Cholas need us even more than we need them. They need markets and they need buyers, and what better place for this than Rome? The Cholas and Pandyas will fight among themselves but, as long as we don't visibly take sides, both of them will continue to do business with us. You run the ship and leave the trading to us.'

'Silvius, let me be clear. You can be sure that the master, the real one, will hear of this – and he will hear it from me. You are endangering the *Minerva* and her crew.'

'I take it it's a yes?' Marcellus spoke up for the first time. Hippalus glared at him, but Marcellus continued without waiting for a response. 'To business. First, we have to gradually bring down the quantity of goods we are procuring from the Chola traders, as they would get spoiled in the warehouses before the next ship gets to

Puhar. Silvius and I have a plan to reduce the perishables we are buying that we'll put into action. Second, the *Minerva* has to be loaded with just the bare minimum without raising any alarm with the porters or port authorities. I will leave this to you and Aafa. The loading of pearls has to happen in Korkai, and it would have to be a night operation as the Chola navy will be on alert then. We will have to talk to the Pandyas about the timing. Three, Aafa says he expects a Roman ship from the eastern islands in a few weeks en route home, so any goods left at the warehouse can be loaded on to that ship as long as we can offload and sell the Eastern wares to the shopkeepers of Puhar. This raises the obvious question of why a Roman ship would offload Eastern goods so far away from home and sell them in Puhar, competing directly with the local traders, and we will need to be ready with a credible response…'

The four of them spent most of the day in the warehouse, chalking out the plan to execute the deal without raising the suspicion of the local traders and port authorities. There were too many things that could go wrong, and they had to account for every possibility. If the three older men were surprised to see a very different Marcellus from the one they were used to, none of them showed it. It was night when Silvius finally rose to leave.

'Gentlemen, I must take my leave as I am expected at the club.'

'Never one to miss the club even if the sky may fall upon us.'

'I am the barbarian here, Captain. I assure you that the sky is not about to fall. In this town, it is important to keep up appearances at all costs. Besides, I am expecting a friend there any time.'

'A friend?'

'From Musiris,' Silvius replied, very carefully avoiding Marcellus's eye.

So there it was, the first warning, Marcellus thought, but he was careful not to react. He'd been waiting for this moment since the day he landed. Silvius was on to him now.

'As a matter of fact, young master, you may know him,' said Silvius, suddenly turning towards Marcellus. 'He always accompanied your father and me back in the day and later took on a job in the Ostian warehouses, where he has been based for many years now. He came with the *Isis* to Musiris, and I invited him here. Bloke by the name of Proteus. Do you know him?'

Marcellus knew the man all right, knew him rather well actually from his time in his father's warehouse.

'Can't say I remember him.' He shrugged.

'That's to be expected, considering your schedule at the Circus every day. On the other hand, Proteus knows you very well as he has often been to the villa. Says he remembers you right from the time you were an infant. I'll bring him home once he gets here. And now, if you gentlemen will excuse me, I'll take my leave.'

Marcellus waited for Silvius to leave and took a deep breath. Hippalus and Aafa exchanged glances.

'You're not going to the club yourself?' asked Hippalus.

'No, I am heading home.'

'Be careful. Would you like Aafa to escort you? We wouldn't want you kidnapped again.'

Marcellus smiled as he stood up. 'I wouldn't dream of taking Aafa away from you, captain. I can manage my way home.' Just as he was about to leave the room, Hippalus pulled out an oilskin pouch from the folds of his tunic and threw it on the stool Marcellus had been sitting on.

'You might want this.'

Marcellus looked at him enquiringly. What now?

'Letters from home. They came on a friend's ship this morning.'

Marcellus picked up the package, nodded at the seamen and left.

16

THREE LETTERS

My dearest son,

Your father sends his regards and I attach his letter to mine so that he can tell you himself how well he thinks you are getting on with the mission entrusted to you. I spoke to Anais a few days ago when he visited us, and he said that he had called on you at Alexandria and that you were not in good health then. I hope you have recovered, and that the sea and the country you have made your temporary home is agreeing with you. As you know, I beseeched your father to send you closer to home – to Alexandria or Anatolia – but he was intent on sending you so far away from me to his trusted Silvius. Wouldn't it have been better if you had learnt your father's trade from within the limits of the Republic – Rome gets her grains, wine and olives from her provinces; for everything else we need, we have armies, ships and servants. So, tell me, what is the need to send you to the other end of the world? I sometimes wonder whether your father sent you so far away from home not for the sake of your education, as he often claims, but so that you can stay away from your true calling. He knows too well that all the riches of his house cannot hold you back when the time comes and that is why he has asked you to undertake this journey. But he should know better – he should know that it is not in his hands that your future rests. Your father thinks of you as a merchant prince, one who is destined to become the king of merchants.

But he forgets that you are my son and hence a son of Rome; and your true calling is inside the empire.

There is talk of unrest and troops everywhere, but on the surface, things are deathly calm. People confer inside homes and baths, and conspiracies abound. It is rumoured there will be a civil war yet again in our city. I was but a girl when the bloodbath happened, and I fear I may not have the heart to see it again. I fear for the future of Rome, and that is why I would like you to make haste and come home as quickly as possible. It is not in my nature to disobey my husband, but in this case I must. I may have married a merchant – a kind one, I will concede – but I am a senator's daughter and my first allegiance is to Rome. Your father, despite everything he has built in this city, will always remain a foreigner, and he thinks it is appropriate for you to hide away in an alien land, while I believe you should be here to fulfil your predestined role. I bid you to come back to Rome soonest, as your life is not to be wasted in a foreign land – especially when the country needs you. Your father says he cares too much about your life to let you return now but let there be no doubt that I am more interested in your destiny.

Good-bye for now, Marcellus.
Your mother in Rome

Marcellus pictured her in his mind – her earnest angular forehead, covered in frowns, forcing a charming smile as she spoke to her husband to make the case for summoning her son back home. If you believed her, Rome was always in danger and her son was destined to play a part in saving it. Only then would she be able to sit with her sisters in her father's house on equal terms. But, unfortunately for her, her husband did not see it that way. His heart was ruled by the necessities of being a successful merchant and he was not easily swayed by principles. Trade succeeds despite politics, as he often used to say, and he had no use for the latter, unless it was to marry the daughter of a respected but not very well-to-do senator, giving him unprecedented access to customers and authorities. Yet, their marriage was a successful one, Marcellus had to admit as someone who had seen it at close quarters in their own home – one from which both parties gained more than they lost. But now, in the matter of their only son, they were at loggerheads.

He wondered if she realized how very much like her Marcellus was – ambitious, patriotic, hedonistic, and a lover of all things Roman – but he had a very different plan to get what he wanted. He was like his father in that he was pragmatic and knew what would be required of a son of a 'foreign' trader to make it in her world.

He opened his father's letter next.

Dear son,

I'd like to assure you at the outset that the debts you incurred have been paid in full, and you will not be bothered by Antonius and his ilk if you refrain from further dealings with their kind.

I trust your journey to Puhar was uneventful and gave you time to think about your future and our trade with Tamil country – away from the distractions of your life here in Rome. Now that you have had an opportunity to see the country, I hope you understand the importance of trade to the continued well-being of the empire that your mother talks of so much. As you are aware, your mother cares for ideas and principles, and she thinks her son is destined for greatness. I am but a merchant, and I like things that I can see and touch. I like pepper. I like silk. I like pearls. I like my son and would not want to lose him to politics or war, or to spectacles in the Circus. This is why I sent you there, against your and your mother's wishes. You will understand Rome better from a distance than from inside it. While I have not seen your mother's letter, I can surmise her message to you and my counsel to you is thus: stay in Puhar until you are ready to come back with something more than what you left with.

Farewell, my son.

He wouldn't have expected anything less from his father. He noticed that Gaius was careful to avoid any mention of the recent happenings in Rome, which only confirmed everything his mother had said about the unrest. He agreed with his father – it made sense for him to stay outside Rome, though he wasn't sure if he was better off where he was now.

There was one more letter from his father, addressed to Marcus, Marcellus's companion. Gaius wouldn't have known at the time of writing this letter that only one of them had boarded the *Minerva* at Myos Hormos. He took his time, turning it around in his hand a number of times before opening it.

Dear Marcus,

It was nearly four decades ago when, for the first time, I found myself outside this city in a trading port in the eastern borders of the empire. I must have been close to your age. I spent many months working with the native runners and traders to establish a safe passage for the silk that had come across the mountains from Thinae. The men of the desert were warm and friendly, and held Rome in awe. Some would say that they were not civilized, and they didn't have roads or dams or aqueducts or the senate, but I didn't see them as being any different from us. We were united by the common goal of moving things from one place to another, from the one who makes to the one who consumes, to bring to a people the things they enjoy – a shawl, a taste, a dye – items they did not know existed were it not for us. Thus, the creation of markets became my calling.

I prospered and I earned a name from my people, and, on my death, it will be written on my epitaph that I was a man who persevered through hard times and died more prosperous than my father and those who came before him. And that I left behind more than what I had inherited. I tell you this because you will have decisions to make of your own soon and I hope this may help you in doing so.

This is all we are here to do – to leave what is given to us in a better state than we found it. While I am afraid I have not always been successful at taking my own advice, I remain hopeful that I may be able to make some amends, thanks to you. I don't for a moment doubt that you will find a way to reach Korkai and fulfil my wishes. Hence, my only other ask of you is to be a true friend and brother to Marcellus, as he will need you more in Puhar than he has ever needed you.

I hope you will understand this one day.

Yours,
Gaius

The patriarch had expressed more in this letter than in all the years his son had known him.

Marcellus settled in to sleep but his thoughts went back to the letters from home. One thing was clear to him now more than ever – the only avenue open to him was to keep moving forward. He could not breach the trust his father placed on him.

17

An Unlikely Visitor

'Where is your dagger?'

Marcellus opened his eyes to see Silvius standing next to his bed, glowering down at him, while Adi searched the room.

'Stay away from my stuff!' Marcellus shouted at Adi.

'Your dagger. Where is it?'

'I lost it; it was taken away from me when I was attacked by the gang the other night. But why do you want to know? What do you mean by –'

'That's enough. How do I know you are telling me the truth?'

'What in Jupiter's name are you going on about?' Marcellus was sitting up now and nothing that was going on was making any sense to him.

'A man, a native Chola man, by the name of Muthu was knifed last night in the Yavana quarters. He bled to death not too far from here. His cousin, Mari, is claiming to everyone who will listen that the murderer was a young Yavana man matching your description.'

'What? Those are the two men who kidnapped me!'

Questions swirled around in his head. Why would anyone murder Muthu? Did he turn on his paymaster? And what was Muthu doing outside prison? Hadn't the Chola soldiers arrested him?

'Great, now you have a motive. When did you get back last night? Did you see anyone?'

'No, I was preoccupied. Did they find the murder weapon?'

'I suspect it won't take long for them to find it.'

'But...I had nothing to do with it!'

'Tell that to the magistrate.'

'How do you know all of this?'

'Adi tracked down Mari. He hasn't gone to the authorities yet, but it won't take long.'

'Wait, I thought they were already in prison. They were arrested –'

Adi spoke up for the first time. 'And how would you know this?'

Marcellus ignored him. 'There was also the bandit girl who was in cahoots with them. She –'

'How do you know this, Yavana lord?' Adi interrupted once again, this time with urgency in his voice.

Marcellus looked up at the boy but did not answer. He had enough things to worry about without being wanted for murder now. He needed to think his way out of this.

'Let me go to the warehouse and –' he started, but Silvius did not let him finish his sentence.

'Hide in the warehouse? The *Minerva*? That's the first place they'll look for you. No, you will listen to me this time if you value your life. You are not leaving this house until I tell you to. We will find out exactly what is likely to happen, and Adi here will see whether he can keep Mari quiet for a while.'

Marcellus nodded. Perhaps his father had been right – it needed a crisis for Silvius to come into form. But another thought struck him. If Silvius was actually worried about *his* life, then...

'Your friend from Musiris? He is not here yet?'

Silvius's eyes narrowed. 'Not yet, but expected any moment now. Why do you ask?'

Marcellus forced a smile. 'Maybe I'll recognize him when I see him.'

Once Adi and Silvius left the room, Marcellus started packing. In a hurry. It was clear by now that whichever way it ended, he was going to be leaving – Proteus would recognize him in an instant. It wasn't safe for him to be in Puhar any more. He was so busy working out his options that he didn't hear the footsteps come up the steep stairwell outside his room. The door opened and he whirled around. A diminutive Chola lad stepped in, dressed as he had been that morning on the magistrate's boat. Before he could say anything, Kuzhali spoke.

'I apologize for the unexpected nature of this meeting, but I do not have much time. I trust you'll understand once I explain the purpose of my visit.'

It wasn't clear what he was more surprised by – the fact that she happened to be in his dwelling, or that she, for the first time, had adopted a formal, almost respectful, tone while addressing him.

'How do you know where I live? How did you get here?' he demanded.

'Don't worry about matters of little significance. I come to you with a request – it is a strange one, I must warn you at the outset. But I hope that you will not refuse me and will think of this as a service rendered to your friend who holds you in the highest regard.'

Marcellus decided to play the game and when he spoke he was as formal as she had been. 'I am indebted to my friend and am happy to be of service. I am also grateful for the opportunity to serve his sister in any way possible. In fact, I have been intending to write to him regarding the facts I happen to be in possession of about the robbery.'

Kuzhali shook her head. 'It is of no concern, and most of the jewellery has been returned. My brother refuses to believe me, but I know who put whom up to it – I must say that my brother is not always careful in his choice of *friends*.'

'But I –'

'It is not you I speak of, Yavana, otherwise I would not be here today.'

'Please tell me how I can be of service.'

Marcellus was intrigued, to say the least. What kind of service could he render for this girl, dressed in a man's garb, that her many servants were not capable of performing? And why him? Not that he needed another thing to worry about, but this was proving to be an interesting distraction.

'I'd like you to take a letter to my brother. It is very important that he receives it and that it falls into no one else's hands.'

'Why? Where has Vallavan gone? Is he not in Puhar?'

He had been so busy with Silvius and Hippalus the past few days that he had not thought of his friend much. The thought of visiting the household had crossed his mind a few times, but an opportunity had not cropped up.

'He is travelling inland, carrying a message to Uraiyur. It is imperative that I send him a message and I cannot trust anyone else,' she said.

Marcellus knew that the king's entourage was camped near the old capital as Karikalan was inspecting the construction of the dam on the Kaveri to divert the excess water to the Kollidam branch. Karikalan had promised a dam to the farmers of the delta if they helped him win the war at Venni, and it was time to keep that promise. An engineer was in charge and construction was under way, but the king wanted to see for himself how the project was coming along. If Vallavan had left for Uraiyur, then he must be carrying a message for Karikalan himself, Marcellus deduced. And Vallavan was no military man, so there was only one reason for him to see the king – a message from the merchants of Puhar. Given what he had overheard in the Manaykan mansion, this wasn't surprising at all.

But what was the urgent missive this girl wanted him to take to her brother, and why did she not trust anyone else with it? She must know that as a Yavana who spoke only passable Tamil, he was likely to stand out in every crowd in this country. How, then, was he to make his way to the anicut without drawing attention to himself? And was he really considering the request? He had to admit that it gave him the perfect excuse to leave Puhar, and it was fast becoming clear he had to do so soon.

'Of what nature is his trip? Will he see the king?' he pressed on.

Kuzhali gave him a dazzling smile. 'How do you expect me to know the reason behind my brother's trip? I am kept away from all business dealings, and I only know he went to Uraiyur because he told me so himself before he left. He also said if I needed help, I should come to you.' If her intention was to flatter him, she was succeeding.

'I am glad to be of help, but please tell me something: other than taking a letter to your brother, is there any assistance I can provide? Would you not tell me what kind of trouble you are in?' Another thought had struck him. That Kuzhali may have a problem of an entirely different nature. What if she was being married off to an unwanted suitor? Or being turned out of her home for bringing bad luck? 'If there is anyone troubling you, I'd be more than happy to sever his hands,' he added.

Kuzhali looked at him in surprise. This boy, her brother's

friend, actually thought she was asking for Vallavan's help to fight off a suitor! In his country did widows have a queue of admirers at their doors? She wondered for the hundredth time whether it was prudent to ask this Yavana to take the message to her brother, especially when it was such an important one.

'I am afraid you can be of no help to me in my current situation. Only my brother can, and I know he will return immediately once he reads my message,' she said, taking out a scroll hidden in the folds of her veshti. She offered it to Marcellus, who took it without thinking.

'I know of the affection your brother has for you and I am asking on his behalf. Please tell me whether there is anything else I should know. Are you comfortable in your home?'

Kuzhali looked at him steadily. 'If that weren't the case, what would you do about it?'

It was fair to say that he hadn't really considered the question. He had simply said the first thing that had come to his mind.

'I will take you with me back to Rome on my ship, just like I got your brother here. I will show you our Circuses and walk with you on the Via Appia. You will see magnificent structures, exceeding even your wildest imagination, and watch great gladiatorial conquests. We will have a house in Rome and one in the country on the hill, and you will have your own slaves. You will drink the finest wine and savour the best meat. Come with me, Kuzhali...and I promise you a world you haven't even dreamt of.'

He knew he had no right to woo her with such obvious falsehoods – she wouldn't give him a second glance if she knew who he really was – and it wasn't clear who was more surprised by his impassioned speech, Kuzhali or Marcellus himself. But he had never shown much restraint in matters of love, and there was no harm in this talk, safely ensconced as they were in Puhar. If it meant he'd get more information out of her, all the better. To his surprise, Kuzhali burst out laughing.

'What does your father think about this proposal of yours? To marry a foreign widow?'

He hadn't actually spoken of marriage and she'd clearly missed that part. 'I have not spoken to him yet, but I will write to him and he will not stand in my way,' he said.

'Let me tell you what he will say. He will say, by all means bring her to Rome. We can always do with another slave in our household.'

That one struck home. In more ways than one.

'I will not let him –'

'Why? He would be right, but even that is besides the point. Why would you assume that a Chola girl would want to leave her home and go with a stranger to a foreign land? Why do you think that I would want to run away and come with *you*, of all people?'

'You do not know the city you reject so casually. In Rome, the world is made and in Rome –'

'But what if the world is not what I desire, Yavana? I am not ambitious enough to seek a place that I cannot imagine. This land, my Tamil country, is enough for me, my brother's friend, and to attain what I want, I need your help. The riches of Rome do not tempt me, especially because I know what I will be in that city of yours.'

'And what are you here, young lady? You are treated as a bad omen in your own house and are not allowed to partake in any festivities. Your younger sister is to be married off at your father's whim to a boy you do not think is an appropriate match. For what? To cement a trade relationship! Just as I am sure your marriage was. What does that make you?'

'Let me put your mind at ease,' Kuzhali said. 'The only kind of marriage I'd be happy to be in is one which leads to something tangible – such as trade, land, power, gold. That, I assure you, Yavana, is the only kind of marriage I know. That's the one I had with my late husband, and neither of us thought anything more of it. What other kind do you have in mind that takes place in your country?'

It was his turn to laugh. It struck him that this was someone his father would be very happy to have as a daughter-in-law. Their views on marriage were one and the same. But he had tried to make a case and he wasn't going to give up so easily now. He considered his words carefully before speaking.

'I speak of love, Kuzhali, the love that a man has for a woman – a love that is pure, unblemished and, until this point, I must say, unrequited.'

'Love? From one meeting? I know of power and duty, but the kind of love you speak of, I am afraid I am not well versed in that. Let us not speak of such things,' she said. 'Now, please tell me you will take my message to my brother.'

'I will gladly be of assistance to you,' Marcellus said gallantly, inwardly feeling very relieved. If she had accepted his impetuous and entirely false proposal, he'd have her on his conscience for a long time. Not that he did not fancy her, quite the opposite, but he was in no position to make a proposal of anything. 'Though you have refused my proposal, I will ensure your wishes are fulfilled to the best of my ability. I will take this message to your brother.'

'My undying gratitude to you, Yavana. Now, I shall take my leave.' The girl left as quickly and surreptitiously as she had come, leaving Marcellus to find his way out of Puhar and into interior Chola country.

~

Hippalus and Aafa were drunk. They had broken one of their cardinal rules: when in a foreign land, at least one of them had to remain sober at all times. But this situation qualified for an exception.

Silvius had visited them earlier in the day – huffing and fuming – to give them news that the bird had flown. Marcellus was nowhere to be seen and he had left no forwarding address either.

'What are we going to tell his pater? That his son fell in love with some courtesan and eloped with her? You will be writing the letter, I presume?' Hippalus asked.

'What son are you referring to?' Silvius snapped.

'What?'

'He is an impostor. If I get my hands on the rascal, I'll wring this neck. No, I'll happily hand him over to the Cholas and see him crushed to death by one of their elephants. Adi is on the case and we'll still find him, I assure you. Whoever he is, he is no son of Gaius. Proteus confirmed that the real Marcellus is a striking image of his *mother*, not his father – and Gaius has only one son!'

There were many things Hippalus had suspected the young man of, but there was no question in his mind about him being his father's son. He had enough of Gaius in him, or so he had made them all think. If Silvius was right, he was one hell of an impostor.

'A *slave*! A companion to the real Marcellus who he must have murdered before he boarded the *Minerva*. You both believed him at face value without a second thought!'

'A freedman,' Aafa corrected him.

'How does it matter? He is a murderer.'

'We don't know that now, do we?'

'You tell me this: where is the real Marcellus? What are you not telling me?'

'He… The impostor… He left a message,' Aafa said finally.

Hippalus turned to his pilot in surprise. 'He left a message for *you*?'

'I don't care which of you he wrote to. What did the bastard say?' Silvius snarled.

'He says that Marcellus, the real one, was on his way to Gaul the last time he saw him. He wanted to join the forces and asked Marcus – our man – to impersonate him.'

'The Hades he did!'

'Well, that's his story, and we can choose to believe it or not. The point is he wants us to go ahead with the plan. He promises to meet us in Korkai.'

Hippalus turned the information over in his mind for a few moments and erupted with laughter. 'You can't fault him for not having the nerve.'

'You cannot be seriously considering this. We don't take orders from a murderer; we have no idea who he is and what he is up to!' said Silvius.

'What's the worst that can happen? We don't load anything at Korkai. In which case, we will come back to Puhar citing urgent repairs.'

'He will hand us all over to the Chola navy; *that's* what he is up to, if you ask me.'

'You are safe. It's we who take the risk, and guess what? If he turns up and it is as you say, we'll throw him back in the ship and take him to Rome, where he can stand trial for murder.'

'I will not allow this!'

Aafa spoke up. 'Your boy, Adi... Let's see what he turns up with in the next few days. We don't have to do anything yet; we have time on our side.'

That seemed to pacify Silvius for the moment. 'We have to be discreet until we know more. I can't ask the merchants for help...

Not yet.' He cursed Marcellus – *Marcus* – a few more times and clambered off the ship.

Hippalus confronted Aafa late that night, once they were both inebriated. 'You say he wrote *you* a message?'

'Only one of us can read and he knows that.'

'You can teach me.'

'We have tried many times, but you don't persist.'

'That's because I am the storyteller. Did Homer read?'

'He sang. Can you sing?'

'You have to be careful of what you say.'

'Speaking of reading...'

'Yes.'

'He may not be Marcellus, but he is Gaius's son all right.'

'Didn't you hear Silvius? Marcellus is the only son.'

'I read his letters before you gave them to him, and one of them was addressed to the real him – to Marcus. So I know enough.'

'Oh, by Zeus, you don't mean to say what I think you mean! The slave girl's son brought up in the same household as a companion, educated and trained with the legitimate child! The standard story in all rich Roman households. I see it now! How did we miss it?'

And once Hippalus started down the track, the missing pieces quickly fell into place. 'Pater sends both off to trade, but one runs away to join the army and the other takes his place. It's no surprise that he is good at this – our Marcus here is no playboy who could afford to spend his time at the races, unlike his brother. He is a freedman who will need to earn his keep. Who wants to bet that he had been working with the old man all these years? No wonder he knows so much about the family business. Don't you ever dare tell him this, Aafa, but by Hades, I am beginning to like the bastard!'

PART II

HIGH ROAD

What Her Friend Said,
criticizing him to give her strength

The drum-footed black elephant's calf,
its crown still soft,
runs and plays
with the gypsy woman's boys,
their bodies all tiny joints,
boys from the seaside
where liquor is plentiful;

is sweet one day
but devours their millet the next;

so too, his games and laughter
turn to hate.

Kuriyiraiyar, *Kuruntokai* 394

Mothers

The old woman's shoulders
were dry, unfleshed,
with outstanding veins;
her low belly
was like a lotus pad.

When people said
her son had taken fright,
had turned his back on battle
and died,

she raged,
and shouted,
'If he really broke down
in the thick of battle,
I'll slash these breasts
that gave him suck,'
and went there,
sword in hand.

Turning over body after fallen body,
she rummaged through the blood-red field
till she found her son,
quartered, in pieces,

and she rejoiced
more than on the day
she gave him birth.

Kākkaipāṭiṉiyār Naccel̤l̤aiyār, *Puṟanāṉūṟu* 278

18

PILGRIMS ON THE HIGH ROAD

In Puhar, life revolves around trade, rituals and royalty, but life in the granary of the Chola kingdom is rather different, or so one understands as we follow two vaguely familiar pilgrims travelling inland, tracking the winding course of the Kaveri. Here in the countryside, the air is clearer, the trees are greener, the people speak their minds candidly and harbour a healthy suspicion for strangers bearing gifts. Grains and pulses are grown by peasants, who till the land perennially, and for whom the only deities that matter are the rain and the river gods. This is also from where the majority of men for the Chola military come – usually the firstborn son – lured by the prospect of bravery and the chance of a better life for their families. Not many from the urban capital venture out into the hinterlands; and the well-travelled traders of Tamilakam may have seen Chang'an and Rome, but they are unlikely to have set foot beyond the first bend of the Kaveri.

Our pilgrims travel on sturdy horses along the main thoroughfare that messengers and middlemen take to get to Uraiyur, before heading down to the borders of the erstwhile Pandya country. The river is in spate as it is nearly the end of the monsoon season. Waters flood the plains, and it is impossible to see what has been planted. The road roughly follows the course of the river, diverging here and there to go through a village or wooded land, but it always winds back to the main riverbank. The two men traverse the road at a healthy pace – a portly, middle-aged Easterner with a single tuft of hair on his head and a tall, striking young man not quite past the first flush of youth, his hairless head glistening under the midday sun.

A few of the folk who observed the pair as they left the city in the early hours of the morning had commented that the younger man was the spitting image of the young Gautama, whose faith he was ostensibly here to spread.

'The disguise seems to be working. We have been out in the country for most of the day and no one seems suspicious of us,' said the young man.

'I'd not be too sure of that. Pilgrims do not gallop on horses; they walk or beg for a ride on a bullock cart. But cheer up, young Roman! Whether your disguise works or not, be assured that your lustrous locks will be put to good use. They will fetch an excellent price in the angadi,' the older man replied with a straight face.

Marcus – he continues to refer to himself as Marcellus in present company, but there is no reason for us to go along with the deception any more – glared at Zhang. The Buddhist disguise was his idea, as a Yavana trader on the main road to Uraiyur would arouse suspicions. But Zhang took it a step too far and convinced him to tonsure his head too. Followers of Buddha, he had told Marcus, never had more than one tuft of hair, and the Yavana would not be identified as a monk if he did not comply. And so Marcus decided to shave off all of his hair rather than travel through this alien land with a single tuft of hair. He wondered whether he had made a mistake in asking Zhang to accompany him. He had to leave Puhar in a hurry and did not have much of a choice. To his surprise, the older man had agreed readily.

'How do we know this is the right direction?' Marcus asked, eager to move away from the subject of his locks.

'We cannot get lost as long as we can hear the river.'

'Have you travelled this way before?'

'I have been this way to debate with Kavunti on a few occasions. This is the woman who peddles the Mahaviran to the merchant families. She lives not far from here.'

'Isn't the Mahaviran similar to your Buddha?'

'In some ways. But now that the Jainas have the merchants, success is getting to their heads. I've always rooted for the underdog.'

'Have you been further south on this road?'

'I can't say I remember.'

'You would surely remember whether you passed this way, would you not?'

'When you have travelled as much as I have, every road seems the same.'

Marcus took this as an invitation to find out more about Zhang. 'Tell me about the roads you've been on. We have all the time in the world now.'

'My story is a common one in my country. I was thrown out of the Middle Kingdom in disgrace.'

'Why were you exiled?'

'If you have to know, I was a record keeper in charge of keeping count of the number of dogs in the garrison. A dog went missing one day and I did not report it, as I knew the soldier who had done the dastardly act. However, the man confessed later, and I was flung into the desert never to return to my country or to see my family.'

'You were a military man? I wouldn't have guessed!'

'A scribe, a dog counter in the military... I did not see any action.'

Marcus pondered over Zhang's story. As far as he knew, the Roman army did not employ dog counters. He could think of a few of his friends who would have been excellent at it though.

'How did you reach Puhar?' he asked.

'After the Wall comes the desert that only few people manage to cross. But I crossed it with the help of a couple of smugglers pilfering silk and a monk who was there to spread the faith of the Buddha. I asked him where I could learn more about the Great One and he pointed to the tall mountains in the distance. So I made my way up and down the mountains, stopping at monasteries on the way and they provided food, shelter and taught me the ways of Buddha. After a few years of wandering, I reached Magadha, where I spent some time learning under a guru. Then I decided to set out to spread the message myself and travelled down to Satkarni's land, and further south to Tamil lands...'

'But why stop in Puhar?' Marcus was at his interrogative best. This was the first time Zhang had volunteered any personal information and Marcus filed it away in his head carefully. It could come of use some day.

'A man has to make a home somewhere and, for now, this country, the city of Puhar, suits me,' Zhang said. Marcus wondered whether it was the appam-seller Rajamma, whom he was rumoured to be living with, who kept him in Puhar.

'Enough of this dog counter's story,' Zhang said abruptly. 'Let us hear the story of the rich Roman – what brings you here, so far away from the empire, when momentous things are happening in your homeland?'

Marcus looked up sharply. For a pilgrim who had settled down in the middle of nowhere, Zhang was a little too well informed. Marcus would have to be very careful about how much he gave away.

'I am afraid my story isn't as exciting as yours. I was neither exiled nor have I found a new faith. I belong to a merchant family in Rome, and my father sent me here to trade and to learn from Silvius.'

'But what kind of trade takes you inland into Chola country and that too in disguise? You wouldn't, by any chance, be looking to buy directly from the peasants and cut out the Chola traders, would you now?'

'I told you the truth when I asked you to come with me. I am going to meet my friend Vallavan and deliver a message. There is no other reason,' Marcus said.

'How did he become your friend?'

'Well, that's a long, boring story.'

'Would it have something to do with him travelling on your ship?'

Marcus nodded.

'I wonder what *he* is doing inland.'

'That I do not know.'

'I hope we find him before we run into the king's retinue. They aren't going to be very pleased with foreigners straying away from Puhar,' said Zhang.

'Aren't they used to seeing pilgrims here? This is a land of many faiths.'

'Yes, but not foreigners such as ourselves. They'll assume we are spies.'

Marcus laughed. He had thought that they would be seen as fugitives, especially since he was indeed one. That they would be mistaken for spies had not occurred to him. 'Why would the Roman empire or the emperor of the Middle Kingdom, who are both so far away, send spies to this small kingdom?'

'Either of them may be considering an invasion. Or aligning themselves with enemies in the north or south to improve their trade prospects. The Chola country may be a small kingdom, but you are here for its wealth, aren't you?'

He had nearly hit the nail on the head. 'We are pilgrims, not spies,' Marcus said hurriedly. 'If we do run into the king, we will convert them to your sect – like that Magadhan king you were telling me about. Then this too will become your Buddha's land.'

This ploy seemed to work, and Zhang was successfully diverted. 'In that case, young Roman, I do wish we meet the king. Perhaps he will give up his plan of conquests like the great Asokan and instead devote his life to the Buddha. Wouldn't that be a wonderful thing?' His eyes shone as he spoke. Marcus nodded sagely. He was much happier with this line of discussion.

Presently, the travellers arrived at a wayside inn – three small buildings surrounded by a coconut grove – where Zhang suggested they spend the night. Marcus turned around and looked uneasily at the road. There was a chance that he was being pursued, and the farther he was from Puhar, the better.

'You are expecting company?'

Marcus shook his head. They had to spend the night somewhere. That, and the inviting aroma of boiling rice and spiced mutton stew wafting from the inn, settled it.

19

AN ALTERCATION

Travellers' inns were one of King Karikalan's more progressive initiatives: a number of such sathirams dotted the north–south highway from Puhar to Kumari for the convenience of travellers. These establishments were manned by a family, usually from a neighbouring village, who received an annual allotment from Puhar, which helped them run the inn in addition to their farm work. The main clientele for these establishments consisted of middlemen carrying goods to and from Puhar, royal messengers, pilgrims, and spies disguised as one of the above. A stone-carved Vazhi Pillayar stood in front of the clearing to welcome travellers and to ward off evil. When guests left the inn, they broke a coconut and offered it to the deity to ensure that they reached their destination.

As we have seen, our pilgrims' timing was impeccable as the inn's guests were just about to sit down for dinner. It proved to be a popular place that evening with a few other parties already seated inside the main courtyard. One group of men sat in a corner talking and laughing loudly. Diagonally across them was a couple – the wife waving a fan fashioned from palm leaves in front of her husband's face.

'Who do we have here at this time? In the name of the great King Karikalan, the saviour of these lands, Maran welcomes you.'

Maran turned out be an old man with a perpetual frown, who'd hurriedly hobbled towards the pilgrims, supporting himself on a walking stick.

'Horses?' he continued. 'Oh yes, we are equipped to deal with them, don't you worry. The stable boy will tend to them. Speak your names and you may step inside.'

Zhang cupped his hands together to greet the man. 'Vanakkam,' he said. 'We are two pilgrims – Zhang and Marcellus – who live by the way of Gautama, the Buddha. We are travelling south to speak of him and his way to anyone who will deign to listen. Please give us shelter for the night and we will, in turn, tell you all about the Enlightened One.'

The innkeeper hastily took a step back before recovering his composure. 'That makes two of you on the same day! We are worshippers of Sivan and his son, Pillayar, who you saw outside. Foreigners are welcome in Chola country, and we will extend you our best hospitality. You are welcome in this inn as long as you are not outcastes. But I must respectfully ask you to pay obeisance to Pillayar and not speak of other gods inside this place.'

'There is no such –' started Zhang, but Marcus interrupted him swiftly. His broken Tamil would serve them better here than Zhang making his case fluently for an egalitarian Buddha. If nothing else, his Tamil would likely not get them kicked out into the night with no shelter.

'We understand, ayya, and we will abide by your wishes while we are under your roof. Neither of us are parayas in our country,' he lied. Freedmen and dog counters were very much the dregs of the societies they came from, but why burden the poor old man with such detail. 'As a token of our appreciation, we hope you will accept this small gift.'

He pulled out a silver coin and handed it to the innkeeper, whose eyes widened. Zhang glowered at Marcus and whispered in Latin, 'Why does a poor pilgrim give away a Roman coin to an innkeeper? If you want to be taken seriously, you have to act the part!'

Whether the innkeeper believed Marcus or not, the coin worked its magic, and it wasn't long before they were seated near one of the large windows that let in the fresh evening air and were served piping-hot rice, goat leg stew, pudding and plantain. Both men ate heartily, and it was a while before they took notice of the other guests. Marcus looked around the courtyard and saw a couple of men in the far corner speaking in low voices, heads bent. The lamplight was dim and he couldn't make out their faces clearly. Unlike the others, these two paid no attention to the new arrivals and were completely engrossed in their conversation.

'The food was heavenly,' Marcus said.

'You have travelled a long way. Anything would taste delicious, but remember, heaven itself is a delusion.'

'Why? Didn't you like the food? You showed no sign of not enjoying it.'

'Those of us who follow the way of the Buddha don't pay attention to such worldly pleasures. Food is merely sustenance to us,' said Zhang. Marcus's mind went back to the first time he had met Zhang and a vivid picture of the older man biting into a piece of fried fish with gusto in Maruvum crossed his mind.

'I'd like to meet the cook to give him my compliments,' he said. And ask for any information regarding Vallavan who may have stopped here a few days ago.

'*She* is the old man's daughter. I don't believe you will be allowed to see her.' Zhang chuckled. 'That, my friend, may take a lot more than one Roman coin.'

'I will thank her father instead,' said Marcus. He walked over to the innkeeper and said, 'I would like to tell you that what you have served today is the most delicious of meals.'

The innkeeper beamed and his frown disappeared for an instant. 'My father used to cook in the house of the general back in his day. We left Puhar before the war, and nowadays, I am just an innkeeper. But I am still my father's son and I am delighted that my daughter follows in my footsteps.' The frown was firmly back in place as he continued: 'But I am afraid that she will not be here long as her marriage will happen after the monsoon is past. I will have to find a new helper once she leaves this household.'

'Are we all invited to the wedding, ayya? Where are you sending your daughter?' shouted someone from the boisterous party of young men who had overheard their conversation.

'All of you are invited! I may be a poor man, but no one needs to teach me how to conduct a proper wedding. I have saved enough to send my daughter with a feast that won't be forgotten for a while. She is getting married to my nephew who lives near Madurai. He runs an inn there, just like us. My daughter will be of great help to him,' the old man said, his voice filled with pride.

'Madurai?' The young man who had asked the question rose and walked towards the innkeeper. He wasn't laughing any more. 'Old man,' he began, his voice distinctly menacing, 'could you not find anyone in Chola land fit for your daughter that you had to find a man in that land of traitors? How could you even think of such a thing?'

His words had hit their mark as the couple in the corner, who had kept to themselves until then, turned around to look at the speaker. The woman stopped fanning her husband.

'But she is getting married to her cousin,' the innkeeper protested. 'My sister married a man from our village, but they moved to Pandya country with his master years ago. The groom is her son.'

'I hope for your daughter's sake that he hasn't turned into a Pandya coward,' said another man from the group, looking askance at the couple. The man in the corner made an attempt to get to his feet, but his wife pulled him back. He shouted to the innkeeper, settling back down, 'Ayya, if your nephew is half as brave as a Pandya lad, your daughter is very fortunate indeed.'

'Brave?' The young men, who were spoiling for a fight, scoffed. 'We all know how you ran away from the battlefield in Venni. An army of deserters, that's what your people are famous for.'

This time his wife did not stop him when the man tried to get up. 'Watch your words, Chola men. I belong to the clan where a grieving mother disowns her own son if he runs away from battle. Our armies fight till the last man standing.'

'There weren't any left standing in Venni! And now, you roam freely in our lands, taking advantage of the magnanimity of our king. Still, your tails wag.'

'You dare to call me a dog, you Chola scum?' shouted the man as he drew a dagger from the folds of his veshti and walked towards the young crowd. His wife ran behind him, but he paid no attention to her. The Chola men all rose, ready to pounce on the lone Pandya.

The innkeeper, sensing that this would not end well for him, stood in between the antagonists.

'Please, this is a house of hospitality, and we are in a time of peace,' he pleaded. 'If you have scores to settle, I request you to take them outside.'

'Move aside, old man. Now that you are going to have a Pandya son-in-law, are you on their side? Are you a Pandya spy?'

'Me? A spy? Please do not speak of such things. My family has served the Chola court for generations and you will not find a more loyal subject than myself!' the innkeeper cried out.

The men, however, were in no mood to listen. Marcus took a few steps towards the crowd, but Zhang placed a restraining hand on his shoulder.

'What do you think you are doing? This is not your battle,' he whispered.

'But they are going to kill each other. We could stop it.'

'Are you looking to get killed as well?'

The Pandya man was by now surrounded by the Chola men, while his wife looked on, horrified; they were circling him slowly while he pointed his dagger at each one of them. Marcus and Zhang watched in morbid fascination, while the two men in the corner paid no attention to the proceedings. The innkeeper looked visibly distraught.

'Please do not fight in my house,' he tried again. 'The king will not allow this to happen.'

'The king will reward us for upholding Chola honour. This Pandya is here to put our lands in jeopardy.'

The Pandya man laughed at this. 'I came to this land in peace, but you have driven me to violence. Wife, if I die in this cursed land, return home and tell everyone what happened here. Tell them how the Cholas mock us after their king told us we would be welcome here. Tell them all that happened in our journey and how I fought these Chola wastrels till my last breath.'

'Don't you belong to a religion of peace? Blood is going to be spilt for no reason and we ought to stop it,' Marcus whispered urgently to Zhang.

'Your family expects you back in Rome. You should not spill *your* blood needlessly here.'

'But how do you know it's needless?' Marcus's fingers reached for his dagger involuntarily before he realized it had been stolen.

The first blow fell out of the blue. One of the Chola men clutched his left arm and screamed in agony. His knife dropped to the ground as he withdrew from the fight and sat with his back against the nearest pillar, heaving with pain.

'Which one of you wants to go next?' the Pandya shouted. Two men went closer just as the sound of tinkling anklets filled the courtyard. A girl of about fifteen – the cook, guessed Marcus – ran inside.

'The tiger flag flies high. The king's messenger is on his way. He travels at great speed, but he will stop here for the night.'

Just as she finished her announcement, Marcus heard the sound of hooves nearing the inn. The Chola men melted into the night through the back door, dragging their injured friend behind them. Marcus did not wait; he was taking no chances with the king's messenger. This could be a soldier on his trail. He slipped inside the dark retiring room they had been allocated and hid from view, next to the window. A moment later, Zhang joined him. Marcus wasn't the only one who didn't want to be seen.

The Pandya man stood alone in the courtyard, dagger drawn, staring at the sky as the king's envoy entered the house.

Marcus sneaked a peek.

Adi!

20

THE ROYAL EMISSARY

The new arrival wore a long veshti with many folds, and a number of holsters on either side to carry messages and weapons. The innkeeper rushed forward to greet him.

'Thambi, welcome! I will fetch you a pail of warm water right this moment and your food will be ready as soon as you have a wash. Will you be staying the night?' he queried.

Adi did not reply as he was staring at the man standing in the middle of the courtyard with his dagger still drawn. His hand involuntarily went to his right.

'Who are you and why are you brandishing a weapon here?'

Adi's voice was authoritative, a tone that Marcus had never heard from him before. The boy had hardly spoken a word in front of Silvius; this was some transformation. In the dark, Marcus could not make out if the older man was as surprised as he was. He'd surely have seen Adi in Maruvum with Silvius.

If Adi was indeed the king's messenger, Marcus was doomed. He knew everything. Well, almost everything, except for the logistics, but Silvius could have informed him about that too by now. He must also know that Marcus was an impostor and that he was wanted for the killing of a Chola subject. If he were to see Marcus here, it would be the end of the Roman.

The Pandya man stared blankly at the messenger, but his wife spoke up from behind.

'O messenger of the king, won't you take this poor woman's message to your lord, though it may not merit the same importance as your other messages? We are but a poor Pandya couple, who are on our way to my sister's house. My husband used to work in the port authority in Korkai, but he hasn't had a job since the war. My sister's husband has promised him work at the port in Puhar, and that is where we are headed. But our journey in your lands has been fraught with troubles, and we have had to encounter untold hardships due to the fact that we are Pandyas. Innkeepers drive us out without giving us food or shelter, bullock carts don't stop for us, people mock us everywhere and it is with great difficulty that we have reached this inn, where this ayya has been kind enough to take us in for the night. But even here, there is no respite, as we are called traitors and dogs by Chola men. Is this what the king promised us when he told the people of Korkai that they would be welcome in Chola country? Is this the famed Chola hospitality? If so, we would have been better off dying in Korkai with at least our dignity intact.'

Adi listened to the woman patiently and took his time before replying.

'Amma,' he said finally, 'if what you say is true, I apologize on behalf of my countrymen. The king will not tolerate their behaviour if he comes to know of it. However, if you plan to deceive me, then neither you nor your husband will be spared. I will give you a letter, which will ensure that you get an audience with the king's minister in Pattinam. You should meet him once you reach Puhar. I promise you that in our kingdom all petitions will be given due consideration.'

The Pandya man broke his silence. 'He doesn't believe you, didn't you hear? He thinks we are here to deceive him. Let us go back to our country where we may starve, but we'll do so with our respect untouched.'

'No, my lord, this is our chance to tell our story to the people of Puhar. Let us see what they say and whether they will offer us what was promised by their king,' his wife replied.

'*Our* king,' Adi said sharply and turned to the innkeeper. 'Sathiram-ayya, do you know the men this lady is referring to?'

'Thambi, I know one of them and he is from our village. The others are not from these parts, and I have never seen them before. In fact, I thought it was strange that they claimed to be our men because they also paid me with Pandya silver.'

'Did they now?' Adi asked, looking thoughtful. 'I think it would be appropriate for you to explain your version to the officers as well. Will you be a witness to this petition, Sathiram-ayya?'

'As you know well, thambi, I am always glad to be of any assistance to the king and his officers. But,' he said, lowering his voice, 'I need to be here, and these are not Chola people we have here –'

'This man and his wife are now the subjects of King Karikalan, whatever their past may have been. The king has proclaimed that in matters of justice there will not be any difference between us and Pandya folk who are loyal to him. We cannot go back on the king's word.'

'I will offer my assistance to the king's subjects,' said the innkeeper promptly. 'But for now, you should rest before continuing on your journey. My daughter has warm water ready for your bath. Will you not wash yourself and partake our humble food?'

Adi smiled and, just for a moment, he transformed into the boy Marcus was familiar with. 'Yes, of course. This is one of the things I look forward to the most in my travels – the hospitality of your household.'

'We should leave,' whispered Marcus as soon as Adi stepped outside. 'He'll see the horses soon enough.'

'I didn't realize you were running away from Puhar! He is but a household slave, is he not?'

'Who also happens to be the king's messenger! I don't know who he is, or what he is up to.'

'He must be Karikalan's spy. The king doesn't trust the official spy networks and he runs his own parallel system. I should have guessed. Why would a boy who looks like that work for your man Silvius? He hoodwinked us all.'

'But he must know –'

'He must know what?'

'Nothing. We have to leave now.'

'He doesn't know we are here –'

'Silvius must have sent him.'

'Masquerading as the king's messenger? The innkeeper knows him, so he's not new here. And if Silvius did send him, maybe he is carrying a message for you...'

'I doubt it, Zhang. I am leaving now... You can do what you want.'

'Don't raise his suspicions, young Roman. He is otherwise engaged tonight with the Pandya couple. Let's remain on guard. If we leave now, he'll follow us immediately.'

Zhang had a valid point. Before they could talk any further, Adi came back into the courtyard. The innkeeper laid out the food for him on a freshly cut plantain leaf. Adi swallowed a large mouthful, clearly ravenous.

'Will you be stopping with us for long?'

'Ayya, I am in a hurry and I need to ride fast. If I leave before dawn, I will be in Uraiyur by midday the day after. My apologies, but I am afraid I cannot stay longer this time.'

'Is everything as it should be in Puhar?'

Adi looked up from his meal and, for the first time, his glance swept the courtyard for any new visitors he hadn't noticed until now.

'Yes, this is just routine,' he said. 'If the young men give you any further trouble, send a message with the stable boy. I'll alert the village authorities on my way out tomorrow.'

'I am grateful to you, thambi. You've always been good to us. I hope you can make it to my daughter's wedding.'

'I hope so too. And now, if you'll excuse me, I'll retire for the night.'

Adi went into the room opposite theirs and closed the door. Zhang and Marcus alternately kept guard for half the night, after which both of them fell into a deep slumber.

The young maiden of the house, meanwhile, spent the night in the kitchen, deeply troubled.

21

THE INNKEEPER'S DAUGHTER

Marcus woke up before dawn and crept outside stealthily. To his relief, the horses were resting serenely and there was no sign of soldiers. He was about to go back inside when he heard a clanking sound followed by that of a pail splashing into a well. This was as good a time as any to speak to the maiden of the house and he made his way to the backyard. In the half-light of the morning he could just about make out a lone, graceful figure drawing water. As the pail came up, she dragged it out and washed her face. She sat down and buried her face in her hands. He paused – should he intrude? He had just decided to go ahead and talk to her when she abruptly stood up and climbed up the safety wall around the well.

He was about to dash over to pull her back down but stopped when he realized it was entirely unnecessary. There was already a rescuer on the scene. Another figure darted to the spot from the other side and, in an instant, pulled her down to safety. She clung to him.

Adi again! Did he know her? He must have because she wasn't screaming for help. As Marcus watched, he led the girl around to the back of the well to the grove, out of sight.

A Yavana's house slave, the king's messenger and now a seducer of innocent girls at wayside inns? And Marcus had thought *his* life was a complicated deception. He knew it would be prudent to head back inside and stay out of Adi's sight, but he couldn't stop himself from following the couple.

'Why did you attempt such a thing? Do you not trust me?' he heard Adi ask gently.

'It's not you, my lord,' she sobbed. 'It is my father. He wants me to marry my cousin in Madurai. He has already arranged the wedding. How will I endure this?'

'You can tell your father that you do not want to go to Pandya lands.'

'Why will he listen to me? It is a good alliance; something he and his sister had always hoped for. Can you not ask for my hand?'

'Not yet, Ponni. I have to finish my mission, but I promise you that on my way back I will speak to your father.'

'You will ask for my hand?'

'I will speak to him.'

'But what will your family say? The house of Vel will never let you marry an innkeeper's daughter,' the girl cried.

'Hush. We will be married even if we have to move out of Puhar. I have a plan, but I can't speak to your father just yet. I'll ask the king to help us – once he grants permission, my family will have to fall in line.'

'Are you really going to speak to the king about us?' A flicker of hope had crept into Ponni's voice.

'Yes. But you have to promise me that you will wait for me and not do anything to harm yourself!'

'Not any more, my lord. You have given me hope when I had lost everything. I will wait for you forever.'

Marcus had heard enough and he quietly left the scene. The

king's messenger in love with an innkeeper's daughter? Even a Yavana like him knew it was a doomed affair; it wouldn't work in the Roman empire and it certainly wouldn't work here in the Chola kingdom. Especially in this case, when Adi was more than just an ordinary messenger – he was a spy and was most likely a double agent.

'Ah, there you are!' Zhang was not only awake but pacing back and forth when Marcus got back to their room. 'I was sure you had made off with the innkeeper's daughter.'

'Whatever gave you the idea? I am not in this kingdom to find a girl to elope with.'

'So you say, young Roman, so you say…'

'What are you doing up at this hour? Who were you meeting?' He wanted to change the topic of discussion at any cost.

'In the course of your stroll I am sure you noticed that two horses have already left the stables – two of the best horses stabled at the inn last night. In fact, they were better than the one the messenger rode on.'

'Who are you referring to? The Pandya couple is still here!'

'That couple didn't travel on horses. They will need to hitch a ride or walk to Puhar. I am speaking of the two men in the corner, who were keenly and quietly observing the proceedings yesterday.'

'Perhaps they wanted to get a head start and reach their destination before the midday sun. Why are you suspicious?' Marcus had not paid much attention to the men the previous night and he wondered what he had missed.

'Why do you think they paid with Pandya coins?'

'I have no idea. How do you know that is how they paid anyway?'

'Because the innkeeper told me, and they were certainly not Pandyas!'

'How would you know that?'

'I know Pandyas when I see them; these men are certainly from the north.'

'If that is the case, maybe they were traders trying to reach Pandya lands. They must have figured out a way to deal with Pandya traders directly, like –' Marcus broke off as he realized he had already divulged too much information. And Zhang had not missed it.

'I don't particularly care for your life, but I am determined to serve the Buddha for a long time to come. What are *you* up to really? Now may be the time to tell me the truth, especially if you are plotting something dangerous,' Zhang said.

'I am taking a message for Vallavan from his family.'

'Does his family know that you have dealings with the Pandyas?'

Marcus evaded the question. 'I hear Adi coming in. We'll have to wait and leave after he does.'

'What, was he out as well at this hour? Don't tell me both of you were wooing the innkeeper's daughter!'

~

It was well into the morning when Marcus and Zhang rode out on the high road, due west. Marcus felt safer now that Adi had left some hours previously, and the risk of him being recognized and arrested had somewhat receded. He turned his attention to the countryside they were travelling through. They were in the beating heart of the kingdom; not the parts made rich from sea trade, but from where the materials for trade came, the granary, and its source of unlimited foot soldiers and peasants. As far as his eyes could see, the land was carpeted with a rich green paddy crop. A few months later, it would be replaced by groundnut and sesame, Zhang told him, but for now, it was all rice. The road was wide enough for two chariots to pass comfortably, though there wasn't much traffic other than the occasional bullock cart and a handful of riders. Peepul and banyan trees lined the road, and occasionally a small side path led to a settlement of a few houses that belonged to the farmers who tilled this land. He could hear them singing in the fields afar as they sowed the grains. Where the road curved closer to the river, the water gurgled in tune with the songs of the people weeding and planting.

'They sound happy. I wish the farmers of my country were this cheery,' Marcus said.

'Don't be deceived. They are as unhappy as the ones in your empire. Singing and dancing are short-term pain alleviators.'

'I hear that the king is benevolent, and he commands their love and loyalty.'

'Like your emperor?'

Marcus laughed. 'You have a point there. Are things different in the Middle Kingdom?'

Zhang shook his head. 'No. Whether they are ruled by a king, god or senate, it makes no difference to the common people. And that's why the only way is the path of Gautama – that of loving your fellow beings, of peace and non-violence, of equality where every man is treated equitably.'

'You cannot actually believe that. How can every man be the same? I am not the king or the emperor or...a slave. Who we are is ordained by a power greater than all of us. It is useless to try and change it.'

'Then we should die trying!'

'Your Buddha can't possibly have said that...'

Zhang did not take the bait and, instead, changed the subject. 'An astute man would have wondered how travellers and pilgrims happen to ride on horses that would have no trouble keeping up with his, but your man Adi did not give them a second glance. Either he knew who they belonged to or he was too preoccupied with something else. And I suspect it's the latter.'

'It was the girl at the inn; there was something going on between them.'

'I thought so, but that couldn't be all. There's something else.'

'He said that he would marry her. But it sounded like he was from a family of different class – Vel or something, he said...'

'A son of the Vels! They are the king's right-hand men; they will lay down their lives for him without a second thought. The family will eat her alive, and if he really does care for her, the best thing he could do for her is to leave her alone.'

'He is going to ask the king for permission so that his family wouldn't be able to do anything.'

'How exactly do you know this?'

'I overheard them...'

'This business with the girl is nothing new for a messenger. He comes, he takes what he wants, and he leaves; that's what boys do. But he is on a mission, likely carrying an important and urgent message to the king. And that's what is of interest here.'

'But is he really the king's messenger?'

'As I said last evening, the king has his own network of spies and messengers. Perhaps we'll find out more in our travels. You don't suppose this has anything to do with your friend, do you?'

Marcus shook his head. He had no inclination of getting involved in the politics of this kingdom. As long as it didn't interfere with his pearls and his visit to Korkai, he intended to stay well out of it. They continued in companionable silence and by mid-afternoon they reached another resting place: a small inn where they stopped to rest their horses and have a bite to eat. Marcus decided to try his luck with the man in charge and went to speak to him. It would be useful to know if Vallavan had passed this way.

'A lot of travellers must stop at your inn,' he began.

'They all do. This is the main thoroughfare to the capital, so everyone must pass this way. However, this is not the season for goods transport, so there have not been many since the king's retinue passed by on their way to the south. That was a sight!'

'That must have been special. Did the king himself stop at the inn?'

'Oh yes! He even spoke a few words to me, thanking me for taking care of the place! He promised to appoint more workers.' The man beamed as the words came tumbling out.

'And not many have been here since then?'

'A handful. But just today, we saw two men in a hurry first thing in the morning, and then the king's messenger – carrying the tiger standard – whizzed past without a second glance. Everyone seems to be in a hurry nowadays. Nobody stops by for the night like in the old days.'

'Why, who else was in a hurry?'

'Two days past, there was a young man who was ill; he was determined to continue his travels. I made him stay a day, but he left the next evening despite my warning him that he was too sick to travel. I hope he is safe.'

'Did he tell you where he was going?'

'I don't know, but he was a trader.'

'How do you know that?'

'One can't mistake a trader. He was interested in the price of everything, but not at all in how they were made!'

'Ha!' That sounded very much like Vallavan.

Zhang had caught up with him by then and he started making enquiries regarding overnight accommodation. He said he was very partial to the food in this part of the country, but Marcus was having none of it. He wanted to continue further, at least until the next inn. If Vallavan had left only two nights previously, there was still a chance of catching up with him before he reached the king. This meant that Marcus could be on his way to Korkai sooner rather than later. However, Zhang wasn't easily convinced.

As they continued to argue in front of the curious innkeeper, they suddenly heard the sound of thundering hooves outside.

'Bandits! Hide!' the innkeeper yelled, rushing to the barn. Marcus followed him, even as Zhang cursed and shouted to his companion to come with him. But Marcus did not turn around. Zhang made straight for the river. He had grown fond of the Roman over the past couple of days, but he'd be of better use to him as a free man, rather than a captive. He knew of a hidden embankment near the river from where he would have a view of the inn. He had barely reached his hiding place, placated his horse and climbed a tree, when he saw half a dozen riders surround the inn. He saw them dismount, rush inside and drag everything of use outside – grains, utensils, stakes, the coin box. They started looking around the inn for people and two of them chased the screaming innkeeper out of the barn. No sign of the Yavana yet.

A moment later though, one of the bandits stumbled out of the barn – he was hurt. The Roman was putting up a fight, but he wouldn't be able to hold out for long, Zhang realized with a sinking feeling. Three men entered the barn this time and a few moments later, a bloodied Marcus was dragged outside, swaying. He was hurt. Zhang's heart was in his mouth and he contemplated stepping out of his hiding spot when he saw the arrows whizzing by – as if by divine intervention, they sailed through the air one after the other but hit no one. The bandits raised their swords and looked around puzzled. As more arrows fell, one of them picked up a fallen shaft and shouted to his companions. They all lowered their swords instantly and, a moment later, a girl – the same girl they'd seen on the road to Maruvum the night of the feast! – came into sight. She ignored Marcus and spoke to the men. Soon, they gathered the booty and tied up the innkeeper. Meanwhile, Marcus, who had been sitting up, shuddered and fell to the ground. He was unconscious. Two of the men lifted him up and placed him on his horse. The group left as quickly as it had come, leaving the girl alone with the Yavana and the horses. She made straight for the forest, away from the river, with the horse carrying Marcus following her obediently.

Zhang considered following them and freeing Marcus, but he knew he was no match for a girl from the hills, especially now that he had confirmation that she was a trained bandit. But if he took the river, he could reach Uraiyur soon enough, where he might get help. He had information that would be useful and, if his intuition was right, the girl was headed in the same direction. He rode along the embankment in search of a boatman.

22

THE APPAM-SELLER OF MARUVUM

Those of you who have had the opportunity to peruse the chronicles of Hippalus would have found the absence of any mention of food puzzling, but there is a valid reason for this: Hippalus never partook of local food during his travels. He stayed away from native delicacies and made do with bread when he had to. But even he made an exception once in a while, an exception that eventually proved the rule. When in Camara, he made a regular appearance every few days at Rajamma's stall and waited patiently for his turn. Her appams served with fried fish were well worth the wait.

'I haven't seen your young master these past few days. Has he gone back to your kingdom?' Rajamma enquired. She was in a rather loquacious mood that day.

'I don't keep track of his movements. I reckon he is spending his days and nights at some courtesan's house in Pattinam.'

'On the contrary, I've heard that he is welcome in some of the richest merchant homes in Pattinam!'

'And where did you happen to hear that?'

Rajamma smirked. 'Do I also have to tell you how I make my appam batter? If I do that, what would I do for a living, ayya?'

'Oh no, I don't want you to run out of business. What else have you heard?'

'A theft – a daring one – from one of the merchant houses.'

'The soldiers came here to enquire I gather?'

'You know how it is. Some idiot's loincloth goes missing in Pattinam and they say we stole it. As if we are here solely to live off them. But, in this case, it's more than just the theft. They say that the thief was murdered here in Maruvum!'

Hippalus pretended to look surprised as was expected of him. 'That's unfortunate! For the people of Maruvum, I mean. You'll have no peace for a while.'

'What's even more unfortunate is that not all the stolen goods have been found.'

'What was stolen?'

'Minor trinkets. A couple of anklets. Oh, and a mirror!'

'Mirrors are everywhere where I come from. Worth nothing.'

'Not this one. This one was held up by a fertility goddess who brings good luck to the house she is placed in. She comes from the northern parts and, from what I've heard, is quite the looker.'

'Hmm...'

'She will bring you and your people luck.'

'And you say *she* is here in Maruvum?'

'How would I know? You talk as if I stole it!'

'Hypothetically speaking –'

'What speaking?'

'What is the thief likely to do with this goddess?'

'A dead man can't do anything with it. It certainly didn't bring *him* luck!'

'Perhaps he hid it before he was murdered. Or perhaps the murderer has her...'

Rajamma looked away as Hippalus pressed on. 'So someone wants to get rid of this goddess?'

'It could be evidence.'

'And how desperate is this person to get rid of the goddess?'

As Rajamma considered his question, Hippalus noticed Aafa making a beeline for him.

'What are you doing here? I've searched all of the harbour for you.' He spoke to his captain in Greek, conscious of the appam-seller's presence.

'A man is allowed to eat, isn't he? Incidentally, my host has been filling me in on a stolen goddess.'

Aafa frowned. 'Careful here, captain. No one can be trusted. You know how things stand.'

'We've done business with her before. It has proved to be lucrative.'

'But not in as precarious a time as this one. I have news of our little master.'

'Our little slave, you mean? What's he been up to?'

'We know where he is headed.'

'That's easy. He must be on his way to Korkai to get away from Silvius and the soldiers. What he hadn't reckoned with is me! Wait until I get my hands on him.'

'But here's the thing: he is not on his way to Korkai.'

'He is not?'

'He is on his way to Uraiyur.'

'Where the Hades is that?' This wasn't surprising, for Hippalus never paid any attention to inland towns. His world began and ended with the seas he navigated and the ports he docked in.

'The dam the king is building. He is heading to the anicut!'

Hippalus started. 'This kid is more trouble than we thought.'

'The rumour is that the vixen of Manaykan's household put him up to it.'

'You don't say!'

'You need to come with me right now. You can discuss your art heist another time. We have some decisions to make before Silvius turns up for a visit.'

~

'But you must believe me, my lady, everything I tell you is the truth and nothing but the truth. I've kept both my eyes open, and this is what I've heard. That Yavana boy… He has been missing for days and they say that he is on his way to Uraiyur. No one knows why he is headed there. They also say he killed Muthu… What do I think? He was very well behaved, and even Zhang the Buddhist took a fancy to him. But, if you ask me, it was all an act. Everyone was taken in, including yours truly. They say the Yavanas are never what they seem, and guess what? They are right. I know what happened when he said he was kidnapped. He wasn't kidnapped at all! It was part of a secret plan for him to meet with the pearl traders of Korkai.

'My lady! Are you all right? I'd suggest you sit down as you hear this. Of course I know what I am talking about. Have I ever given you false information? He met the Pandya traders and agreed to buy pearls from them. I have no idea how he thought he'd give our navy the slip. Perhaps that's why he killed Muthu. Because Muthu knew of his trading plans.

'And perhaps he was also the thief who stole from this very household, and diverted the suspicion towards Muthu. You don't believe me? Was he not here at the feast that night? Can you account for his movements when the robbery took place? Oh, can you really? Then I wonder...

'They didn't find the goods on him because he had already got rid of them. Did anyone ever search his rooms? Here's more evidence: even his own people are angry and are looking for him. They don't know where he is and they think he has run away now that he is wanted for murder. It doesn't add up, does it? I can't help you there, my lady. I can only tell you what I see and hear. I'll keep my eyes open, and I'll come and tell you if the boy ever turns up. Now, before I take my leave, here are some appams. You can pay him all the silver in this world, but your cook can never make them taste like mine!'

23

ANGAVAI

When he regained consciousness, Marcus found himself sprawled on his horse, his face resting on the beast's neck. He looked up groggily to see another horse in front of him, but he could not make out the rider. He had no idea where he was and could not hear the river any more. This reminded him of water and he realized he was very thirsty. He let out an incoherent cry. The horses stopped and, a moment later, a girl came into view, carrying a jug. He took a few grateful gulps from it and promptly slumped back on his horse's neck.

The next time he woke up, darkness had fallen and he couldn't make out anything. The girl reappeared with more water. He passed out again. When he finally became fully conscious, it was light again. He was lying on a bed of grass this time, under a tree. An earthen jug stood within reach. Two horses, untethered, grazed a few feet away, but there was no sign of the girl and he wondered if he had dreamt her up in his delirium.

As his mind cleared, he thought of Zhang and wondered whether the older man had survived the bandits, and if so, whether he was looking for him. It did not matter any more; he was on his own now. This was nothing new for Marcus. He was used to being on his own and working by himself. But how was he to get to Uraiyur and then to Korkai? The river had been his compass, but he seemed to have moved away from it. His story would end in ignominy: he had failed his father, both in trade and otherwise, failed to get a message to a friend, and had been kidnapped somewhere in the hinterland of a small kingdom so far away from Rome! He tried to rise to his feet but winced in pain and collapsed on the ground again.

'Drink the water. It has herbs that will help with the pain and your bruises.'

He looked up to see the girl from his dream holding a dead rabbit and a couple of palm fruits, still ensconced in their shell. For the first time, he took a proper look at her. She was taller and darker than the Chola women he had encountered. She wore a skirt that reached just below her knees and her upper body was covered in beads and necklaces of various shapes. Her hair was tied in a bun on top of her head, well out of the way of her bare shoulders on which hung a quiver full of arrows. He knew he'd seen her somewhere before.

'Who are you?' he asked after a while. She had borne his inspection in a proud silence.

'I am called Angavai and I expect gratitude for saving your life.'

'Saved my life? You kidnapped me!'

Angavai laughed – a loud, full-throated laugh rarely heard from a woman. No sign of coyness or modesty. *Here is a woman,* Marcus thought, *who does not care what the world thinks of her.*

'You seem to be the man to kidnap these days. Does your dear father love you so much that he will keep paying ransom after ransom to get you back?'

'If ransom is what you are after, let us make a deal – you take me to the site of the Kallanai, and I will give you as much Roman gold as you desire,' he said quickly. If she thought he was valuable, there was no reason to disabuse her of the notion. What point would telling her the truth, that there was no silver or gold, Roman or otherwise, available in return for his freedom, serve now? In fact, his freedom itself was in question if he ever found his way back to Rome.

Angavai ignored him and kindled a fire. She sat down and took out a knife from the folds of her skirt. Marcus inched back instinctively. She held the rabbit upside down and started skinning it methodically, starting from its leg.

'Yavana, I don't need your permission to relieve you of your gold.'

'I will find my own way,' he said, and attempted to rise once again, only to cry out and drop back down.

'You plan to find your way out of this forest? These woods are full of beasts, far wilder than your imagination,' she said, without looking up. 'I've always wondered what you do with the animals you buy from the traders of Puhar. The poor beasts my people barter away for a pinch of salt and rice. Do you sacrifice them to the sea goddess?'

'No, we take them to Rome where we put them in cages and let them loose in a ring.'

The girl's eyes widened. She wasn't sure whether he was serious or not. He continued, 'The whole city watches them in action, fighting it out between themselves and sometimes fighting it out with human prisoners... Sometimes against slaves. It is a sight like no other.'

'Then you wouldn't mind fighting a couple of them on your way out of the woods. You are sure to find at least a few animals waiting to meet the people who take their kin away for perverse entertainment. These creatures are not dumb; you shall hear them soon enough.'

Marcus hesitated. Nobody had called him a coward before, but he wasn't reckless either. They couldn't be too far away from human habitation; he knew that the forest next to Maruvum did not have any wild beasts and it was likely that this one did not either. And it was still daytime. He was inclined to take his chances. He took a few gulps of water from the jug next to him.

'But here you are, roaming freely in this forest full of dangerous beasts, eating their prey,' he said. The rabbit was roasting on the fire now.

'They are used to me.' She shrugged and turned her attention back to the rabbit.

'Right.' He did not believe her. He rose slowly and limped towards his horse. Just then a screech rent the air and he stopped dead in his tracks.

'When you meet her, tell her how her mate, the one you took back to your country, misses her. You never know, she may want to come too and, soon, you'll be the best of friends.'

Marcus gulped. And suddenly he was incredibly hungry. He turned around and looked intently at the rabbit roasting on the fire.

'I will leave after I have had some food,' he declared. 'That looks tasty!'

'Rabbits are tastier in the wild; they taste much better here than in the rich houses of Pattinam.'

He sat back down and considered his next move. The girl carved out a chunk of meat and carried it over to him. Marcus gobbled down most of it in one go.

'You are not just a good hunter, but also a great cook,' he said. 'You must make your husband very happy.'

'I don't intend to cook for anyone but myself!' she said sharply.

But still, she knew how to skin and roast a rabbit, and that must count for something.

'If you change your mind, you'd be welcome in the merchant houses of Rome.'

'Are you proposing to take me with you, Yavana?' she demanded, and he realized how he must have sounded.

'If that is what you wish, why not? You can be part of my... father's household,' he said quickly. This was the second time he had offered to take a Chola girl with him back to Rome. Where it was likely he'd be sentenced to death for pretending to be his father's legitimate son – but she didn't know that.

'Part of your father's household as a slave girl? This is sounding interesting – what other services would I have to provide?' she asked. Not a question that Kuzhali had asked him, but she was from a different world. He wondered how best to extricate himself from the question, when Angavai laughed at his discomfiture.

'I am not a housemaid. Now, eat up, we have to leave soon.'

'Where are we going?' he demanded. 'Take me to Uraiyur, or even to the riverbank and I'll make you very rich.'

She didn't deign to respond.

'Did the bandits put you up to this? Are you with them?' He should have seen it earlier. She was taking him because they'd ordered her to do so. Perhaps she was afraid for *her* life.

'You are so like your friend, you know that? No, I am not with them, Yavana, I *am* them. The boys who almost killed you yesterday are the ones *I* trained'

A Roman freedman masquerading as a merchant scion captured by a bandit chieftain in a barbarian kingdom. And the leader of the bandits happens to be a girl, who wasn't much older than him. Now, if that wasn't material for one of Hippalus's fanciful histories, Marcus didn't know what was. Who did she think she was? Boudicca?

'Doesn't the king provide for all of your people?' He knew the answer to that one, but he still had to ask. After all, being a bandit wasn't just a profession one decided to pursue out of interest. 'Why do you do this?'

Angavai's eyes flashed. 'You know nothing of this land. The wealth of the people is mined and stolen away from us by the merchants and priests, and sold off to you for a profit. The king gives this racket protection because he needs their gold to conquer other lands. He gives away the land and hills of my peoples as gifts to these daylight robbers, and we have no choice but to become bandits. To reclaim what is rightfully ours! But no, you would not understand – you are a merchant prince in your country... How would you even begin to understand what I am talking about? So let's not waste any more time. My men would have finished you off had I not arrived on the scene. I spared your life because you once helped my friend and we have a common goal – at least for a little while. After that, let's see what we should do with you.'

Marcus decided to stick to the cover story he and Zhang had designed. There was no need to confirm her suspicions of him.

'What do you know about my goals? A bandit like you, given to violence, and a pilgrim like me, who has taken the path of ahimsa, cannot have common goals. I've embarked on a pilgrimage to the southern lands. Unless you are a follower of the Buddha, I must insist that our paths are divergent.'

'You are a follower of the Buddha and my innermost desire is to be a slave girl in Rome! Yavana, shut up. I know you are carrying a message and I am looking for the same man.'

So that's what it was: Kuzhali had engaged more than one messenger. That explained how Angavai knew who he was and where he had been in Pattinam.

'You can inform your mistress that she doesn't need to worry about my ability to carry out the work entrusted to me. I'll deliver her message to her brother.'

Angavai looked confused for a second. Then she got up and walked over to him. She brought her face close to his and spoke in a low voice. 'I am tempted to leave you here as a feast for the wild beasts, but I don't wish to displease your friend, who holds you in high regard. A word of warning – from now on, you will not mistake me for a maid of any kind, least of all as a maid of that vixen in Pattinam who thinks she can run the world hiding in the safety of her mansion.'

There was no love lost between the two, which meant this girl had nothing to do with the mission Kuzhali had entrusted to Marcus. But in the process, Angavai had inadvertently revealed useful information. Marcus kept quiet and busied himself with the rest of his meal. If this mysterious girl was a friend of Vallavan's, however strange that idea may be, he was safe for the moment. It made sense to travel with her and see if she would lead him to Vallavan.

Once they finished eating, he mounted his horse – the pain was now tolerable – and followed her obediently out of the clearing and into the woods.

24

A RESCUE

They rode in silence for a long time, stopping only for a quick meal of fruits and nuts. Marcus had not seen a water source yet, but Angavai seemed to have enough water in the jugs tied to her horse. From what he could make out, they rode south most of the way before turning west. Finally, just as the sun was about to set, Angavai dismounted and put her ear to the ground. She got back up on her horse and turned right on the narrow path.

'Why are we not going to Uraiyur?' He was tired of second-guessing her intentions.

'He did not reach the anicut. He took a detour – a shortcut, he thought – but it was a trap. Harm has befallen him, and I'll get him out of danger.'

'How do you know that? And why are you so intent on helping him?' He pressed on to see if he could gather more information for he still didn't quite believe her. The people most likely to entrap Vallavan were her people, the bandits.

'I met Vallavan sometime ago, when he was making an inland trip. Merchants don't usually travel to the hinterland and he was unprepared for what he would experience there. I saved his life first from a rhino, and then again from my own friends and, since then, I have taken it upon myself to make sure that he stays alive. Besides,' she said, smiling broadly, 'he is worth a lot of gold, and I am, after all, a dacoit.'

She was taking great pains to tell him about herself, but the question in his mind was different: what was she to Vallavan? He'd never mentioned her in their conversations on the *Minerva*. Vallavan wasn't the type to go after girls from the hills – there were enough courtesans in Puhar to keep him happy.

'Why would anyone other than your own people kidnap him?'

'He is a rich merchant's only son. Moreover, I am not the only one who could get a good price if I catch him. I know he was followed from Puhar and, whoever they are, they don't want him to reach the king.'

'Why not?'

Angavai shrugged. 'That is not my business and I don't particularly care for his dealings with the king.'

Marcus switched tracks abruptly.

'Have you really fallen for my friend's fair and handsome face? I must tell you that there is no hope, none whatsoever. I know for a fact that he is engaged to marry his cousin and that he is deeply in love with her.'

'I don't intend to get married at all. I also don't remember asking for your advice, Yavana. But since you gave it so freely, I can also confirm that he is indeed engaged to his cousin. Whether he is in love with her or not, it's not for me to say. That is not how marriages work in Puhar.'

This was the second time a Chola girl had schooled him on how marriages worked in this kingdom. In addition, this one was insinuating that Vallavan, instead of being in love with his beautiful cousin, was in love with her.

'Which caste do you belong to?'

'I don't belong to any caste. Like you, I stand outside it and... *hush!*' She stopped suddenly and listened carefully for a few moments.

'I am going to tie the horses to this tree here so that we can continue on foot,' she whispered. 'They are not far away, the men we are looking for. Vallavan will be with them. I can take them by surprise. But first, we need to find out how many are there and whether they are armed.'

'You are going to fight a bunch of men? Now I can see why you dragged me with you. You cannot do this by yourself!'

'Are you really this dumb?' she snapped. 'You think I chose *you* instead of one of my well-trained men? I don't need you for any of this. What good are you anyway? If you are anything like your friend, you will have no idea how to hold a bow.'

'I am trained in sword fighting. Archery is not my strong suit,' Marcus admitted reluctantly.

'Great. So if you want to help me, you lure them out and I shoot.'

'How do you know Vallavan is with them?'

'Trust me, he is,' she said, as she swiftly climbed up a tree. A few minutes later, she came down as stealthily as she had gone up. 'Here's what I saw: one man in the camp next to the fire. We can assume that he has had a good meal and plenty to drink, which makes our job easier. There is another man sitting beside what looks like a makeshift palanquin, and I suspect Vallavan is inside that. There may be a third man, I cannot see from the tree, but at most we have three men to worry about. This should be easy!'

Marcus liked how she had switched to using 'we'. Whether she liked it or not, she was counting on him.

'Are they armed? If they have swords and daggers, it is no trouble. I can easily fight them,' he said. He could handle four men, even with an injury.

'With what? You don't possess a sword!'

'I can be dangerous with a dagger but...' He trailed off when he remembered he didn't have his dagger with him; it was probably in an evidence tray in Puhar at the moment.

Angavai bent down and fished out a dagger from her linen sack. She handed it to him. 'Just in case. But we stick to my plan. Yavana, these men are not the clowns of Chola land who kidnapped you in Puhar. They are trained killers and spies. We have to lure them out one by one, and once they are within shooting distance, I'll take care of them. We can't afford to get any closer without them noticing us. Here,' she said and this time she took out something tightly wrapped in a small sack. 'This is an anklet that will jingle as loudly as a temple bell. One of them will come out to investigate and you lure him to this spot, right here by this rock. I will have a clear shot from the mound over there. We wait for the moon to come out as I need light.'

'What if they come in twos?'

'Then you will have to deal with the other one until I can get to him. Use the dagger you keep threatening to use. There are two palanquin-bearers –'

'In addition to the three? But you said –'

'They are locals and they'll run as soon as the racket starts. They wouldn't want any trouble. A strange jingle in these parts after dark is not a good omen.'

'What if the palanquin-bearers are also spies?' Marcus was beginning to doubt Angavai's reconnaissance mission.

'I have sufficient arrows if the need arises. I'd rather not have them on my conscience, but if they are not what they seem, that's their problem.'

'How do you know Vallavan is in the palanquin and these are his kidnappers? What if you are wrong?'

'You ask too many questions, Yavana. You have to trust me. The only people who come into this forest are those who have something to hide or are running away.'

'We aren't doing either!' protested Marcus.

'Aren't you? You can leave if you like; I am not holding you prisoner. I can handle these men.'

Marcus resigned to the task at hand and started to unwrap the anklets.

'Not here,' Angavai hissed. 'Walk over to that tree there, chant the names of all your gods and goddesses, and then do it. That will give me sufficient time to get into position.'

'I have no god but the Buddha any more.' Vallavan may have told her about his Roman friend but that didn't mean he couldn't have seen the light of the Enlightened One and become a monk.

'Then chant his thousand names.'

She pushed him forward gently and turned away. She vanished in a moment, and Marcus walked steadily to where she had pointed and crouched behind a tree, with a good view of the camp. He started chanting the names of gods – he started with Jupiter, but as he got to Vesta, he decided to invoke the Olympian gods as well. He started again, this time with Zeus and just before he untied the bundle, he prayed to the Buddha too and then opened his eyes.

A man was warming himself in front of the fire, drinking. The two palanquin-bearers were fast asleep to the side. Only the sentry in front of the palanquin seemed alert, his eyes scanning every movement in the forest. There was no third man.

This should be easy, Marcus thought, but just as he was about to sound the jingle, the sentry shouted, 'He wants water!'

'Give him a little. We don't want him too healthy, though,' said the man drinking by the fire.

The sentry grabbed the jug next to him and unlocked the door of the palanquin. He stuck his head inside with his hand offering the jug. A moment later, he screamed and pulled back. His hands covered his face in pain as the jug dropped to the ground. The man by the fire rushed towards him and the palanquin-bearers opened their eyes groggily.

'This is enough! No more water until he behaves!' snarled the man who was clearly in charge. He pulled out his baton and struck inside the palanquin blindly. Marcus heard a cry – Vallavan! In his shock, he dropped the anklet he was holding, the sound of which echoed through the camp.

'What was that?' asked one of the bearers, immediately alert.

'Bees. Let me take care of the prisoner first and then we worry about the bees,' said the sentry, nursing his bloodied face. He was about to go inside the palanquin when the other man stopped him.

'The instructions are clear; he is not to die. He must be alive and in reasonable health.'

'It is ridiculous that we have to treat him like a royal guest,' the sentry said. 'I don't understand why we cannot get rid of him and be on our way. This is an utter waste of time!'

Marcus had heard enough. Angavai had spoken the truth. He picked up the anklet and jingled it again.

'Oh no, we should never have come into this forest. It is full of ancient spirits,' moaned one of the bearers. 'We told you we could take another route, but you didn't listen and see what we have done now! We have angered the spirits of the forest. We are doomed!' He turned to his companion. 'We helped the Pandyas kidnap one of our own and we hid him in this forest; there is no hope for us!'

'Shut up. There are no spirits or ghosts here. You keep quiet and watch the prisoner. We will have a look around and see what the racket is about,' said the man with the baton.

'Are you sure?' asked his sentry. 'We cannot leave the prisoner with these two bearers.'

'I will guard the prisoner. You check it out.'

The sentry pulled out a dagger and walked towards where Marcus was crouched.

'Pandya-ayya, we don't want to get involved with spirits. We are leaving!' cried out one of the bearers.

'Where will you go in the dark? Wild animals will get to you before the spirits can. In any case, you cannot leave without returning the gold we gave you as an advance.'

Marcus jingled the anklet once again and slowly started walking towards the next tree.

'We will return the gold!'

'Nobody is going anywhere... Hush,' said the man as he followed the sound. The crackling of the fire and the intermittent jingle were the only sounds heard in the camp for a while. And then, suddenly, a man's scream. Angavai's arrow had hit its mark.

The two palanquin-bearers decided to risk the beasts. At least the beasts were predictable and familiar. As the Pandya man pondered his next move, the bearers took the opportunity to gather up their bundles and make a quick exit.

'You lazy cowards, come back!' the man shouted, but he did not pursue them. Instead, he took a few steps towards where he had last seen the sentry.

He took one of the fire pandams and walked towards the tree from where the jingle had come. He had barely taken a few steps before Marcus shook the anklet again. The man gave a start and rushed back towards the camp to check if there was any movement from the prisoner. None. He turned back towards the tree. Another jingle, and he hesitated. He made a split-second decision and ran back towards his horse. He had just mounted it when Marcus burst into the camp, bells ringing, dagger drawn.

'Go!' the man screamed, giving his horse a kick. Marcus was almost upon him when the horse decided to obey his master. The dagger nicked the man's arm and tore his sleeve, but the horse did not stop. The man managed to kick Marcus before the horse dashed out of the clearing.

'You fool!' Angavai ran into the clearing, bow still drawn. 'We could have lured him and attacked him just like the other one. You let him escape!'

'He was going to leave, and I wanted to stop him!'

'He would have killed you first!'

Angavai rushed towards the palanquin. She unlocked the door and pulled the curtain aside. Inside lay a tired, bedraggled Vallavan. He was gagged. They lifted him out slowly and Marcus pulled off the gag. Angavai fetched the water jug from the ground and gave Vallavan a few sips from it. He was barely conscious, and Marcus cradled him in his lap while Angavai checked to see if he was hurt. There were a number of bruises on his arms and legs, but nothing looked very deep. Once she finished examining him, she pulled out a few herbs from her pouch and held them under Vallavan's nose. He opened his eyes, looked at Angavai and smiled.

'Am I in heaven?'

'I am not going to let you escape from earth so easily!'

'You are awake! I shall offer prayers to all the gods of Rome and your Chola gods,' shouted Marcus.

Vallavan looked up at Marcus in surprise, but his expression rapidly turned to anger.

'You betrayer! You extend your hand in friendship and then stab me in the back! What are you?' he asked loudly before fainting. The outburst had cost him his consciousness.

'What is he talking about?' Angavai asked.

'I don't know,' said Marcus, though he had a pretty good idea what Vallavan was talking about. His deal with the Appans was not a secret any more. He did not know how his friend had been informed of the pearl trade. Angavai gave him a long searching look but did not push further.

'We need to get him out of the woods. I know a physician by the river. Help me lift him up, and if we take the horse they left behind we could be there in a couple of hours,' she said.

'Travelling at night?'

'I know every tree, every animal and every spirit in this forest. No harm will come to us from animals, but of men I cannot be certain. The sooner we leave this place, the better.'

Angavai whistled and their horses came trotting out into the clearing. 'You ride the captor's horse. We will load Vallavan on to yours.'

Marcus helped Vallavan to his feet. His head leaned heavily against the beast's neck, but the horse did not complain. A few moments later, the three horses left the camp. Angavai led the way with a burning fire taper illuminating the thick grove of trees; Vallavan's horse was behind hers and Marcus brought up the rear. She started singing as they made their way out of the forest and towards the river.

25

BEFORE DAWN

'A dip at this hour! You'll catch a cold. The morning fog is not to be trusted,' said the physician, looking up as Angavai walked up to the house from the riverbank, dripping wet. The older woman handed her a cloth, which she took wordlessly. She towelled herself dry vigorously and reached for her clothes, which were hanging on the wooden rail attached to the wall.

'I'll need other clothes,' she said, and gestured towards Vallavan. He was fast asleep on the straw mattress in the other corner of the room. 'Their clothes...'

The physician nodded. 'We have some in store. I'll bundle them up along with your food. But you aren't going to look like them just because you wear their clothes.'

'It'll have to do.'

She sat down on the floor next to her quiver. She took it out and examined each arrow before carefully putting them back in.

'He is in no shape to travel,' the physician began.

'He'll be fine. He is desperate to reach the king. You heard him yourself.'

'He is delirious and not right in his mind.'

'Seemed all right to me. He wants to get to Uraiyur and I'll make sure he gets there.'

'And they are going to let you in to see the king just like that?'

'We'll see about that when I get there. I just need to get as close to him as possible.'

'You and everyone else!'

Angavai grinned. 'Karikalan has no dearth of enemies. The Pandyas, Cheras, Satkarni himself, and even his own priests and merchants want to get rid of him. Too many people ready to do the deed.'

'It comes with the crown. But what about this young man here?'

'What about him? He is a loyal subject. He'll deliver the message he came to deliver and be on his way back to his family in Puhar in no time.'

'Will he though?'

'I'll make sure of it.'

'Why do you need him?'

'To get close to the royal entourage.'

'That's it?'

'What else could it be?'

'How about the Yavana in the hut?'

'Ah,' said Angavai. She looked up at the physician. 'He isn't needed any more.'

'Why did you bring him here?'

'Because I didn't know whether he'd be of any use to me. We tracked him in Puhar for a while, as he was an unknown then, and Karikalan's foreign enemies showed a lot of interest in him. But now I know that he has nothing to do with...all this. It is also clear that Vallavan wants nothing to do with him and I have confirmation that he is carrying a message for Vallavan from the vixen of Pattinam. She probably wants her brother to return as quickly as possible, which is not what we want now, do we? The Yavana did help me in rescuing Vallavan, so I suppose he's not entirely a waste of space.'

Vallavan turned in his sleep; Angavai rose from the floor.

'I'll be back,' she told the physician.

'No!'

'Why not?'

'You said that he wasn't involved. He has nothing to do with this!'

'Thaai, he lives on borrowed time. Vellayan and our boys would have finished him off at the inn if I hadn't intervened.'

'Angai,' the older woman said gently, 'we all live on borrowed time.'

'Well, he has outlived his utility.'

'Child, we don't kill indiscriminately. If we do, there's no difference between us and them!'

'You are going senile in your old age. If he escapes, it's dangerous for us. He knows this place, he has seen us –'

'So has your friend here.'

'That's different!'

'How?'

'Vallavan won't remember you or this place. Thaai, we cannot let the Yavana escape –'

'He won't... He won't be able to find his way out of the forest.'

Angavai looked at the older woman for a moment and asked, 'You think it's all right for him to get lost in the jungle and be eaten by a wild creature? It is more humane to finish him off now. Don't stop me!'

'No, Angai. No more innocent blood on your hands! You've spilt enough... This young man is stirring – you leave with him and I'll take care of the Yavana.'

'*You?*'

'You don't think I am capable of it?'

'Of course not. You taught me everything I know!'

'Did I? Have I really made you into...this?'

'No, thaai. You taught me how to shoot, but you didn't make me this person. You know *who* made me *this*. Yes, I know you can finish him in a flash if you wished to. But he's not your problem. You didn't bring him here. I did!'

'The Yavana is *our* problem. I'll deal with him. Now hush, this one is waking up. Get him ready, and I'll go see to the horses.'

26

THE PHYSICIAN

Marcus woke up to the gurgle of running water. For a moment he thought he was back at his father's villa in Aventine Hill, where, around this time, Nubia would drain the water from the fountain and shout at him to get on with polishing the mosaic. He hadn't been to the villa in years – not since the day his master told him that his manumission had been processed and that he was a free man. He wasn't ever likely to set foot in the house again, and, at the current time, whether he'd even make it back to Rome was in question.

He rose from the mat on which he had spent the night and walked groggily towards the door of the one-room hut. They had reached the physician's home in the dark of the previous night, and he had no idea what the place actually looked like. Now he saw that the hut was perched precariously on top of a hill that sloped, rather steeply, down to the river. It was hot and well past noon, he surmised, as he looked up at the sun. His recollections of the past couple of days were hazy at best. He looked around for signs of habitation – there were a couple of huts and a stone building further along the bank. His bruises had more or less healed, but his entire body was aching with exhaustion and he decided to have a wash first. He walked cautiously down to the river, taking care not to slip, stripped and stepped into the water. It was cool and refreshing – just what he needed. He waded a few steps further into the river and felt the ground slope beneath him. He ducked his head underwater, held his breath for as long as he could and came back up for air. He swam two laps to the far bank and back. The fog had lifted from his head.

Marcus, a Roman freedman masquerading as his half-brother, a rich merchant named Marcellus, and now disguised as a Buddhist pilgrim, was lost somewhere deep inside the Chola kingdom – swimming away in their sacred river. He was wanted for murder in the kingdom's capital – a crime that he did not commit. He was the mastermind behind an illegal trade deal that would result in him – and his fellow partners – being executed without a trial if they were caught. And if this wasn't enough, he had to fulfil a mysterious errand for his father in Korkai, where his ship may or may not be waiting for him. On top of that, he was also carrying a message for a friend, who, with good reason, considered him a traitor. However, Marcus felt no guilt in this regard. What he had done was fair and to be expected in trade. If their roles had been reversed, Vallavan would have done exactly what he had. Perhaps he was giving Vallavan too much – or too little – credit. If his sister had been in his place, she'd have done exactly what he did. All Marcus had to do was keep his promise and deliver her message to Vallavan without delay. And then he could be on his way. He couldn't afford to get mired in the local political situation. He swam to the shore with renewed vigour and stepped out of the water. The sun dried him in no time. He shook out his clothes, put them back on and was about to put his scabbard back in place when he saw it.

The dagger! It fitted perfectly into the scabbard just as it had in his hands the night before. With a shock he realized that it felt familiar because it was his! This was *his* dagger, the one his attackers had taken away from him that night in Maruvum. And Angavai had handed it back to him when they were rescuing Vallavan. He had assumed that his dagger would be in an evidence room somewhere in Puhar, confiscated after Muthu's murder, but instead it had been with the self-proclaimed bandit queen all along! This meant that it was her men who had ambushed him in Maruvum. How Angavai was involved in this business he couldn't say, but he immediately understood that extricating himself from Chola country and reaching Korkai wasn't going to be easy.

First, he needed to find Vallavan and speak to him. He walked towards the stone building where the old physician had led Vallavan and Angavai to before he was offered food and shown the way to the hut. He stood in front of the house and said loudly, 'Amma, vanakkam! I am looking for my friend. How is he today?'

The old woman slowly shuffled out and looked at him in surprise. 'Welcome, thambi. You don't look like you are from these parts, but you're welcome here, of course. Who is this friend you refer to?'

Marcus smiled. 'It was dark last night, amma, and maybe you did not catch a good look at me,' he explained. 'I came with Angavai and Vallavan, and you gave us food and shelter in your hut. I have come to thank you and to enquire after my friend who is in your care.'

The woman looked bewildered. She came closer and rubbed her eyes. 'No one came here last night. In this corner of the country, we don't get many visitors. Where do you come from, thambi?'

It was Marcus's turn to look confused. 'But I saw you last night!'

The physician looked thoughtfully at the hut in the distance and turned back to Marcus. 'Did you say that you came from that shack?' she asked in a low voice.

'Yes, you gave me food and a place to sleep in, for which I am grateful!'

'You cannot have slept there, thambi. That hut is haunted. We take our dead there before we cremate them, but other than the bodies, no one ever goes in there. It is a place filled with the spirits of the dead. You cannot have spent the night there. Unless...'

Marcus was now concerned for Vallavan's well-being. This woman wasn't quite right in the head. He should not have trusted Angavai.

'Amma, are you feeling all right? Is there anyone else at home I can speak to?'

The woman shook her head. 'No one lives here but me. They do not bother me unless there is a death. I take the dead to the shack to cleanse them of their sins.'

'Amma, will you let me come into your house and give me a drink of water?'

'I will fetch water, but you cannot come inside. Not when you claim to have spent the night in the dead people's hut!'

'I know this is difficult to believe, but two of my friends are in your home. Perhaps they are there without your knowledge. Vallavan, Angavai!' he cried out at the top of his voice, hoping to catch their attention if they were still in the hut.

'Thambi, sit down here and rest a while. There is no one else here and your shouting is not going to bring anyone. Are your friends spirits of the dead?'

'No! I insist that I left my friends here last night. The girl brought us here because she said you were a doctor and would help my friend who was hurt. Where is she? Where are the horses?'

It hadn't been easy to hide the horses the previous night, but now they were nowhere to be seen.

'There are no horses here. What is your name and where do

you come from? If I know that, maybe I can help you.' She bent down, picked up a jug and handed it to Marcus. He drank from it gladly. The water tasted sweet and cool.

He sat down on the thinnai. Without Angavai and the horses, he was at a loss – how would he proceed now? He had to think of another way to get out of here. The old woman sat down next to him. She was toying with a long stone pestle, which he hadn't noticed before.

'My name in Marcellus and I am a citizen of Rome, the greatest city on earth,' he told her.

'Why did you leave this great city of yours to wander about in this wilderness? What brings you to this country?'

'I came to trade,' he began before he realized he had forgotten his cover. That would not do. 'I came to trade, but I was converted by a follower of Shakyamuni into a Buddhist,' he said quickly. 'Now I travel in this land and spread his faith.'

'I have not heard of such a god. Is he like our Mariamma or is he like the Brahmanas' Vishnu Perumal? How does one please him?'

'He is unlike your gods, or mine for that matter. He does not want to be pleased.'

'How else will he grant your wishes?'

'He doesn't grant any wishes!'

'How is he a god then, this Shakyamuni?' the old woman asked, sounding puzzled and genuinely interested.

'He said no one, not even a god, can make all your wishes come true. In fact, I think he doesn't believe there are any gods to begin with.' Marcus wasn't entirely sure if this was the case, but he was certain that he had heard Zhang say it a number of times. In fact, a lot of things Zhang said were contradictory, now that he thought about it. He wondered where Zhang was and whether he had been able to get away.

'Thambi, why do I – or anyone else for that matter – need a god like the one you speak of?'

Marcus thought about it for a while and came to the conclusion that the old woman was right. What was the point of a god who not only could not fulfil your desires but also assured you that the only certainty in this world is the destruction of your mortal body? But Zhang seemed to find it useful; in fact, it was what he claimed had given him a new life.

'Because he teaches us that everyone is equal. There is no difference between king and slave, or between a Brahmana and an outcaste,' Marcus said.

The old woman started to laugh. 'Then it seems to me that your god does not understand the ways of this world. Let us not waste time on this, let's instead talk about you. Tell me, son, why are you really here?'

Why was he really there?

It was time to get it off his chest.

'I am here because my father – my master who is also my father – asked me to come here and help his son – his real, legitimate son – with trade and to take a message to a woman in Korkai. My brother had other plans and he went off to Gaul, while I pretended I was him and came to this country...'

Even to his ears his story sounded too strange to be true.

'Did you live with your master and his son?'

'I was born into the same household.'

'And your mother?'

'I never met my mother.'

'How did you know who your father is then?'

'The other slaves told me. It was evident to me as well as I grew up – I was his favourite slave and, needless to say, his wife's most hated.'

'It must have been hard for a little boy –'

'No.' He shook his head. 'I was treated well and educated, along with my half-brother, as his companion. Once I was of age, my master gave me my freedom and a job at his warehouse. Then one day, he sent me on this journey across the seas with a message –'

'Who are you taking a message to in Korkai?'

An old woman in the middle of nowhere was going to do nothing with this information. So Marcus told her.

'A woman. I need to give her a parcel that I've carried all the way from Ostia.'

'Do you not wonder who this woman is?'

'A long-forgotten love perhaps. But women don't mean much to him. It is more likely that she is a trader of some sort... I don't know, but first, I need to get out of your kingdom and –'

'It is not my kingdom,' she said abruptly.

'Is it not?'

'My people were killed, our girls raped, our men enslaved, our lands conquered and our wealth plundered by the king's soldiers. Not because we were a threat, but simply because the king wanted to show his people that he owns all of this land you see around you. Because he wanted to feel powerful. Because he wanted our men for his army. But all that is past –'

'You are not Pandya?'

'No, we are not Chola or Pandya or Chera. We are the free people of the hills and we go about minding our own business, living in our mountains and forests. And even here, they don't leave us alone. Every king wants us to be his subjects, but we are nobody's subjects and that makes them unhappy. So they come to murder us...'

And so your people put up a resistance and became dacoits. Marcus didn't need to hear more. This old woman had to be Angavai's accomplice. The empire sent its armies into barbarian territory, but they kept fighting back. And they'll keep fighting until the last one is dead. This was a familiar story in his part of the world too, but not one in which he had any part to play. The question remained as to why they would attack a Yavana so far away in Puhar's harbour town or rescue him and bring him to this place, and he wasn't going to get his answers from this woman.

'Amma, my friend and the girl...' he tried once more.

The old woman looked at him for a long moment. She seemed to have come to some sort of decision. She put the pestle down.

'I don't know anything about your friend, thambi. If you walk along the path here for a few pagams, you will reach a boatman's house before sundown. Tell him that I sent you and he will offer you help. Take you where you want to go. Go to Korkai and fulfil the promise you made to your father!'

'But I promised to deliver this message to Vallavan –'

'Your business and your life belong back in your country, and not in this pilgrimage, the spreading of a faith you do not understand. Nor does it lie in following a friend who does not share the same charitable view of your friendship. Go home, thambi. Your city and your family await you. Mariamma's blessings will be with you.'

Marcus took his leave as he saw no point in staying further. She wasn't going to give him more information, and it was highly improbable that Vallavan and Angavai were still there. The only explanation was that they had left while he was asleep. And, for reasons of her own, Angavai had decided to spare his life. It was time he took his leave and made his way to Korkai. There was but one path that led along the river and he walked down that.

The old woman watched him until he was well out of sight. She had dealt with him the best she could, and Angavai would have to live with that. She went back inside her house.

After a while, Marcus saw the boatman's hut in the distance. He sighed in relief – he wasn't entirely certain that the old woman hadn't sent him on a wild goose chase – and checked his *bursa* to take out enough to pay the man, when he caught sight of the scroll. The one that Kuzhali had given him. Now that Vallavan didn't want it and Marcus didn't intend to take it to him, what was the point in carrying it? He took it out and was about to fling it into the river when a thought struck him. He broke the seal and unfurled the scroll. His knowledge of written Tamil was rudimentary at best and it took him a while to decipher the message.

He sat down.

Marcus had a decision to make and he knew what he *should* do. If the contents of the letter were true, then the warring kings and merchants were going to have their hands full for the foreseeable future. There may not even be a king for a while; a power vacuum was imminent. This was the ideal time to take the pearls and dash back to Rome before anyone suspected anything. No one would be looking for or going after a rogue Yavana ship at a time like this.

But as he walked into the boatman's hut in the darkening twilight, he shouted, despite himself, 'Uraiyur! Get me to the anicut as fast as you can!'

DELTA

That month
in that white moonlight,
we had our father,
and no one
could take the hill.

This month
in this white moonlight
kings with drums
drumming victory
have taken over the hill,

and we
have no father.

Pari's Daughters: On the Death of Pari, *Puṟanāṉūru* 112

Your bards are wearing lotuses
of gold

and the poets
are getting ready to ride
fancy chariots
drawn by elephants
with florid brow-shields:

is this right,
O lord, rich in victories,

this ruthless taking
of other men's lands

while being very sweet to protégés?

Nettimaiyar, *Puṟanāṉūru* 12

IN PRAISE OF A CREMATION GROUND

The jungle spreads.
Cactuses grow.
Owls hoot even by day.
And haunted by she-demons
gaping in the light of crematory fires,
this ancient smouldering cremation ground
looks fearful.
Lovers' tears
wept from the heart
quench the burning white
ash and bones.

This ground,
it is the end
of everyone in the world,
looks upon the backs of all men,
and hasn't seen anyone yet
who will look upon its back.

Kataiyan Kannanar, *Puṟanāṉūru* 356

27

SPIES IN THE DELTA

The small village next to Uraiyur where King Karikalan had set up his camp was situated along the river's southern branches that were of supreme importance to the Chola people. It was along these tributaries that the most fertile fields of the country lay; this was where water turned grain into gold. A dam that would channel the water to the lands that relied on it along the southern branch was a dream that had been talked about for many generations and, finally, here was a king with the will to make it come true.

The king's entourage had taken over a large area close to the river. The royal quarters were at the radial centre, which housed the king himself, and his servants and personal guards. The construction workers lived in shacks further west, while an army battalion was stationed at the east end of the camp. The prime minister's temporary dwelling was between the royal quarters and the barracks. He had reached the camp a few days ago and was speaking to his informer at the moment.

'If what you say is true and the bandits are brazenly attacking inns that have the protection of the king, then they are preparing for battle. This has to be construed as an attack on the king himself.'

'If you have any doubts about the veracity of my account, the king's messenger can corroborate it. He was slightly ahead of me but would have definitely heard of it too. News travels fast along the high road,' said the informer.

'The king's messenger is here? I wonder who sent him. I don't seem to have a message from the general in Puhar…' mused the prime minister.

The informer kept quiet. He wasn't going to volunteer any information on this matter as he had no intention of coming between the king and the prime minister.

'No, I don't doubt you,' the prime minister continued. 'You have proved yourself trustworthy. It is time to send the army out into the forest to quell this problem once and for all. They need to be taught a lesson they won't forget.'

'That's what the king said when he first took his army into the hills –'

'You forget who you are speaking to…yet again!'

'If I may say so, it would actually be prudent to keep the army here until the ceremony. The bandits will attempt to make their presence felt during the pujai.'

'But they cannot attack the royal camp! Where would they hide? We'll know as the peasants and villagers are on our side!'

'Are they?'

'Do you have any information to suggest otherwise?'

The informer shook his head. 'No, but the bandits must have some support from them; perhaps from the villages along the northern side…'

'It's not the peasants who worry me. Our intelligence report says that Pandya spies have been in touch with the bandits and are actively abetting them. The bandits have gone beyond looting – this is treason and they will pay for it!'

'This information may be of use then. Before I left Puhar, I ran into the thieves who stole the jewellery from Manaykan's house.'

'You *ran* into them?'

'I found that the thieves have had dealings with both bandits and foreign spies.'

'We know who put them up to it. They confessed when they were apprehended – a bandit ghost who claimed to be from Pandya land!'

'A Pandya bandit ghost seems unlikely.'

'Not if they are in cahoots!'

'A ghost in cahoots with bandits and Pandyas? That sounds like one of the things your priests come up with to scare the people into performing expensive rituals.'

'*Zhang!*'

'I speak the truth, Your Highness. Once you see the path of the Buddha, you will see the truth about the priests.'

'I shall not tolerate further discussion about the priests!'

'If I were you, I'd be more suspicious. Why can't the priests be in cahoots with the bandits?'

'The bandits hate the priests. Even you can't believe otherwise…'

'Then the bandits have more sense than I had given them credit for. I am curious – if the thieves were arrested, how come one of them was found murdered in Maruvum later?'

The prime minister's eyes narrowed. 'They escaped.'

'They escaped from the dungeons of Pattinam?'

The prime minister sighed. 'All right, they were let out so that our people could follow them and see who they met. As bait…'

'Didn't look like it worked if one of them was murdered. Or did it?'

'Zhang, I suggest you keep your nose out of *that* business!'

'I also saw northern spies on my way here. Satkarni's men.'

'Are you certain?'

'Yes!'

'Because you are...were one of them?'

'I never spied for Satkarni!'

'So you say…'

'And you believe me. Whatever they are doing in inland country, it cannot be good.'

'It has to be routine work. They have bigger fish to fry up north. A whale, if I am not mistaken.'

'But it strikes me that the Chola navy will be of great use to Satkarni if his problem is a whale. He doesn't have a navy to speak of!'

'This is idle conjecture. Let's focus on the bandits for now. I'll keep the army here as per your advice, but the day after the *pujai*, they are going straight into the forest.'

Zhang nodded and then hesitated. 'I have a request.'

The prime minister frowned. 'Go ahead.'

'My fellow traveller, a Yavana, was kidnapped by bandits. I'd like to take a couple of your men and go look for him.'

'You want two of the king's men to rescue this Yavana companion of yours?'

'Yes.'

'Who is he to you?'

'His father is an important man in Rome.'

'Why would that matter to us?'

'We don't know what alliances we may need in the future. Traders can be useful.'

'Can they?'

'I understand that a trader from Puhar brought a message to the king. This man I was travelling with was looking for that trader.'

'I am not aware of messages from any merchants. I need the

Romans as much as I need your Middle Kingdom! Time for the truth – now, why do you want to look for this man?'

Zhang evaded the question. 'If you grant my request, I will not try to make you see the way of the Buddha.'

'Do you also promise not to bad-mouth the priests?'

'Not in front of you!'

'Granted. You can take them after the *pujai* is over.'

'But –'

'We are short of men here. I can't spare anyone at the moment.'

Zhang nodded. He didn't have much of a choice as he stood no chance of rescuing Marcellus by himself. He needed the prime minister's men, and he would wait for them. He just hoped that the young man wouldn't come to harm. He covered his head with a scarf and rose to leave.

'Easterner, next time, please use the ring I gave you. This is becoming ridiculous. Every time I see an old woman, I think it must be you!'

~

While Zhang was closeted with the prime minister, the king's messenger was finally granted an audience. King Karikalan was tired after a long day of supervision at the site, but Adi didn't usually ask to meet him without reason and so an audience was granted.

'What news do you wish to bring to our attention today?'

'The general in Puhar sends his greetings, Your Majesty.'

'And?'

'I am not here on his account.'

'We appreciate your personal initiative. Proceed!'

'Your Majesty, the merchants of Puhar have conspired with the bandits and the Pandyas-in-exile to bring you down.'

'It's not the first time I've heard of such a thing, as you are well aware. But never before has it come from a reliable source. Why would the trading guild do this? After everything I have done for them. What do they gain?'

'Monopoly over trade, Your Majesty!'

'They have it today.'

'In name only and some would say it's not enforced.'

'Who dares to disobey my orders?'

'A Yavana trading family has made a deal with the Appans of Korkai.'

'The Appans? Is the magistrate of Maruvum aware of this deal?'

'I don't know, Your Majesty.'

'There must be a reason for you not making him aware.'

'That would have blown my cover, Your Majesty.'

'And you are here, traipsing around the kingdom, claiming that the traders of Puhar know this. Why haven't *they* gone to the magistrate?'

'I don't know,' Adi admitted. 'It may be because they don't believe any action would be taken. What I do know is that the guild is funding the Pandya exiles, who, in turn, are encouraging the bandits to foment more trouble.'

'Have you heard of a burglary at the Manaykan residence?'

'It was to make the point that the king is not in control of Puhar.'

'Are you suggesting that they employed burglars to rob from one of their own houses?'

'I... The burglars confessed to being put up to it by Pandya gho...spies.'

'But you think the traders are in cahoots with the Pandyas? Why would the Pandyas want to rob their partners?'

'A distraction, Your Majesty. They want to divert suspicion away from themselves.'

'Boy, your story is so convoluted that if I narrate it back to you, even you may not find it plausible.'

'With due respect, Your Majesty, I maintain it is the truth. A conspiracy is being hatched to –'

'I don't doubt that. I merely question who is involved and how they are planning to take me down.'

'I don't know how, but I mean to find out!'

'How?'

'I have reason to believe that people in the royal circle are involved.'

'You make serious allegations!'

'And I don't make them lightly. I will come back to you with evidence.'

'Who are you referring to?'

'I am afraid I –'

'You've broken protocol and come here with a message that could easily have been sent with an official messenger. He'd have made it here faster. There could only be one reason for doing so. Speak now and tell me who you suspect!'

'The prime minister, Your Majesty. He was seen leaving the Manaykan residence –'

'Where he was invited!'

'From where he was supposed to have left early, but he didn't actually.'

'There could be a thousand reasons for that.'

'A man, one of the burglars, was murdered before we could find out who he was meeting. The other went into hiding immediately.'

'And you think the prime minister had them killed?'

'He was the only one in the administration informed of the plan to release and follow them…'

'You'll have to do better than that if you accuse him of treason!'

'I'll be back with evidence, Your Majesty.'

28

TROUBLE AT THE QUARRY

Angavai and Vallavan made good time on land since they had joined the high road to the south earlier in the day. By mid-afternoon, signs of urban life started cropping up in the form of inns, tanks, dwellings, bullock carts and people. This place had been a rural backwater just a year ago, but since the start of the construction of the anicut, people flocked here from across the kingdom looking for work. At this junction, the riders moved away from the high road once again to avoid unwanted attention, and took a narrow trail between the road and the western hills. Angavai was on alert as always, but Vallavan's energy was flagging. His wounds had not yet healed and they had to stop often so that he could rest.

'The Yavana came to see you with a message from your sister. Why did you spurn him?' Angavai finally asked. They had not spoken about Marcellus all day.

'Do not speak to me of that traitor. I thought he was a true friend and I trusted him, but I was a fool. How do we know that he came with a message from Kuzhali? He could have simply said that to suit his nefarious purposes, whatever they are!'

'But you could have at least read the message. I'd have, if only

I knew how to read.' She could mention it now that there was no chance he'd read the missive.

'Why would Kuzhali send a message through him of all people?'

'Because you were so enamoured of your friend and couldn't stop singing his praises.'

'I was not enamoured... Wait, do you... Did you really think...?'

'It does not matter what I thought of your relationship with the Yavana. What matters is that your sister sent you an important message and now we are never going to know what it was.'

'Even if she did send a message, he could have changed it. Now that I know what he is capable of, I don't doubt that he tinkered with the message.'

'Learned he may be in his own language, but I doubt he can read or write in Tamil any better than I can.'

'Why are you so interested in Kuzhali's message? You don't even like her.'

'But she is your sister and she may need your help,' Angavai said, watching him carefully.

'You don't know my sister! She doesn't ask for me when she is in trouble. She wasn't happy that I was sent to take the guild's letter to the king. Perhaps she is trying to stop me. I respect my akka, but this is not the time to deal with women's intuition and whatever new theory that has caught her fancy. The Chola trade is at stake; and more importantly, the king's life is in danger and I have confirmation of that from my kidnappers. I have far more important things to do than to rush back to Puhar right now. Marcellus may well be involved in the treachery against the king. He has made a deal on pearls with the Appans of Korkai; what's to say he has not conspired with the Pandyas to assassinate our king, who had decreed that he cannot trade with them? I thought of him as a dear friend and yet...'

Vallavan spoke with a combination of anguish and rage. Angavai looked at him, concerned. Since his rescue, he had been intermittently delirious and was barely able to walk without assistance. The physician's advice had been clear – Vallavan needed a few days to recover, but that was neither in his nor Angavai's interests. Vallavan spoke of a Pandya conspiracy to assassinate the king and establish power over Chola lands. He'd gathered this intelligence while in captivity as he said his captors weren't particularly discreet.

None of this was news to Angavai. It was common knowledge among the hill peoples and delta villagers that Pandya spies roamed the land trying to induce people to rise in revolt against the king, and that the young Pandya prince was secretly being raised and groomed in the hills near Korkai. At the physician's residence, Angavai had offered to take the message to Uraiyur herself, leaving Vallavan behind, but even in his weakened state he wouldn't hear of it. He pointed out that she stood no chance of getting close to the king. He, on the other hand, hailed from an important trading family in Puhar, and was carrying a message from the very people who funded both the king's wars and his peacetime projects. She could not disagree with that, especially since she'd counted on him saying precisely that. She stood a much better chance of getting close to the king if she was with Vallavan. There was also the question of what to do with the Yavana, but Vallavan had not asked after him until she had brought up the topic. He had a knack for blocking out anything or anyone he didn't want to deal with.

'For whatever it is worth, I believe he is devoted to you. He helped me rescue you,' she said. If the Yavana's blood was going to be spilt because she'd ordered it, the least she could do was clear Marcellus's name with his friend. Even bandits had a code of honour.

Vallavan halted and stared at Angavai. 'I am beginning to think that he has made an impression on you! He is very deceptive. The Romans can be charming and convincing, but remember, I am your only true love!'

'I'll remember that especially when you are about to be married to that mousy cousin of yours,' she said sharply.

'I am not getting married to Mythili, whatever people may say. You are my only love, my protector, my goddess –'

'Stop it...that's enough! I am happy to be your everything, but you must not promise what you cannot deliver.'

'Yes, you are right,' he said despondently. 'My family will never allow it, but perhaps my akka will understand. She had married of her own accord.'

'Your akka?' she asked, her words dripping with disbelief. If he, even for a moment, thought that Kuzhali would bless his union with a girl from the hills, he was clearly not right in his head. 'Did she really? But look what happened to her. He died!'

'And now she wants to marry the king!'

'Widow remarriage... Isn't that sacrilege for your people?'

'That never stopped her doing anything she wanted.'

'You say she wants to marry the king?'

'My sister will marry whoever helps further her ambition. And right now, there is no one better than the king himself.'

'Then I wish her luck.'

They both laughed and for a brief while were transported back to happier times, in the Pari hills where they first met and in the grove behind his house where for a few stolen moments revenge, conspiracies and trade all lay forgotten.

A shout rent the air.

They turned to look and saw several men in the distance. What were they doing on bare rock under the scorching sun? Curious, the travellers left the trail and led their horses through the trees to get a clear view. As they neared the hill, they could make out a long line of men carrying huge rocks on their backs. It was a stone quarry and the workers were being supervised by guards. One of the workers, a frail-looking elderly man, had dropped his load and was begging for water.

'Water...' He could barely speak. A guard walked over to him.

'Lift the rock and you can have water.'

'Please, I can't. Just some water,' the man pleaded.

'Can you see the path there? If you walk some distance, there is a stream over there, where you can quench your thirst. But you cannot go there leaving the load here.'

The line of workers behind the man looked at the guard with unconcealed hatred.

'What are you staring at?' the guard growled. 'This is not break time, and none of you are getting water if you don't get the rocks to the site. Keep walking!'

The train of workers started moving forward slowly, past the guard and the old man. He dropped down to the ground, utterly exhausted.

'Thambi, have some pity. I will go to the stream, quench my thirst and I'll come back for the rock. Where else can I go?'

The guard laughed. 'No, this rock is your responsibility, and it cannot be separated from you until you reach the anicut. Those are the rules. Take your load and you are free to get water. Here, let me help you lift it.' He walked towards the rock. 'Come here.'

At this, the old man prostrated on the ground, next to the guard's feet. 'Please, I will die if I carry this. Kill me if that is what you desire, but do not make me suffer like this.'

'I'd rather you die doing something useful.' The guard laughed.

'Who knows, the gods may take pity on you and you may even go to heaven then.' He removed his belt from around his waist and cracked it down on the rock next to the old man. 'Let me see if you can lift this or not,' he said and lifted his arm.

Angavai did not wait to watch any further. 'Wait here. Whatever happens, don't come after me,' she said and dismounted swiftly.

'But you can't –'

'You'll find out that I can. The last time I waited in the shadows they dragged my mother and my sister away. I never even saw their bodies. You wait here, merchant lord.'

She broke cover and rushed towards the guard and the old man. The train of workers turned around in shock.

Angavai of all people knew the futility of getting involved in this situation. She and her men dealt with this kind of assault, humiliation and harassment every single day. It was why they were what they were in the first place. But that hadn't stopped her from intervening before – other than the one time it really mattered to her family – and it wasn't going to stop her now.

'You! You leave him alone. Does your king know this is how his workers are treated?'

'These are not workers!' exclaimed the guard. 'They are prisoners from the lands our king conquered. They are here to do what we tell them to do. Who are you to interfere with royal works?'

'I am from the hills over there, where we take care of the old and the infirm.'

'Really? Did you hear that, old man? Shall we show her how we take care of you?' asked the guard and brought the belt down on the old man, who screamed and writhed in pain. Angavai did not hesitate. Before the guard realized what was happening, she stood in front of him, bow in hand, ready to shoot an arrow through his heart.

'Now, pick him up and give him water,' she said coldly. The

guard stood paralysed. He had heard stories of bandit men and women who'd come in from the woods to pillage entire villages. If she was here, it was likely that her band was nearby, waiting to strike. He had to call for help and he looked around frantically for his fellow guards, but they were already well ahead.

One of the workers came forward to help the old man up.

'Give him water. Take the jug from that thug there,' Angavai instructed. 'Don't worry, he won't move – not with this pointing at him.'

The man took the jug from the worker and gave it to the old man, who was sitting up now. He gulped down the water thirstily.

'Now listen, all of you. It won't be long before the guards come to check what's wrong here, and if they know what happened here, you'll all be dead.'

'Better that than this life,' croaked the old man.

'It won't be an easy death, take it from me. So this is what you are going to do: I can see two of them coming this way. When they get here, you are going to tell them that bandits came and they attacked the guard. You lot had nothing to do with this.'

'But the guard will tell them –'

'Hey... What's wrong over there? Why is the train not moving? Hurry up!' a guard in the distance shouted.

The guard opened his mouth to cry out, but only a croak came out. Before anyone could react, the arrow went through his chest and he fell. The prisoners sprang back in fright. Some of them dropped the rocks they were holding.

'The guard won't be around to provide his version of events. I am leaving now, but remember this: one day, we shall be free! Don't give up hope!'

By now, two guards were hurrying back to the train as they'd realized that something was wrong. Angavai rushed to where she had left Vallavan, but he had broken cover and was walking towards her.

'Get back –'

'You killed him. *You* killed the *king's* guard... How could – ?'

'I am a bandit! That's what I do. Now, come with me.' She tried dragging him back, but he pushed her away and started walking towards the guards.

'They'll take you prisoner!' she shouted.

'I am the king's subject and the sooner I am taken before him, the better. As for you...'

She looked back – a few guards were running towards them. She wouldn't be able to fight off all of them by herself, not in plain sight. And she couldn't afford to be caught. She made her decision.

'Good luck to you, my love. Farewell!'

29

THE KING AT THE HOLY ISLE

Oblivious to the various parties of messengers, Yavanas and potential assassins rushing towards the anicut, the object of their collective attention was at that moment ensconced in the priests' quarters in the river island of Vellithirupatti. The Kaveri split west of the island, its southern branch retaining the name of the main river and the northern branch becoming the tributary called Kollidam. The dam site lay to the east and work was nearing completion. Before the Kallanai could be declared open, Lord Ranganathan, who reclined in the isle, and his fiercely protective priests had to be propitiated. The shrine's rituals were clouded in secrecy and even the king was not allowed beyond the priests' quarters. No one other than select priests and novices had ever been in the presence of the reclining lord, and it had led to rumours that the god wasn't even there in the first place. But this was of no account to the king, who was here to seek the deity's blessings and gain foresight.

Karikalan had spent the past few days in relative peace, inspecting the progress made on the construction of the dam, meeting local farmers and artisans, and visiting the odd village around his grand project. But the recent messages he had received from his military officials and spies gave him cause for concern. His days of idealism were well past and he knew that peace wasn't a permanent state of affairs. It was the time to gather troops before the start of another war. Every king spoke of peacetime as the end state to strive for, but every one of them knew it was a lie – they only wanted their people trained and rested before they'd be called to fight again, in another conquest or to defend the kingdom. Mankind wasn't meant to be peaceful, and as men of this world, Karikalan and his people could not afford to stand still. That would be suicide.

Yet, for the past two years, he had kept his attention focused on building dams and roads across the kingdom, bowing to the wishes of the common folk. He had given the traders free rein as he knew that sooner or later he'd need them to contribute to the war chest. When he came back home victorious after the battle at Venni, and then again from the successful foray into Yalpanam, he had planned for a few months of peace to help him rebuild his infantry and cavalry. A strong navy alone would not do for the northern conquest he had in mind and he'd have to build a formidable army to carry out his plan. And for this, he needed the support of the Cheras and the Pandyas to present a united front, but he did not have friends in either kingdom. He was seen as the conqueror, the usurper who'd defeated their kings and humiliated their people. The Pandyas hated the Cholas, while the Cheras, who had recaptured some of their territory, were discreetly developing their relationship with the Yavanas at Musiris and fending off the pirates on the western coast. He couldn't count on them supplying strong men for his army.

Karikalan intended to capture lands from the very powerful Satkarni of Amaravati and he wanted to catch him unawares – for the northern king was fixated on lands further north and west. But recent intelligence pointed towards Satkarni looking south – he especially seemed to have realized the importance of Yavana trade. The war that Karikalan wanted could come sooner than expected, but he wasn't prepared for it. He did not have the numbers to take on the full might of the northern army if it came down to that. His navy could destroy the opposing navy in a matter of days, but he knew he was weak on land – his infantry and cavalry would not be able to withstand the onslaught. To make matters worse, the very traders he protected with the might of the Chola navy were now engaged in a conspiracy to unseat him. Traders had no allegiances, and everyone knew they only followed the gold. A war – now, they would not want that as it would be detrimental to their business, but would it stop them from supporting a coup? He could not be certain. And now, Adi had come with the news that the prime minister himself may be involved in the plot.

He hoped Ranganathan would provide some resolution to his troubles. An endorsement from the priests would be useful in cementing his standing with the Vaishnavites. Entering this shrine, even though it technically belonged to him, had cost him a small fortune in the form of gold, flowers, saffron, ghee, rice and cane. The origin of this temple was shrouded in mystery from what he remembered of the stories he had been told as a child – was this where Vishnu decided to make his home as Vibhishana could not carry him any further or was this really the shrine of the Asura lord that these priests razed down to make room for their god?

'I apologize for the delay, Your Highness,' said a young novice as he hurried towards the king. Karikalan knew this young man well as he had been at the forefront of most of the rituals over the past several hours. 'One of our priests has unexpectedly taken ill and the chief priest is meeting with a suitable substitute from Madurai.'

'He cannot meet him later?'

'No, Your Highness. Because his services are needed for the

ceremony tomorrow and the chief priest wants to ensure that the anicut pujai goes ahead without incident.'

The king nodded absently.

Soon, a withered old man appeared, barely able to walk. He was clothed in a bright saffron robe, and wrinkled tattoos of naamams filled all the visible areas of his skin. The king rose to greet him.

'Sit down.' He spoke without formality. The king noted that there was no reverential address. The priest's voice was clear and strong, surprising for a man his age. 'We are glad you have come here to meet us after all this while. Ranganathan has been waiting for you!'

'I did not mean to keep him waiting.' The king tried his best to sound apologetic, which was not exactly his strong suit. 'If I had been aware –'

'It is not his duty to make his subjects aware of his wishes. That is my duty and in that I have failed!'

'How have you failed? I am here, aren't I?'

'Yes, but only because you wish to know the future as you have lost all hope.'

'But I haven't lost hope; not at all!' said the king. 'On the contrary, you will be pleased to know that the kingdom is enjoying a glorious period of peace and prosperity.'

'Even so, the signs are everywhere. Spies roam freely. Foreign gods take root in the land of Vishnu Perumal. The Yavanas and traders are a religion unto themselves!'

'Swamy, tell me what you see and I promise to make this temple the most famous Vishnu temple in all of the country,' said the king, getting straight to the point.

'Do you propose to dedicate this island to the lord?'

'Yes!' Karikalan did not hesitate. He'd come prepared. He knew the priest's blessings and tacit support came at a cost – one that he was willing to pay. If the Vaishnavite priests wanted to claim this island as their own, it was fine by him. The people would get their dam, and they wouldn't complain either.

'Will you give up Sivan?' the priest pressed on.

'No, of course not!' The king gave an involuntary start. 'I will elevate Ranganathan to the same level as Sivan in all of my lands. Of that, I give my word.'

The priest's eyebrows shot up. 'Ranganathan does not desire parity. He is the only truth and he needs to be recognized as such.'

Karikalan wasn't sure he'd heard right. 'Are you asking me to give up all other gods?' he asked slowly.

'Not just you. Your kingdom has to accept Vishnu and his avatars as their only true god.'

'That will not be possible. My subjects are welcome to their gods. I will not force any one god on them.'

'But you come seeking Lord Ranganathan. Why?'

'To know my future!'

'Ranganathan is not a street astrologer! You can ask your court astrologer or the maadan's priest for that.' Since he had ascended the throne, the king had not been spoken to in so rude a manner, but he ignored it for the moment.

'I was told that Ranganathan knows best and I came to see if it was indeed true. Am I mistaken?'

'No, you're not.'

'Tell me, what do the omens portend for my kingdom?'

'What the lord sees, he does not like. Things are not what they used to be. The rains will fail this year as the sun is not happy.'

'What have we done to anger him?'

'Your enemies have propitiated him, and he is pleased with them. Beware of the sun – he will not let the rain clouds in this year.'

'What can I do to change his mind?'

'The sun is the least of your worries, king. All around you, darkness is creeping in. Heat and darkness together.'

'What darkness do you see?'

'I can only see what the lord shows me, and he has shown me the darkest of nights. You have shown the Pandyas mercy and you have made their gods – yes, *their* gods – yours. But they are ungrateful wretches: they want more and in an effort to please the Pandyas you have angered Ranganathan. You've let Buddhists and Jainas roam this country as if it is theirs for the taking, while Yavanas frolic in your capital. Who gave these foreigners permission to make this their land? They can bring only darkness with them. What else did you expect?' the priest asked. His voice was low and patronizing, that of a benevolent parent scolding an erring child.

'Yavanas come to trade, but they do not ask us to adopt their gods or their way of life. They adhere to ours for as long as they live in our lands!'

'Take a look at the temples they have built in Musiris and you'll understand their real intentions. And what about the Buddhists and the Jainas who seek to convert our people to their vile religion? They put ideas into people's heads; they say the king and the peasant are equal.'

'They can say what they want, but our people trust me and our gods.'

'Not any more. King, wake up before it is too late! If you continue to give free rein to foreigners and foreign gods, this kingdom will be forfeited. It may already be too late –'

At this, Karikalan sprang up, furious. This had gone on for long enough.

'Swamy,' he said, struggling to keep his voice calm, 'this kingdom was forfeited years ago, and I came back from certain death to claim it. I made it what it is today, and what I have built will not be lost. As long as I live, the tiger standard of the Cholas will fly high in Puhar, in Madurai and on this island of your lord.'

'That may indeed be true,' the priest said, nodding thoughtfully.

'So you agree with me?'

'I pray for your long life, king.'

'I see. What does the future hold for me?'

'I cannot see into your future. I can only see what he deigns to show me. But for the sake of this kingdom, I ask you to banish foreign gods –'

'Just foreign gods or the gods of the hill peoples too?'

'Especially the asura gods. They are not true divine beings; they're the superstition of an uncivilized people –'

'And yet, they say that the people of the hills built this very structure you stand upon. You claim it for your god, but did your people build it?' Karikalan could not resist speaking the words. This priest may be powerful but *he*, Karikalan, was still the king of the land.

For the first time since the start of the meeting, the old priest's face showed emotion. 'You do not understand what you speak of. With this kind of talk you encourage the very bandits who seek to destroy you. I warn you against such sacrilege. Do not dare to question Ranganathan's power!'

The king did not speak for a few moments. Finally, he asked, 'What would you have me do?'

'Perform the pujai tomorrow, go back to Puhar and outlaw the false gods. Dedicate this island to the lord – henceforth, it shall be known as Srirangam. Do not let foreigners near you!'

The king thought over matters for a while. Two could play this game and he didn't have to give anything away just yet. 'I will see you tomorrow at the pujai,' he said quietly.

Karikalan left, no more knowledgeable than when he had come into the temple. That his kingdom was surrounded by people who wished to conquer it and steal its wealth was not news to him. Foreign religions didn't necessarily concern him, but he made a note to ask the chief administrator to look into it. The king's view on gods and faiths was simple: he wanted to propitiate as many of them as he could so that they would all be pleased with him. If his people were to follow many gods, it could only be better for the kingdom. Who could defeat him if he had so many gods on his side? But the priest was forceful and something had to be seen to be done regarding foreign gods. He'd see through the pujai and ask for a report on Buddhist and Jaina pilgrims. That should keep the priests happy for a while.

As the king and his party were leaving the temple compound, they caught sight of two men from the chief administrator's office rushing towards them.

'See what they want,' the king told his bodyguard, and the men were brought to him immediately. They bowed low and stepped back.

'A message from the chief administrator, Your Majesty. A man has been arrested under suspicious circumstances in the quarry. He was with a bandit woman who murdered one of our guards in broad daylight. The man claims to be a trader from Puhar and says he carries an important message for you. He refuses to give this message to anyone but the king. Our master has put him in the prison enclosure.'

'Traders and bandits! He could be the assassin we were warned about,' Karikalan's bodyguard whispered. 'He is the one we were waiting for.'

'You think they sent a trader boy to finish me off?' the king asked. 'But you are right, this requires investigation.'

'The chief administrator would like to execute the man immediately. In light of –'

'I am surprised at the administrator's incompetence! I think his senses have been numbed by his affection for me. We have to find out what this man knows and who his accomplices are before he is put to death!'

'Yes, Your Majesty, we will interrogate him thoroughly and put him to death today.'

'He is a Chola subject and he will have a trial. I will be the judge!'

'Your Majesty, the chief administrator has heard him and pronounces him guilty.'

'Then why did he send you to tell me this? I wish to see this man before he is hanged. If he wished to harm me, he will be hanged in a public square in Puhar, not here in Uraiyur, where they can't see what happens to those who conspire against the king.'

'We shall bring the man to you immediately, Your Majesty,' the man said, bowing again.

The royal priest, who was travelling with the king's retinue, cleared his throat softly. 'Your Majesty, you cannot meet criminals until tomorrow's pujai is complete. The gods are clear about this. You are not to perform any state duties until tomorrow evening,' he reminded Karikalan.

The king thought it over for a moment. He had angered enough gods already and could do without angering any more. Karikalan wanted to speak to the captive, but it could wait. He wasn't going anywhere.

'Keep him in the prison camp,' he instructed the men. 'I will question him tomorrow night.'

The two men bowed again and turned to go.

'You said there was a woman? A bandit?'

'Yes, Your Majesty, a girl from the hills.'

The king frowned. 'Has she been questioned?'

The men looked at each other sheepishly before answering. 'We think he picked her up on the way and she is of little consequence. While we were apprehending him, she escaped...'

The king glared at them, his anger mounting once again. 'When I question the man tomorrow I want the girl to be present. If she is not there, I expect the chief administrator not to be administering anything in the future. Will you make this clear to him?'

'Yes, Your Majesty,' the men said in unison and withdrew.

30

An Unwritten Letter

My dearest kutti,

The guards have refused my request for a scribe. Nor are they willing to consider providing a scroll and stylus, as they believe that I will use this as an opportunity to send a message to my co-conspirators. They are wrong. I am no conspirator, and the king doesn't have a more loyal subject than myself in this kingdom. But such is my fate and I must endure it.

When our amma visited the Navallur astrologer before she fell out with him, he'd told her that the wicked spell Shani had cast on me was coming to an end, but I am afraid that the planet has a final showdown planned for me and I am not sure I'll be able to escape his clutches this time. There is one last hope: that of an audience with the king. Everything I know of him tells me that he will listen and judge me innocent. But if I don't get to see him, then they'll come and tell you that I was a traitor, that you should disown me. Don't believe them. Even if this unwritten letter never reaches you.

Our akka says that I am careless in my choice of friends. Kuzhali has been proven right yet again. (Has she ever been wrong?) The Yavana Marcellus who I thought was a true friend turned out to be a cobra in disguise. Not only has he cut us out on the agreement with the Appans, he and the rest of the Yavanas are in league with the Pandya exiles to overthrow our king. This I learnt from the men who kidnapped me and who took great pains to keep the information from me. The magistrate of Maruvum was right about the real motives of Marcellus and his crew, and that's why the charges were brought against them. The magistrate recognized a snake when he saw it, but I, who spent forty days and nights nursing and befriending this creature, did not. And ayya gave in to my wishes and let him go free – but as a result, I lie in a prison in our own kingdom, accused of a coup against our beloved king.

You may be young, but you have seen enough to know by now that I've not been the son that ayya wanted me to be, or the son I should have been. I'd always, even as a boy, wanted to serve the king – either in his administration or in the military. Bravery and valour against all odds are the traits I value above all, but I, unfortunately, was born a merchant of Puhar. Ayya has never let me forget this: we don't serve the king. The king needs us, needs our gold, and we can never be servants to the king. He sent me to distant lands to keep me away from Puhar. I obeyed him and performed my duty to the family. I got the guild what they wanted in the hope that when I returned I'd have proved myself in trade and be allowed to pursue a role in the king's administration. When the opportunity to take a message to the king arose, I jumped at it, but look where it brought me. Oh, the irony!

I told you that I've erred in my choice of companions and by that I didn't mean just the Yavana. There is someone else: a girl. You, my kutti, will never understand it and I don't expect you to either. I don't understand it myself. She is not a courtesan who only knows how to sing, dance and entertain men. Angavai can shoot an arrow from one end of Nagarathar Street to the other, and her aim will be true. She saved my life once and I fell in love with her. It was an impossible love from the start, but I didn't think that she'd aim directly for the king and his men. I'd always thought she was made to do what she did. However, that wasn't the case. She killed one of the king's guards with impunity in front of me and that's when the scales fell away from my eyes. She wasn't the victim of circumstance; she was what she was because that's who she wanted to be! Go on and laugh, Kannaki; your brother in love with a bandit woman from the hills! And where did it get me? In prison, waiting for an executioner!

Here is a truth that no one will tell you, but one that you should know: our king, the great Karikalan, is not loved or revered by our people. We cannot say this out loud, but it is true. They believe that he is dangerous. He doesn't give in to the wishes of the priests like the other kings were wont to; he maintains his own set of spies and messengers; he doesn't grant all the demands of the guild; he keeps us at arm's length and doesn't show us his cards. He doesn't even listen to his own ministers, if rumours are to be believed. The guild worries about this, and they'd like someone more predictable and amenable to be the ruler of the kingdom. But the very trait that our people hate in the king – the fact that he has a mind of his own – is his strongest weapon. He is a self-made king, and he'll do what he thinks is right for the people of this kingdom. If he were to die, could the person replacing him guarantee the safety of the kingdom? The Pandya heir in exile is hardly more than a child; the Cheras can't ward pirates off their coast. Could it be Satkarni and his ilk, who don't even speak our language, let alone understand our way of life? Or the ambitious ministers and countless royals, none of whom can command the respect of the people? There is no one but Karikalan!

There is one other person who knows this and who sees the situation as I do. Or maybe I see it this way because she does, and she can be very persuasive. Kuzhali and I are usually on opposing sides, but in this one respect we agree: we want Karikalan to remain the king of Tamilakam. The prosperity of our kingdom and our family depends on it.

But why am I, in what is possibly the final few hours of my life, boring you with politics and trade? Whatever happens to me, you have an entire life to look forward to – a life with a dutiful husband, sons and in-laws who'll cherish you as much as we do. You, my dear Kannaki, have an advantage over me – you've always had it – our akka was never in competition with you. She has never forgiven me for being the son of the house, but you she loves. In fact, if there is one person Kuzhali loves unconditionally, it is you. So here's my final piece of advice to you, kutti: have a good life. Don't pay too much attention to straying husbands – they'll come back. If you ever get into trouble, don't run away. Run to your sister. She'll find a way.

Your unfortunate Anna

31

MONKS REUNITED

'Once we turn that bend, you'll see the campsite and the settlement. I have to stop soon after as boats aren't allowed upriver after that point until the dam works are complete.'

Marcus looked up towards where the boatman was pointing. This was the rice bowl of the Chola country, and beyond the reeds and trees along the riverbank, all he could see were endless paddy fields. The bend reminded him of a similar turn of the Tiber a few *mille passus* before it reached Rome. His master – well, father – had a house up on the hill and the family used to go down to the river for picnics in the summer.

'You must get a lot of customers due to the construction work,' he said absent-mindedly.

'Only in the short run,' the boatman replied gloomily. 'This anicut will be the death of my village!'

Karikalan's dam was being billed as a lifeline for the people of the delta. *But this man is telling me that it will harm his village,* thought Marcus. Seeing his surprised expression, the boatman continued, 'It all depends on which side of the river you are from. My village is on the banks of the Kollidam, the northern branch. This dam diverts excess water from the Kaveri, where it splits, so the water will then flow to Kollidam instead. Floods wreak havoc here even in a regular year; once the anicut is in operation, we'll drown. The farmers in the south have most of the land, so no one cares about us.'

'Your people can petition the king. He –'

'And how do you propose we speak to him? What are a few villages in the service of the mighty Chola kingdom?' he asked in a matter-of-fact tone.

'But –'

'Don't worry about us, Yavana. We'll find a way. Are you going to see the pujai?'

Marcus nodded. 'Do you know what it is for? And when it's supposed to take place?'

'It is a cleansing rite to Vishnu, asking him to ensure the safe completion of the work. Vishnu wasn't happy with the previous pujai as it was offered only to the earth goddess. The project has seen many accidents in recent weeks and the king is now trying to appease Lord Ranganathan. You have reached just in time. The country folk are arriving from near and far, and there will be singing and dancing today. I am expecting a lot of rides. Whatever we think of him, it's not often that you have the king here in Uraiyur nowadays. Long gone are the days when this was the Chola capital!'

Marcus had an uneasy feeling in the pit of his stomach. The festivities sounded like the right kind of distraction required for an assassin to carry out a plan. This day would not end well. It was much harder to do the dastardly act in Puhar as the king would be well guarded. What better time than when everyone was distracted by the pujai? He had to warn the king or at the least warn his bodyguards. But how he would reach them or make his story sound believable, he hadn't quite worked out.

The boat, meanwhile, turned the bend and headed steadily for the bank. A woman was washing her face by the river.

'This is as far as I can take you, Yavana. Head in that direction over there. You can hear the sounds already!'

Marcus leapt out and paid the man generously, who thanked him and pushed the boat back into the river before jumping into it himself. The woman had now walked back to her basket by the riverbank and was watching him intently.

'Ayya, would you like to buy some sweets? You won't get sweets like this anywhere else... Try some?' she asked loudly. Marcus was suddenly ravenous, and he bought a little bit of everything in her basket and gobbled it down. He started walking towards the din. The groves on the bank hid the camp from view, but he could see smoke rising from beyond the first clump of trees. As he walked on, he heard the beat of drums and the hum of voices grow louder. Soon, he started seeing groups of people cooking or milling about, laughing. Children played hide-and-seek in the grove, and behind a thick bush, he saw a couple stealing a private moment away from prying eyes. He screamed as a young girl nearly fell down on him from a tree above before he realized that she had been found out by the seeker and was just making her way down hastily. A festive atmosphere pervaded the place as he walked on purposefully towards the centre, where he hoped the king and his men would be.

As Marcus emerged from the grove, he saw groups of people roughly spread out in a semicircle around the centre, from where the smoke was rising up to the sky. He understood there were hundreds of people around – almost as many people as he was used to seeing at the Circus. Until then, he hadn't seen any of the king's men, but here the army's presence was perceptible as armed men ordered people out of the way and broke up petty quarrels among the populace. Vendors of dolls, incense, savouries and sweets were doing brisk business as children dragged their parents towards them. Soon he realized that the crowds were gathered in concentric semicircles, and with each circle, the military presence went up a notch. He thought of stopping one of the soldiers and asking if he could meet the king. But he dismissed the idea as soon as it occurred to him – he would have to explain himself, his disguise and what he was doing in the woods, and even then he wasn't sure when the assassination would be attempted or how.

Then there was also the small matter that he was wanted in the capital with regard to a murder case. The soldiers would throw him in jail or brand him crazy – he would have to find another way to reach the king.

'Hey, you, stop right there. Who are you?'

This was the last thing he needed – being stopped by a soldier.

'I have come to see the pujai –' Marcus began, when the soldier cut him off.

'That's not what I asked. Where are you from?'

'I am a follower of the Buddha.' He decided to stick to the script this time.

'Did you know that Yavanas are not allowed here during the ceremony? Chief administrator's orders!'

'I was not aware of such an order –'

'You say you are a Buddhist. But you are here to offer prayers to our god. What is your real business here?' The soldier was getting more and more suspicious of him.

'I told you the truth! I was passing by and a boatman told me about the pujai. I'd like to see it just like everyone else here. I was told that in the Chola kingdom everyone is welcome.'

'Not in these times. There are spies and assassins everywhere. You'd better come with me.'

'Where are you taking me?'

'You can stay in the prison encampment until the pujai is over. We will interrogate you properly after that. If you are guiltless, you have nothing to fear!'

'But you are not listening to me. I am an innocent pilgrim, come to see the rites and join in the festivities. You cannot arrest me! I haven't committed any crime!'

'Come with me, Yavana, or I will have to drag you all the way.' The soldier reached out and held his wrist in a vice-like grip. Before Marcus could decide whether to bolt or stay, a commotion behind them caught the soldier's eye. Two men were arguing loudly and a group of onlookers had surrounded them.

'You dare to come here to this sacred place, where we offer our prayers to Vishnu Perumal, and say that your god is better?'

The soldier moved forward to get a better view, and his grip loosened. Marcus was about to take his chance when he saw who the question was directed to.

But of course!

'You are not listening to me. I did not say my god is better. I said that the Buddha, the enlightened one, said that rituals are of no use. They are not going to help you,' Zhang proclaimed loudly, with his characteristic enthusiasm.

Marcus relaxed. The ever-resourceful Zhang had managed to escape the bandits unscathed. And here he was taunting the crowd with his unique brand of sacrilegious talk. He wondered how this particular foreigner had not been arrested by the king's soldiers yet.

'Another follower of the Buddha, an Easterner!' the soldier muttered. 'This place is growing foreigners. And this one makes fun of our gods!'

'Hey, you, come here! Who are you?' he shouted loudly. It was perfect timing. A number of men in the crowd were just about to attack Zhang when they saw the soldier.

Zhang looked up and beamed as he caught sight of Marcus. 'I am a Buddhist pilgrim like the one standing behind you. In fact, what a coincidence! He happens to be my disciple!'

The soldier swung around in surprise and looked at Marcus. 'You did not tell me your guru was here!'

'That is because we were forcibly separated near Nachiyar Koil while on our way here.' Zhang laughed. 'Thanks to you, we are now reunited. We are grateful to you and –'

'What were you doing in Nachiyar Koil?'

'Just what we are doing here. Telling people about the Buddha.'

'They cannot do that,' the man who was arguing with Zhang cried out. 'They come here and mock our gods. They should be banned from the Chola kingdom!'

'I am not mocking you. I am just showing you that there is a better life for you if you care to see it,' Zhang said patiently. 'Tell me this, why can you not go into the pujai pandal?'

The man hesitated before answering, trying to figure out if this was a trick question. 'Because the priests perform the pujai and no one else is allowed in?'

'And who made the priests the agents of your gods? Why can you not speak to him yourself? Does he not understand Tamil?'

'This man is questioning the authority of priests!' the man shrieked. 'He should be imprisoned immediately!'

The crowd around them roared in approval.

'I have committed no crime!' said Zhang.

'You have desecrated our gods and there is no greater crime in this kingdom. This man should be put to death!'

The soldier interrupted at this point. The crowd was getting out of control and his primary job today was to ensure nothing untoward happened. He had a mandate to maintain peace during the ceremony, and he wasn't going to let a lynching happen on his watch.

'Calm down. I am taking these men, the guru and his disciple, to the chief administrator and they will be tried over there.'

'We demand justice now!'

'Justice will be served in the land of Karikalan the unconquerable, but the king does not believe in street justice. Both of you, come with me right now!'

There was no point in trying to make a run for it, Marcus decided. It would be a case of jumping from the frying pan straight into the fire as the crowd wouldn't let them get away. He'd have to take his chances with the chief administrator now.

32

ARRESTED AGAIN!

The soldier pushed the two men past the crowds – people promptly gave way when they saw the guard's uniform – and into the inner circle which housed a few large tents. From here, Marcus could see the much-talked-about anicut, which extended more than halfway across the Kaveri. It was made of large stones fitted together with limestone to form a formidable barrier. Near the river was a raised platform, inside which a homam fire was burning. The smell of incense filled the air along with the chants of the priests, who were sitting in a circle atop the platform. Helpers went around fetching offerings. The king and his bodyguards were nowhere to be seen.

'You wait here,' the soldier said to them at the entrance to one of the tents. Turning to the doorman, he instructed, 'Don't let them out of your sight. They are not to be trusted. I am going to meet the chief administrator.'

The soldier opened the screen and slipped inside.

'How did you escape the ambush and get here?' Marcus whispered to Zhang.

'Trust in the Buddha,' said Zhang quietly.

There was no time to waste and Marcus came straight to the

point. 'I need to get a message to the king. His life is in danger. I have news of a conspiracy to assassinate him while he is here. Can your Buddha help me get to him?'

Zhang's expression did not change. 'Who are the assassins?'

'Spies have been dispatched from Amaravati to kill him. The trader guild in Puhar is implicated.'

'How did you happen to learn this?'

'It was in the message I was carrying all along!'

'Did you tell your friend?'

'He didn't want to meet me. I don't think I'll ever see him again.'

'I wouldn't give up so easily. He is here.'

'Vallavan reached here safely?'

'Depends on what you mean by safe. He is in prison under arrest. They tried to arrest the bandit girl too for murder, but she escaped.'

'But Vallavan was carrying a message for the king,' exclaimed Marcus.

'Shut up both of you. Or there'll be nothing left of you by the time you get to the chief administrator!' The doorman flashed his sword to ensure that they understood. Both men went silent and, after a while, the soldier came out of the tent.

'Follow me, and remember to show respect. You are in the presence of the chief administrator, after all!'

The chief administrator was a sombre-looking man whose most prominent feature was the number of weapons he had on his belt – Marcus counted four daggers and a sword. He sported a thick moustache in the manner of all Chola soldiers. Marcus noted that he wasn't alone in the tent as there was another man in the corner, hidden in the shadows.

'These are the two I mentioned, Your Lordship. They were inciting unrest in the crowd and disrespecting our gods.'

'I didn't –' started Marcus but the chief administrator was in no mood to let him finish.

'Where do you come from?'

'From Puhar we came south to spread our faith and stopped to see the pujai,' Zhang replied.

'Do you expect me to believe that?'

'You can ask anyone in Maruvum, Your Lordship. I am Zhang, the Buddhist, and everyone knows how dedicated I am to the Buddha!'

'In that case, let's ask someone about it before we proceed,' the chief administrator said and turned to the man in the corner who stepped forward into the light.

'He is right. Everyone knows Zhang. The question I have is for his companion. When did you dedicate yourself to the Buddha, *little master*?'

'Adi!' cried out Marcus. 'I know we haven't seen eye to eye before, but believe me, the only reason I am here today is to deliver a message to the king. This is important!'

'You too?' The chief administrator sounded incredulous. 'How many assassins are out there?'

'I am not an assassin. I came all the way here to warn the king!'

'He came to warn the king! Marcellus – no, that's not your real name, is it? Marcus, little slave, why are you here?'

At this, Zhang turned to Marcus in genuine surprise.

'I told you why I was here. I was carrying a message for my friend Vallavan –'

'He is an accomplice of the two murderers. Where is the bandit girl? Answer me now!' roared the chief administrator.

'I don't know who you are talking about!'

'Throw him into prison. He'll be tried with the trader and executed. He must be the mastermind –'

'Your Lordship,' Adi interrupted, 'I suggest more caution in this matter. We'll need to investigate this further before –'

'What's there to investigate? He says he came to warn the prisoner... What do you know about him?'

'He is a trader from Rome. No, he is a charlatan – a slave who pretends to be the son of a prominent Roman trader!'

Marcus noticed that Zhang had lifted an eyebrow at this.

'And now he pretends to be a pilgrim,' the chief administrator snapped. 'Isn't that sufficient?'

'He is wanted in Puhar for the murder of a local citizen. I also know that he had illegal trade dealings with the Pandyas –'

'And you want to investigate further? This man here is an assassin sent by the Pandyas to kill the king. He is already wanted for murder in Puhar. Soldier, throw him in prison and we'll bring them before the king after the pujai. Take these men away right now!'

'But I haven't killed anyone. The king needs to be on guard,' screamed Marcus.

'The king is guarded by *my* men. He'll be safe. Once you are in prison, he'll the safest he has ever been.'

'Your Lordship.' Zhang spoke up. 'I only accompanied him as he said he wanted to follow the Middle Path. I've no other interest in this matter. Surely you'll show this poor pilgrim mercy?'

'No, the king will decide what to do with you.'

'In that case' – Zhang's tone changed in an instant from servile to authoritative – 'if I may, Your Lord, I have an insignia that I would like you to see.'

Adi and Marcus looked at Zhang in bemusement. *He had what?*

'We shall see it.'

Zhang put his hand inside his robe and pulled out a scroll and a ring that he handed over to the official. The chief administrator's face changed as he read it and he looked at Zhang with a sudden respect. 'I was not aware that you are acquainted with the prime minister!' He turned and showed it to Adi, who had suddenly become very quiet. 'You shall not be troubled any more, but you may be needed to provide evidence during the hearing.'

'Thank you,' said Zhang and withdrew swiftly from the scene. Marcus was led away by the guard to the barracks.

33

DRAMA IN PRISON

'No, you can't meet the king at this time. No one is allowed inside!' The king's guards stood their ground.

'But I have an urgent message for –'

'Everyone seems to have an urgent message for the king.'

'I am not everyone!'

The guard shrugged. 'I don't care who you are. My orders are my orders. The king is forbidden to speak to anyone before the pujai is complete.'

Though officially lower in rank, the king's personal guards controlled access to Karikalan and were very protective of him. Even undercover spies such as Adi, as highly regarded as he was, didn't stand a chance against the guards. He could have spoken to the chief administrator and got access to the king, but this matter was too delicate and he wasn't sure whom to trust.

'What if this is an emergency?'

'If it's an emergency, we expect the prime minister to be here. He has delegated authority at this time.'

This was far worse than he had thought. The one person who had access to Karikalan was the one who shouldn't have any access to him now. Adi finally had the evidence he was looking for – Zhang the Buddhist was the prime minister's spy. The insignia was proof. And Zhang had accompanied Marcus, who was in league with the Pandyas, which could only mean one thing: the prime minister was a traitor who had aligned himself with the Pandyas to kill the king and usurp power. *He should be executed for treason before he gets the opportunity to put his plan into action*, Adi thought frantically. *Zhang must be the connection between the prime minister, Marcus, the trading guild and the Pandya exiles.*

Adi looked across the prime minister's tent to see if there was any movement, and right at that moment Zhang emerged. 'Traitor or not,' Adi muttered to himself darkly, 'the prime minister has more sense if his spies have access to him at all times.'

But then, he noticed that the Easterner was behaving strangely. He looked around to see if anyone had seen him and walked around to one side of the tent and hid himself behind a pole. This was laughable as he was too portly to be really hidden, but no one else seemed to have noticed him. Adi moved away from Zhang's line of sight and kept an eye on the tent. He didn't have to wait long. The prime minister stepped out soon enough and he had taken some pains to make himself look inconspicuous. A long cloth was wound around his head, which covered the lower half of his face. Adi checked to see if the king's guards had noticed him. No such luck. They were all looking towards the pandal from where endless chants and clouds of dark smoke were emanating.

The prime minister didn't stop to look if he was being followed. He walked swiftly towards the barracks. Adi waited to see what Zhang would do and, sure enough, after a few moments, the Buddhist followed at a discreet distance. Why was Zhang following his patron, wondered Adi. The best thing the spy could do in this situation was to keep the prime minister and his emissary in his line of sight and so he did not hesitate. He followed the prime minister and Zhang as the evening sun sparkled over the Kaveri.

~

Imprisoned for the second time in this alien kingdom, Marcus calculated his chances of getting out alive. He had been certain that the first night in Puhar had been a misunderstanding that would be cleared up by Vallavan. It turned out he was wrong. It was no misunderstanding and he had only ended up stepping off the ship alive thanks to Kuzhali – if she was to be believed. This time, there was little reason for hope, especially since he had no proof whatsoever; Kuzhali's letter was taken away from him before he was thrown into the cell. The evidence against him included, among other things: a murdered man in Puhar with whom he had a history; an illegal trade deal he had signed, despite having been warned explicitly that doing so would result in death; and the presence of the king's spy and messenger, who could confirm that he was impersonating another man.

Against the above evidence, in support of his case, all he had was a letter from a widow in Puhar, outlining an outrageous plan to finish off the king – and this was assuming the letter hadn't been destroyed. The only unknown was Zhang: he had pulled a rabbit out of his hat with that insignia he'd shown the chief administrator, but it wasn't clear whose side he was on. From whichever angle Marcus considered it, his chances of being acquitted were extremely low. He had to consider more unorthodox options to escape. With this in mind, he looked around the makeshift prison, which was until very recently a stable.

That's when he noticed the other inmate sitting in the opposite corner.

'Vallavan! Is that you?'

'Stay away from me. I am glad that you have been apprehended. I shall await your trial gladly!'

'My friend, listen to me. I swear I haven't done you any harm.'

'Do you deny that you conspired with the Appans of Korkai?'

'I deny that I've done any wrong by you!'

'I should've left you behind in that inn and let the Arabs finish you off in Cana.

'The only reason I am here is that your sister sent a message addressed to you. I know what it is about – it talks of an assassination attempt on the king!'

Vallavan laughed. 'And she sent it with you, the prime conspirator himself? My sister never puts her faith in the right people, and that includes me! But I don't understand your motive. What do you gain by working with the Paṇdyas to kill the king? You gain far more by trading with us than –'

'Hear me out, Vallavan! I am not conspiring with the Pandyas to kill the king. It is King Satkarni of Amaravati and members of your own trading guild who are involved in the coup!'

'Are you throwing suspicion on the guild now that you've no way out? How dare you?' Vallavan raised his voice.

'I am only relaying what I read in your sister's letter –'

'And pray tell me, where is this magical letter? Let me see it!'

'I...I don't have it. The soldiers took it away before they locked me up here.'

'You are far more cunning than I ever imagined. But I've heard it from my own abductors... They were Pandyas who were on the way to Uraiyur to kill the king.'

'Did you not wonder why they chose to kidnap you, but not kill you? They were using you! Can you not see it? They wanted you to hear what they said; they wanted you alive so that you could throw suspicion on the Pandyas! Your sister implied as much in her letter.'

'That's the most convoluted thing I've ever heard. You'll say anything to save your skin. But you'll not succeed as long as I live. Be certain of that, Marcellus!'

Marcus remained silent for a while. 'That's not my name,' he said finally.

'What?'

'I am not Marcellus. My name is Marcus.' As Vallavan stared at him open-mouthed, he continued, 'I am a freedman who works for Gaius in his warehouses in Ostia.'

'Why are you telling me this now?'

'I am telling you the truth, and all the truth and nothing but the truth. I'm telling you this in the hope that you'll believe me.'

'And where is Marcellus?'

'He wanted to fight in the war. Our...his father would not let him, but he was desperate to go to Gaul. He asked me to impersonate him and left.'

'You're the slave who abandoned your master's son, the real Marcellus, are you not? Tell me the truth, what did you do with your master?'

'I am not a slave... I have not been for a while and I did not abandon Marcellus. He wanted to make his mark in Gaul – he wanted to join the army and serve the empire. He had no interest in coming to Puhar. *He* asked me to take his place. I thought I'd do him a favour. And so I did.'

'It is my fate! It must be!' Vallavan cried out. 'I am destined to fall in love with ungrateful lowlifes. A Roman slave who gangs up to assassinate *my* king. And the bandit girl who kills the king's guards without a second thought! Oh god, I've sinned just as the priests had predicted. I promise you that I'll repent and perform all the rituals to cleanse myself. I will not stray below my station ever again!'

Marcus took a few steps back. He sat down on the damp floor and sighed heavily.

So there it was again. Abandoned as soon as they understood where he was from. A former slave, a freedman from Rome, who hung around the edges of society and was ignored except when he may be of use. Even his own father had not, and would never, acknowledge him as his son. Well, he could escape from this prison, but what after it? He'd be arrested the moment the *Minerva* landed in Myos Hormos – Hippalus would make sure of it – or, if he was lucky, he could make it back to Ostia somehow. But again, what after that?

Perhaps it was better to die here in this foreign land, orphaned in death as he was in life.

But he didn't have time to wallow in self-pity, for at that moment the stable door opened and two soldiers stepped inside.

'Which one?' demanded one of them.

'The Yavana, that one with the shaved head.'

'I was told that the trial would be held after the pujai?' Marcus said.

'Guess what? You are lucky, unlike him over there. No trial for you as the orders have come straight from the prime minister himself!'

Hope fluttered in his heart for a moment. Zhang may have convinced the prime minister that he was innocent, after all. But something about the soldiers and their tone made him wary. He still had his dagger on him – they hadn't searched him when they brought him in, only asked him for the letter, which he had handed over.

'A painless death, immediate execution. As I said, you're very lucky!' continued the soldier.

'You're going to kill him?' asked Vallavan, not comprehending what the soldier was implying. Marcus's hand went to his dagger by reflex.

'Your time will come soon, don't you worry. But the king wants to see you first, so I suspect yours will be a public affair. This one, we were ordered to be discreet about. Avert your eyes, trader,' the man said as he turned to his partner. 'Shall we get it over with? You want me to do it?'

'What about my last wish?' asked Marcus.

'You are funny.' The executioner pulled out his sword. 'Bend! We haven't got all evening.'

'You cannot do it here!' Vallavan cried out. 'Not like this. This man deserves a trial!'

'Stop talking!'

'No, you can't. He...he...is my friend,' said Vallavan. Marcus looked up in surprise as Vallavan rushed towards the soldiers, putting himself between him and the soldiers.

Oh, my friend!

'Get out of the way or you'll be collateral damage.' With his free arm, the soldier shoved Vallavan out of the way and raised his sword. Marcus sidestepped him nimbly and pulled his dagger out and threw it at the soldier. The man was quick, however, and the dagger only grazed his thigh and landed harmlessly on the floor behind him. He charged towards Marcus, swinging his sword. His partner had stepped behind the Yavana, and he grabbed him and held him down as Vallavan watched on in horror. Marcus waited for the right moment and with a swift heave, flipped his captor over. The sword came down on the soldier's stomach and he howled in pain and fell to the ground.

'Yavana swine!' screamed the attacker. He pulled his sword out from his partner's body and came after Marcus again. He was up against the wall by now and had nowhere to run. The sword – dripping with blood – was going to slash him any moment now, when suddenly the soldier's eyes opened wide. He took a step backwards as his weapon fell to the ground with a loud clang. The soldier's body followed a moment later. The dagger – Marcus's dagger – had caught him on his neck.

Adi stood calmly in the doorway, while Zhang muttered away next to him, holding up a scroll.

'Forgive us all, Buddha, we know not what we do. Sometimes, the situation demands it. I hope you understand. Forgive us!'

34

THE ASSASSINATION

'Marcellus, or whatever your name is, you'd better come with us. We need to meet the king before the prime minister does,' ordered Adi.

'The king wants me dead!'

'The king doesn't know you exist. The prime minister wants you dead and we foiled his plan, but we have little time. Your Buddhist friend here was too trusting of his patron when he shouldn't have been. Now, with you both in tow, I have all the evidence we need. Hurry!'

'I don't trust you, Adi. That's my dagger that killed the soldier over there!'

'I abhor violence of any sort. If that's your dagger, you must've killed him.'

'Just like I killed Muthu? I remember you trying to pin me down for that one too.'

'I had nothing to do with it. But if I am right, that was ordered by the same man who ordered your execution today. The prime minister. *That* murder is what put me on to him to begin with.'

'Adi, I know what you are up to. You want me executed for murder. I know you –'

'You don't know me at all, Yavana'

'Boys, this is not the angadi in Maruvum. Enough!' said Zhang. He turned to Marcus. 'Roman, he is on the same side as us.'

'And which side would that be, charlatan monk?'

'The side that doesn't want the king of the Chola country dead. Adi and I overheard the prime minister give orders to kill you once he read the letter you were carrying. I admit that I have been misled. He must have known of the Satkarni plot all along and must have even actively abetted it. He was trying to throw suspicion on the Pandyas and bandits, and I should have seen it earlier. All of us were taken in – Adi here thought it was the Pandyas until he saw the letter. Come with us now...we need to get to the king fast,' said Zhang.

'If you say so,' said Marcus. He didn't have much of a choice here and Zhang's story sounded plausible enough. 'But what about...?' He turned towards Vallavan.

'I don't understand who you all are... If you are plotting against –' began Vallavan, when Zhang cut in. 'Trader, would it help if you saw your sister's letter? It is burnt on one side, but we saved it in time. The message is intact.' He handed the scroll over to Vallavan, who unfurled it and began reading.

My dearest brother,

Forgive me, but this is no time for formality. I am sending this urgent message through your Yavana friend because I don't trust our usual messenger network.

Things are not as we thought; the guild is unwilling to wait to see whether the king will side with us against the Pandya traders or not. Sudar-mama and his cronies have already made up their minds and have made a pact with King Satkarni of Amaravati. There is someone else involved, but I cannot write who he is. King Karikalan's life is in danger. The Pandyas will be blamed and suspicion will not fall on the guild, as you and your message are evidence that the merchants are peaceful and would like to discuss their concerns with the king. In the confusion arising from the king's murder, when attention is focused on the Pandyas, Satkarni's man will be installed on the throne here in Puhar. His troops are already camped along the northern border. The guild has been promised control over trade in all of the current Chola and Pandya territories, as well as over a portion of Satkarni's lands in return for their support. They plan to catch the king off guard while at the anicut. Ayya is aware of the plot and has refused to join them, but I must say with the greatest regret that he is not willing to take any action against them either. I believe that the guild has made a suicidal decision, and I know that in this matter you'll agree with me. This will not end well for our people and our business interests. We may have our differences with the king, but there are far better ways of making him see what is good for the kingdom and for the guild. Warn the king and return home immediately. We have work to do –

'But this cannot be true!' cried Vallavan. 'The guild can't do this... You...you must have faked this letter. You are all traitors –'

'Trader, that's enough,' snapped Adi. 'I am the king's informer, and I am no traitor. If anyone should be tried for treason, it is you and your guild.'

'I am the king's most loyal subject –'

'Do not talk to me about loyalty. I belong to the house of Vel!'

Vallavan's demeanour changed in an instant from indignation to cautious respect. 'You're a son of the valorous house of Vel?' he asked softly. 'The ones who stood by the king even when he was imprisoned! I shall come with you. Please forgive me!'

Marcus shook his head sadly. Vallavan was proving to be both predictable and fickle. A high-born man such as Adi *had* to be brave and loyal, according to his friend. Marcus, on the other hand, had given the man a safe passage home and had given himself up in friendship, but he was still just a low life, a slave, to Vallavan. He would not be believed, just as Vallavan's own sister wouldn't be believed unless backed by a man claiming to be from a high-born house. That was just how Vallavan saw things. But, despite all this, Marcus had to admit that his friend had not hesitated to put himself between the prisoner and the executioner. That counted for something. He could live with that.

'Let's go. But you have to be careful. No one other than the guards saw Marcus being brought in, but you are well recognized as the prisoner from the quarry,' warned Adi.

The group left the barracks for the riverbank, where the pujai would now be well under way.

~

'Where are the soldiers?'

'Establishing peace in the fairground. There are hundreds of people out there. There was news earlier of a bandit attack in a village up north and a contingent has gone up there to investigate. And that turned out well for us as we would not have been able to get you out otherwise. They were the only two guarding the prison. We'll have to split as we get closer. I'll see if I can find the chief administrator. He is in the clear and he'll help us get to the king. You stay out of sight!'

Adi melted into the crowd with that. For a moment, Marcus couldn't spot Zhang, but then he saw him. Or her, rather. The monk had, by some magic, changed into an old woman craning her neck to see the pujai, with her hands held together in prayer. Vallavan inched his way towards the centre and Marcus stayed close behind him. He saw that no one was guarding the king's tent.

Instead, all the guards conglomerated around the raised platform. The smoke surrounding it made it difficult to see, but the king was visible as he sat in the centre on a low wooden plank, his back proud and straight, wearing a jewelled crown which glistened in the light of the setting sun. He was surrounded by priests chanting hymns and pouring ghee into the fire in the middle of the platform.

And then, everything happened at once.

'The priest! He is an impostor!' Vallavan screamed. 'That's one of my kidnappers. He must be the assassin!'

Marcus looked at the priest Vallavan was pointing to closely: he recognized him as the man who had ridden away from the camp during the rescue, the one whose thigh had been grazed by Marcus's dagger. In a flash, he also remembered seeing him in the inn – one of the quiet men in the corner who had stayed out of trouble. The man now stood next to the king holding up a knife. The king held the sacrificial lamb in place, ready for it to be slaughtered.

A shout. Vallavan had been spotted.

'The prisoner has escaped! The assassin is loose and is running towards the homam!'

Vallavan did not stop; he scaled the low wall around the platform and jumped. Arrows rained down around him, but he remained miraculously unharmed. At that exact moment, the priest raised the knife in his hand and went for the king's throat instead of the lamb's. But he, like everyone else in our narrative, had underestimated Karikalan. The king let the bleating lamb go and twisted the knife out of the priest's hand in one swoop. He raised it high and made a swipe at the assassin's neck. The head severed clear from the rest of his body.

Everyone froze, even time remained suspended in shock, except for the king. He waited for the body to stop trembling and once he was certain that there was no life left in the man he picked up the head with his left hand and held it high for everyone to see.

'The priests told me that a lamb would be sufficient, but Ranganathan must have willed this. So here it is: a human sacrifice for Lord Vishnu!'

He was not done. 'Let this also be a warning. If anyone is planning to finish me off and steal my kingdom, this fate awaits you too!' he roared to the crowd. He had led and won enough wars to know what worked and what didn't.

He turned his attention to the priests next. The chief priest cowered in front of him.

'King, I had no idea... It was a last-minute change as we couldn't... The priest who performs the sacrifices fell ill –'

'Speak only when you are spoken to, priest. I hope your lord is now pleased. But mark my words, next time an assassin infiltrates your ranks and pretends to be one of you, this will become a mass sacrificial ground. My people want water for their crops, not blood. Don't make me turn the holy Kaveri into a river of blood. Now, go back to your hymns!'

The king held up his hand and the guards stepped back from the platform. The priests positioned themselves to begin chanting again, but hardly any words came out of their mouths. That's when Marcus saw – no, rather felt – the reflection. He looked up for the source. The glint seemed to come from the river; or was it from the island in the Kaveri, from a mound atop the holy isle?

The arrow left the island and sped towards its mark.

Angavai. It couldn't be anyone else!

But Marcus wasn't the only one to have spotted it. In the blink of an eye, Vallavan was atop the platform, standing in front of the king, in the direct path of the incoming arrow. He fell to the ground just as Angavai's scream rent the air.

'For my sister! For my father! For my people!' she roared, her voice reverberating across the riverbank.

The king was the first to react again. He fell to his knees and cradled the dying man in his lap. Marcus was on the platform a moment later.

'Marcellus... My dear friend...'

'Oh, what have you done, Vallavan!' screamed Marcus.

'I wish you to know that you were always my friend... I... Tell my akka to take care of the family. My father will be too broken-hearted, but she...she'll know what to do. Kannaki...my kutti... tell her too. And... An...Anga.' And then, a deep shuddering breath later, he was gone.

The king stood up and barked orders to capture the brigand.

Oblivious to the world around him, Young Marcus sobbed inconsolably.

35

AFTERMATH

The king's company left for Puhar the day after the pujai. Vallavan was cremated on the banks of the Kaveri, where the king himself paid his last respects to the trader before he left for the capital. Two regiments were sent into the forests in pursuit of the bandits. The orders were clear: don't take prisoners; burn the woods if needed.

Marcus felt duty-bound to go back to Puhar to offer his condolences and an explanation to Manaykan and Kuzhali, but he had his own troubles to deal with. They'd no doubt hear that Vallavan died in the service of the king and kingdom, and there wasn't much else for him to do. The right course of action was to continue on to Korkai, where, he hoped, the *Minerva* would be waiting for him. He'd have to take his chances with his own father back in Rome.

'Zhang, what'll you do now? Where are you headed?'

'I'll do what I have always set out to do: propagate the teachings of the enlightened one.'

'And what about the prime minister?'

'He is nowhere to be seen and some say he has been executed, but I don't believe it. The king will want to go after the merchants in

Puhar. I don't think he will finish off the man until that's complete and when it happens, it will be a public spectacle,' Zhang said, his tone unnaturally subdued. Marcus knew that the Buddhist had taken it badly. He'd trusted the prime minister. 'I...' he paused, before starting again. 'The prime minister was too ambitious. He wanted to be king and I didn't see it. I should have!'

'Was it just him?'

'I have no idea who else was involved. They have ruled out the priests for now.'

'Even though the assassin was one of them?'

'A change at the last moment that the priests here weren't aware of? Yes, I believe them.'

'*You* believe the priests of the holy isle?'

'Put yourself in their place. What do they gain by switching allegiance to Satkarni, who is known to patronize all faiths? Nothing at all. They want other faiths outlawed. No, they'll stick with King Karikalan and see what they can do with him.'

'But will they...will the king spare you?'

'Our boy Adi seems to have some influence in the matter, so I am safe for now. I'll have to stop meddling in things other than that of the Buddha,' he said, seemingly chastised.

'Well...about that. We need to talk.' Adi had silently entered the quarters where Zhang and Marcus were housed for the night.

'I am returning to Puhar with the king. He has an assignment for you that he'd like you to consider. Your friend here,' he said, pointing towards Marcus, 'is free to do as he pleases as long as he does not create further trouble in the kingdom.'

'You can tell him that I am at his service.'

'But can he trust you to be loyal?'

'My allegiance is to the Buddha, and as long as your king is his patron in this kingdom, he'll command my loyalty.'

'That's the problem. Satkarni is your god's most famous patron and you have spent many years in that kingdom. And yet you claim your loyalty is to the king of Chola lands and that you were not involved in the conspiracy. You could well be the conduit between the prime minister and Satkarni.'

'I plead not guilty. The Buddha has a foothold in the lands of Satkarni. My work is to make sure he has one south of Amaravati as well. The Buddha wouldn't want to do it by force, and I wouldn't want it that way either.'

'The assassin didn't seem to think so…'

'He is not a Buddhist. For the final time: I am not in cahoots with Satkarni!'

'You expect the king to believe that?'

'He already does. Otherwise I'd have been dead by now!'

'You presume too much, Easterner. I'd be careful if I were you.'

'What is the assignment?'

'Our intelligence sources mention a runaway Yavana ship that will be setting out from Puhar any day now,' said Adi, looking pointedly at Marcus, whose eyes were fixed on a speck on the ground. 'The Yavanas plan to undercut our merchants and buy pearls directly from the Pandyas. We don't have the evidence to confirm the suspicion…' Marcus looked up at Adi, but he gave nothing away as he continued. 'And neither do we know which merchants are involved in the transaction. We'd like you to go to Korkai and ascertain the state of affairs there. Our information is that the ship will be marooned off the coast until the night of the new moon. You will find out who owns the ship and who they are dealing with in Korkai. We are not making any arrests at this point. We'll await your intelligence.'

'What if –' Zhang began, but Adi had anticipated the question, so he cut in.

'If the ship's inmates are seen in Korkai, they will be arrested by Chola officials immediately and sentenced as per our laws. The Yavanas have received a warning once before, so it will be execution without trial. If any Pandya is seen conspiring with them, they will be arrested as well. The navy will be there at the port if you need them.'

'But is it prudent to arrest Pandyas inside Korkai, given the current situation?' Zhang asked slowly, choosing his words carefully. 'There is no love lost for Chola soldiers in the town...'

'That's not your concern. You leave today. The stables will provide you the horses you need. I have to now catch up with the king's party. I'll expect you in Puhar,' said Adi, and left without a second glance at Marcus.

Later that day, as they walked down to the stables, Marcus attempted to broach the subject one last time.

'In the Buddha's name, who do you work for?'

Zhang smiled. 'I work for everyone, but mostly just for myself. And the Buddha, of course! I met the prime minister a few years ago when I helped him with information regarding spies in Maruvum. Since then, I've worked as his eyes and ears and provided him with useful information. I hoped that one day I'd be able to convince him, and thereafter the king, to adopt the teachings of Shakyamuni.'

'But to do so, you have to indulge in acts that go against his teachings! This is rather convoluted. Did your god deal in intrigue the way you do?'

Zhang shrugged. 'You can be certain that Shakyamuni would have considered all options to avert bloodshed, and it is my duty to do the same. But we have all the time later to discuss his teachings and him. You heard what Adi said? Here is what he didn't say: you will not be allowed to go back to Puhar, but they will let you leave the kingdom quietly. If I am not mistaken, they want you back on your ship, and for the ship to leave quietly and quickly.'

'Zhang, Adi knows of all my plans, thanks to Silvius. They don't need anything more to arrest me and the only reason they want us to go to Korkai is so that they can catch my crew red-handed too.'

'No.' Zhang shook his head. 'You are in the king's favour just now as you've provided the evidence and testimony for the Satkarni conspiracy. They are now going to use your trade deal with the Pandyas to make a point to the merchants of Puhar – that without the king's patronage, their business will be in tatters. Karikalan would not dare execute all of them, as he still needs their gold to fund his wars. But he can put the fear of death into them and he'll make the point that Yavanas will be allowed to trade with whoever they wish to. They'll turn a blind eye and let you go free. Whether you will be able to return to these lands ever again, I cannot say.'

'You expect me to be grateful? The king imprisoned Vallavan and caused his death. And I should be grateful for my freedom now?'

'You forget it was Angavai who killed your friend. She had it all planned, that girl. The Pandyas, the traders, Satkarni and her own men providing distraction, while she found the right opportunity to finish him off. You know what I think? I don't think she'd have let the northern assassin kill the king. She'd have finished him off had the king not. I think she wanted to do the deed herself!'

'It didn't work...'

'No, but that doesn't mean she won't try again.'

'They'll finish her and her people off before that!'

'I wouldn't be so sure of that. She wants revenge, and she'll stay safe until she can find another opportunity. Karikalan killed her father and burnt the hills that were her home. I am sure he didn't think much of it, as kings are wont to do – they conquer territory and show people that they are powerful. Is your Caesar any different?'

'And she hasn't been found yet?'

'Not as far as I am aware. She won't be easy to find!'

'She loved Vallavan. Despite everything she did, she loved him. This must hurt her…'

'Roman, that girl is more than what you imagine her to be. Lover killed by her arrow or not, she'll not rest. Of this I am sure. I suspect that this is not the last time we'll hear of her in this kingdom. But here we are, choose your horse, boy, and let's be on our way. Let's get you home.'

36

MEANWHILE IN PUHAR

Malathi Ammal was in denial. She kept saying that it could not be true that her only son was dead, and she went on to behave as if everything was normal. Kannaki made things worse by encouraging her mother.

'Didn't we all think that he was lost to the sea when the ship returned without him? Anna is coming back this time too,' she said, agreeing wholeheartedly with Malathi Ammal.

Kuzhali had had enough of this.

'Amma, he is dead! It was the king's men who brought the news. They not only saw him die, they also cremated him. His ashes are there... In front of the Mahaviran!'

'You were always so cold, even as a child. You'll never know what it means to lose a son. I refuse to believe it!'

It was a low blow, but her mother had always made it abundantly clear where Kuzhali stood on her list of favourites. And she had to concede that her mother had a point. What would she, a childless widow, know about the loss of a child? It was her father's reaction that had pained her more. He was heartbroken, as was to be expected, and he had shut himself in his office refusing to see anyone. When she had barged in, he'd asked her, 'Are you happy now? This is what you wanted, isn't it? You resented him and wanted him out!'

She left without a word and went back to her quarters. She may have resented Vallavan, but she had also loved him. She hadn't wanted her husband to die, she hadn't wanted her brother to be killed, but that was the hand that fate had dealt her. She had no choice in the matter. If Manaykan thought she had something to gain from Vallavan's death, he was losing his senses.

Kuzhali knew why she was welcomed back to her parents' household after her husband's death, instead of being left to age and die in a forgotten corner of his home. Because Vallavan had stood his ground and asked his father to do so. She was grateful for the kindness he had shown her, and she recognized what Vallavan's presence meant for her own life. As long as he was alive, no one would turn her out of the house she was born into. They were also right when they said she was guilty of ambition that was far above her station, but they failed to see that without the male figurehead, her ambition would come to nought. So she'd loved Vallavan because he was her brother, because he was kind to her, because he was malleable and because she needed him to further her own aims. But she wasn't ready to mourn him. The time for mourning would come, but not yet. She had unfinished business to attend to first.

For one, no one actually knew how he'd died. Just that the arrow was meant for the king and he was brave enough to give up his life to save Karikalan's. But who had shot the arrow in the first place? Kuzhali didn't believe that the bandits had any agency. As far as she was concerned, they were puppets pulled by strings controlled by someone else. The rumours spoke of Pandyas, Yavanas, Satkarni, and even the prime minister was mentioned, but no one said anything about the merchant guild of Puhar proper. But then, as the day went on, news spread like wildfire from grove to grove along Nagarathar Street. Since the morning, nine merchant homes had been raided. Sudar-mama's was the first. The men of the household were taken away and no explanations were given. Kuzhali waited for a raid at the Manaykan household too, but it never came. In his death, Vallavan had made sure his family was safe.

Marcellus was mentioned in passing in some of the whispers. That he was there when it happened. Had it been wise to send the message through him? Since she'd learnt of the pearl deal with the Appans, she knew that she'd made a mistake in trusting him. Marcellus was not what he seemed; she had misjudged him as he was her brother's friend – she believed that he would be as gullible as Vallavan. What she couldn't believe was that he'd killed Vallavan; after all, Marcellus had saved his life by bringing him back from Cana. But what if Vallavan had found out what Marcellus was up to with the Appans? Did he have her brother killed before he was exposed?

'A woman from Maruvum to see you, my lady. She has been waiting in the grove for a while and says that you'd know her.' Kuzhali looked up as the maid spoke.

Rajamma! She could have news that would shed light on the subject. Kuzhali flew down the stairs to meet her.

'My lady, my child, look at you!' Rajamma cried out on seeing her. 'I am so sorry for your loss. First the theft and now this. How will your poor mother take it? And what's going on in Pattinam today? The town is under curfew and soldiers are everywhere. I had to jump – in my old age – from grove to grove to get here. They say the king has returned, but no one seems to have seen him!'

'So I hear,' Kuzhali said, giving nothing away. 'What news do you have for me?'

'The Yavana ship you were so interested in… I have a feeling that it is going to leave our city soon. It could be tonight.'

'Why do you think so?'

'The Yavanas always wait till the last couple of days to buy certain things.'

'Such as?'

'Fine Chera jewellery, Kanchi linen, the odd good-luck idol, you know...'

'Why?'

'They think they get a better price that way.'

'Do they?'

'Depends on who the seller is.'

'Did they buy anything from you?'

'What could a poor appam vendor have that they want? But sellers talk and Rajamma listens as she serves them hot food. The captain and the crew have been buying a few items discreetly, which leads me to believe they'll leave the port soon.'

'Have they loaded the ship?'

'The porters weren't particularly busy...'

'Does the magistrate know that the ship is planning to leave the port?'

'You can't ask me what the magistrate knows or doesn't know! How can I answer that? But I have a feeling that he may be otherwise engaged. The navy has been training intensely over the past few days. People think there's going to be another war soon.'

'I'll write a message... Will you take it to the magistrate?'

'You want to get me killed, child? I will do nothing of the sort. They'll cut my throat and throw me into the water if they see people like me in the vicinity.'

'There is only one option in that case.'

'Which is?'

'You'll go with a companion. Wait here and I'll be right back.'

KORKAI

What Her Girl Friend Said

to him

Near the salt pans
the clusters of *neytal* and blue lily
are closing for the day.
The sea restlessly
brings in the lapping tide,
the side-pincered crab
surfaces from its wet nest
of black clay,
and the seaside falls silent
in the absence of users.

Don't ask the charioteer
to yoke the thick-legged donkey,
　　　　used to the crooked plow,
to your chariot strung with bells.

And for our lovely girl's sake,
her eyes cool as rain,
stay tonight
and go on tomorrow,
　　　　man from the great waters.

In that shining big sea,
fishermen with big boats
　　　　careless of the killer shark,
dive for the right-spiralled oyster,

sound loud
the conch shells
that contain voices,

are met and welcomed
by bustling Korkai city
as they disembark on the long sandy coasts.

There
you'll see
our good little town.

Centaṉ Kaṇṇaṉār, *Akanāṉūṟu*, 350

37

KUZHALI

When they entered what was once Pandya territory, Marcus waited for the landscape to change, but he was disappointed. Other than Chola guards at the border, there was nothing different about this land from the one he had just come from. There was no apparent sign that this was once a separate country. The plains were as fertile as the ones in the Kaveri delta, water rushed in abundance from the monsoon-fed streams and the great Vaigai and Tamaraparani rivers, and the villagers and innkeepers they met in Pandya country were as friendly and hospitable as the ones in the Chola kingdom.

'They are the same,' Marcus remarked.

'We are out in the countryside, where it is always the same. They grow their rice and send their sons to the army. It hardly matters which army they are sent too. Does the Roman army employ slaves?'

'I was never in the army, if that's what you are asking. For a slave, I led a rather sheltered existence. I was freed when I came of age.'

'Ah, a generous master! You are fortunate. But will he spare you when he finds out that you impersonated his son?'

Marcus grinned. 'Marcellus asked me to, and he wouldn't have come this far anyway. He is too much of his mother's son. Besides, I *am* Gaius's son.'

'You can't possibly still... Wait, do you mean to say what I think you are saying?'

'I never saw my mother. I've always wondered if he sent her off to die somewhere in the countryside on the promise that I'd be taken care of... My father is known to keep his promises!'

To his surprise, Zhang burst into laughter. 'You Romans! You say you grew up in the same household?'

'As Marcellus's friend and companion! Even received the same education as him.'

'What about Gaius's wife?'

'Hates me and ignored me for the most part. You are right... I was...am rather fortunate.'

Some time later, Zhang and Marcus found themselves near the coast once again as they entered what was the prominent port city of the once-mighty Pandyas. This was the city of pearls and fish where, if one was to believe rumours, the crown prince of the defeated Pandya king was being raised after being driven out of Madurai. But that is a story for another time.

They skirted around Korkai, cautious, before heading towards the harbour. The port seemed much smaller than the one Marcus was used to in Puhar, with mostly fishing vessels and rowboats docked. The few people they passed by looked at them curiously.

'Look down and walk on. We don't want to attract attention. The port officials work not too far away. The pearl fisheries are over there... We should be able to find the ones you are interested in.'

'I...' Marcus paused. 'I need to find someone. I need to make some enquiries.'

'Out with it, Roman, what's this about?'

'An errand. My father has a message, a gift, I think, for someone in Korkai. I need to find her and deliver it.'

'How does your father know this mystery lady?'

'I don't know. He requested me to deliver it in person and made me promise I'd do so before I left Korkai.'

'You're so full of surprises that I have no idea what you'll say next. If any Chola soldier catches sight of you, you'll be back in Puhar in no time on charges of illegal trading. There's only so much Adi can do and he's not letting you go free because of the goodness of his heart. You cannot go in search of any woman at this time. Here's what... Wait, who's that man rushing towards us? Do you know him?'

Maruthappan!

'Lord, I didn't recognize you at first. What have you done with your hair? I hope it's an offering for Murugan!'

'He has taken a vow to follow the Buddha,' said Zhang.

Maruthappan glared at Zhang.

'Not quite, but, Zhang, this is a trusted friend. He knows about... what we are up to,' Marcus reassured him.

'Along with half of the kingdom,' Zhang muttered in Latin.

'Has the *Minerva* arrived?'

'Yes, but we were expecting you on the ship. Why didn't you come with the crew?'

'I thought it'd be better if I came by land. So that it wouldn't arouse suspicion.'

'A brilliant idea! Your arrival is timely. We have some –'

'Maruthappan, first I need to ask you this. I have to meet a lady – her name is Kannamma. Do you know anyone in this town by that name?'

Maruthappan's expression changed instantly. 'What...what name did you say?'

'Kannamma. She is a diver and that's all I know. You know her, don't you?'

'Yes. Why do you want to meet her?'

'I have something for her. From my mast – er, father – I have to give it to her myself. Could you please take me to her?'

'She...she... I am sorry, young lord, but this Kannamma you speak of, she is no more. She died some time ago.'

'Are you certain? Maybe this is another lady... My father was here so long ago –'

'Yavana lord, I know who you are referring to. She was, for a time, in your father's employment. I know…used to know her well. This was a long time ago; well before the war when he spent his time between the emporium here and Puhar. I am sorry, but you can't meet her.'

'Does she have a family?'

Marcus had deduced that his father must have harboured some feelings for this woman many moons ago and was making amends in his old age. It had also occurred to him that it was plausible that this woman was no more, in which case he intended to deliver his father's gifts – he assumed that's what it was – to her descendants.

'She has two children.'

Meanwhile, Zhang, who was listening to this conversation with some interest, had his own doubts for he was a sceptical man and had been around longer in the world.

'I'll give my father's message and gifts to them. Where do they live?'

'I am afraid you won't be able to see them. They are out diving, and won't be back until much later,' said Maruthappan stiffly.

'I can wait…'

'No, you can't! The ship needs to leave tonight – the navy is on alert and we've heard that something happened in Uraiyur a few days ago. The Appans want you gone from our waters, and things have got complicated for us.'

'Has the ship been loaded?'

'We loaded through the night yesterday, thanks to Lord Murugan. We finish the final round as soon as the sun goes down. Your captain is looking for you. There are...some issues…a particular issue that needs resolving.'

'What's wrong? If it's Hippalus, I can take care of him,' Marcus said, exasperated. It was just like Hippalus to come up with something at the very last minute.

'I'm afraid it's not him at all!'

'What's the problem then?'

'The captain has found a stowaway on the ship and he wants to leave the stowaway with us. It is impossible! We cannot get involved... That would be suicide.'

'A stowaway on the *Minerva*?'

'You'd better come see for yourself,' Maruthappan said. 'They're at the warehouse. This way.'

Marcus puzzled over the new development as they followed Maruthappan through the alleyways of Korkai. Zhang took the opportunity to speak to the Pandya.

'We heard news of unrest and an assassination on our way here. What have you heard?'

'Muruga! No! We do not wish the king dead. Not when he has agreed to listen to our petition to trade on better terms. If the Chola kingdom were to fall into someone else's lands, we'll have to start all over again.'

'The king is safe,' Marcus assured him. 'We saw him in Uraiyur.'

Maruthappan's jaw dropped. 'You saw the king?'

'It's a long story.' He paused and looked towards the sea. A rowboat was slowly making its way towards land. 'How far?'

'We're nearly there. Up these steps, please. The captain is there with our Appan-ayya and the...the stowaway.'

No sooner had the three of them entered than a loud snort erupted from the atrium – Hippalus stood in the far corner, glaring malevolently at them. Marcus saw the old man from the mandapam – the senior Appan – seated on the step, while his brother, Veerappan, paced up and down the courtyard.

'Here he is finally, his highness! The accusation would have fallen on the unscrupulous Greek, as always! The kidnapping villain! Let's hang him, for he is just a Greek man. But here he comes, the *real* villain, making an appearance now that it is all over – hoping he can just sail off into the sunset. Not so easily, lover boy. You tell me, what are we to do with this girl of yours?'

'Girl?'

Marcus looked around in confusion. Even the imperturbable Zhang looked stumped at the turn of events. Then they saw her behind Hippalus – a lean figure with her hands bound behind her back, dressed in man's clothing, a disguise familiar to Marcus.

'Kuzhali!'

The girl kicked hard and tried to say something, but her gag made sure no one heard. Hippalus removed the strip of cloth from her mouth, saying, 'Ah, lover boy. We await the reunion. First the brother and now the sister – you have charmed the entire family!'

'Hippalus, untie her now!'

'Are you sure, little master?' he asked but untied her hands nevertheless. In a flash, she threw herself at Marcus with a force that made him stumble and fall to the ground. Hippalus started laughing.

'That's a strong kind of love, that one,' he remarked to no one in particular.

'You traitor!' Kuzhali screamed as he picked himself off the ground. 'How did my brother die? Did you kill him?'

Hippalus whistled. The Appans looked at Marcus curiously, waiting for him to respond.

'No! Your brother died a martyr. He saved the king's life!'

'I've heard that, but who shot the arrow?'

'A bandit girl. Angavai.'

'They told me that. I want to know who *told* her to do so?'

'No one! She was aiming for the king; she wanted to avenge her family.'

Kuzhali looked at him for a long time before speaking. 'Did she really?' Marcus detected a note of respect that had crept into her voice.

'Yes! I saw Vallavan willingly sacrifice his life to save the king. I'd have saved him if I could.'

'That is why you are smuggling pearls from under Chola eyes? Is that what he'd have wanted you to do? Yavana, you'll do no more business in this land –'

'Stop right there, you little liar,' Hippalus cut in. 'You told me that you were in love with him and he deceived you, which is why you were on the ship.'

'He deceived all of us, captain, but that's not what I am here for. As for love, what world do you live in?' Kuzhali snorted.

'Girl, I don't have time for this. I have to sail a ship across a couple of dangerous seas and we're leaving now!'

'Not so fast. The Chola navy waits not far from where we are. What makes you think they'll let you sail away so easily?'

'They were too busy in Puhar and they haven't seen us here yet. We'll be away before they realize where we've been.'

'Unless someone alerts them to your presence…'

'Are you suggesting that you're going to walk out of here and report us? I'd like to see you do it. Go on, I'll wait,' said Hippalus, stepping back as he crossed his arms.

'I am not a fool, captain. I wasn't the only stowaway on your ship. Your security is pretty lax, I must say. My companion stands next to the navy base at this moment, awaiting my arrival. If I don't make it there by sundown, she has a letter from me that will alert them.'

'You expect me to believe that?' asked Hippalus, though it was clear from his tone that he wasn't sure of what to believe.

'Kuzhali,' said Marcus quietly, 'if you make it safely to your companion, are we free to leave?'

'That depends.'

'On what?' he asked, tentative. This girl was always a step ahead of him and he'd no idea what she was up to now.

'She means us, Yavana lord. She wants to talk to us,' said the senior Appan, speaking for the first time. 'Come to me, child, and tell me –'

'I am not your child, ayya.'

He sighed. 'No, you are not. What do you want?'

'A partnership.'

Veerappan spat on the ground. 'What did you say? You steal our wealth and tie our hands behind our backs, and then call it a partnership?'

'Let the girl talk, Veerappan,' said the older Appan quietly.

'We trade together and split the profits equally. We'll be the conduit to Yavanas, and to the eastern and northern kingdoms, for your pearls. You know we can!'

'Yes, and we pay the price for that,' the older Appan pointed out.

'Not any more. I'll say it again – equal profits.'

'What's the catch?'

'There is none.'

'Now you are patronizing *me*, girl. I know what your guild –'

'You are mistaken. We're not talking about the guild here.'

'We're not?'

'You deal with me and my family alone. The guild will not be involved and will not take a share in the profits.'

'You can't take unilateral decisions... Not without the guild agreeing to it.'

'Things have changed. You'll soon see that I can.'

'What madness is this? And why should I believe anything you say?'

At this point, Zhang cut in. 'If I may say so, I can confirm that things are changing in Puhar. You'll find that the guild is not as powerful any more, as a number of them are likely to be implicated on charges of treason against the king.'

'How do you know this, stranger?'

'Appan-ayya, you don't need to believe me or this man here. You can send your men to Puhar and see for yourself,' said Kuzhali. 'All I need for now is your word. I have come a long way for this. I am told that your word is as good as Lord Murugan's.'

'In return for my word, you'll let the Yavanas go and not report us?'

'This time and only this time, yes. I'll not let this man trade in this kingdom ever again, but this time, he'll be spared. I'll even forgive his captain – this uncouth excuse for a man – who has brazenly stolen my family's good-luck goddess, a gift for my sister, and has the audacity to display it on his ship.'

'I've done *what*?' sputtered Hippalus. 'I *bought* her fair and square from that woman, the appam-seller who –'

'You bought it from Rajamma?' asked Kuzhali. Then she laughed viciously. 'That wily bitch! So, what do you say, Appan-ayya?'

'If it is an equal partnership you're offering, you have my word. I feel this is the beginning of a lucrative association.'

'In that case, we're done here. Captain, you have till dawn to clear out.'

38

ENDINGS AND BEGINNINGS

'Why are you following me, Buddhist?' Kuzhali asked. She was walking along the beach, towards the navy quarters.

'I am travelling to Puhar, the same as you. It may be safer to travel together.'

'Safer for whom?'

'For a young lady from a rich merchant house in Puhar. There are bandits along the way, not to mention opportunistic villagers waiting for a chance to take revenge against any Chola who crosses the path.'

'I can take care of myself.'

'This disguise may not always work. If, on the other hand, you are disguised as a pilgrim and are travelling with a monk –'

'Do I have to get rid of my hair?'

'That doesn't suit your name, if I may say so, my lady.'

'Would you want me to change my name too?'

'No, all I'd like is to accompany you back to Puhar.'

'Thank you for your concern, but I...'

Kuzhali looked around in surprise. Sure enough, Rajamma was gesticulating wildly at them from behind a clump of trees. They walked towards her.

'Oh, there you are, amma! You frightened this poor appam-seller to death, and I had no idea what to do. All I meant to do was take you to the magistrate's residence, not snoop around for evidence on the ship that left with us stuck inside. I thought they'd kill you, or, worse, take you as a slave once they found you... Your family would have killed me if they ever found out I was involved. But thank Aiyanar that you're safe and... Zhang! You infernal Buddhist. What are you doing here? You left without news and without paying my dues. I'll never forgive you. You'd better find this lady…I mean, lad...a palanquin to take us back to Puhar immediately, or actually a boat will get us there quicker!'

Kuzhali was too exhausted to say anything to this strange pair. She was needed back in Puhar. It was time to go home. It was time to mourn.

~

After sundown, Hippalus and Marcus rowed out in a dinghy into open waters, towards where the *Minerva* was waiting. Aafa stood on the deck, supervising the final round of loading and working out an appropriate time to leave.

'What do you propose to do with me?' asked Marcus quietly.

'I will get you and that shipload to Myos Hormos in one piece.'

'Even though I am not –'

'That's not my problem, little mas...whoever you are. I even intend to make a trip across that dastardly sea of yours. I'll accompany the cargo all the way to Ostia to make sure it doesn't vanish along the way. Besides, I need to meet a publisher in Rome.'

'A pamphleteer?'

'A literary thing, nothing of importance, I assure you. And have to meet a couple of antique dealers in Pompeii, as I am sick of trading with the middlemen in Alexandria. As for you, your father and the judges may want to send you into the Circus to play with the lions, especially if your brother doesn't turn up –'

'And you want to deliver me to them personally?'

Hippalus sighed. 'You know the problem with you young people? You don't listen. I said I'll ensure that the cargo doesn't vanish along the way. I never said anything about you. You may want to think about that.'

'Thank you, captain. It has been a pleasure.'

'Oh, we're not done. Not yet. It's a long way home.'

EPILOGUE

The woman sat in front of her hut, staring at the horizon, hoping to catch a glimpse of the Yavana ship that would be on its way home by now. She couldn't see it – maybe the *Minerva* had already left familiar waters – but she conjured up the ship in her imagination anyway. She hadn't thought about it for a long time, but there was a day, a very long time ago, when she had sat in the same place staring at another Yavana ship that was making its way steadily towards Western shores. She had cried that day, and the grief that struck her then did not leave for many seasons. But all that was several moons ago, and life had moved on. What mattered to her now was much closer: near the shore. She watched as a catamaran rode on the waves on its way back to land.

'You should have met him – he is a striking image of you!'

'Is he really?'

'They told me that he looked exactly like his father before I met him, but that isn't what struck me. He takes after you – no one can mistake it. Why did you not want to meet him? His father sent him to you, after all.'

'So that he could meet the woman who abandoned him when he was an infant? The woman who gave him up for what she knew would be certain death? His father warned me that there was a small, a very small, chance that he'd make it alive to Rome and, yet, I let him go. I put my faith in Kadalamman and let him go with his father because I couldn't counter the shame of raising an illegitimate child here. He'd never forgive me if he met me.'

'But he survived! Oh, you should have seen him. The young master, they call him, and he commands so much respect from his crew.'

'All the better I did not see him. My bad fortune is contagious. His life is better off without me!'

'He brought this for you. From his father. I told him I'd give it to your children.'

'Is Gaius-ayya offering me gold? I hope not! I made it clear that it was the last thing I wanted.'

'Open it.'

She carefully untied the string around the oilskin pouch. She slid her hand inside and pulled out a...

'Mirror! After all these years, he remembers the one thing I used to covet in those days. But what's the point now, Marutha? Why does this old woman need a mirror any more?'

'Amma!' She looked up at her children dragging the catamaran into the beach. The boy and the girl ran to her, their hands full of the day's catch of oysters.

'Look how much we've got,' shouted the boy joyfully. 'And we saw another Yavana ship today heading south. It's raining Yavana ships in Korkai!'

AUTHOR'S NOTE

The Grand Anicut is a work of fiction, but there are very good reasons for the story of young Marcus panning out the way it does. Here are five references in the tale that are true:

1. If one were to travel in our time along the old Appian Way, south of Rome (make sure you take loads of water with you), one can still see a tombstone marker, which has been standing in this place for over two thousand years. It reads:

   > Stranger – stop and look at this mound to the left. There lies the bones of a good and compassionate man, a friend of the poor. I ask that you, traveller, do nothing bad to this tomb. Gaius Ateilius Euhodus, freedman of Serranus, pearl seller on the Via Sacra, is preserved in this tomb. According to my will, it is unlawful to preserve or bury anyone in this tomb except those freedmen to whom I have granted and allowed this.

2. A couple of hours south of Rome, at the National Archaeological Museum in Naples, the traveller can see the rather inappropriately named 'Pompeii Lakshmi'. Zhang calls her the Eastern Venus in this story, but none of the descriptions do justice to this ivory lady. She was found in 1938 in Pompeii, near one of the houses, and has been dated to the first century CE. From the time I first

saw her a number of years ago, I've always dreamt up stories of how she could have reached Pompeii from southern India.

3. The first century CE document *Periplus of the Erythraean Sea* served as a guide to trade and navigation in the Indian Ocean. The map on p. vi is based on the descriptions in the book. The authorship is unknown, though I'd have quite liked Hippalus to have dictated it to Aafa.
4. Back in India, Karikalan's Kallanai, or the grand anicut, that famous dam across the Kaveri, stands to this day, a few kilometres from the city of Tiruchirapalli. It has been built and rebuilt many times over and it is fair to surmise that the current version may look nothing like it did in ancient times. The dam exists, but whether there is any water for it to channel is a different question altogether.
5. All poems in this work have been taken from the corpus of Sangam literature. There is one on this list which is of special importance in that it is the only one, among the hundreds of poems, that is attributed to women, Angavai and Sangavai, on the death of their father, the chieftain Pari (scribe: Kapilar). This poem, my opinion, also has one of the most beautiful first lines ever written in the Tamil language: '*attrai thingal annilavil*', which A.K. Ramanujan translates to, 'That month, in that white moonlight'.

Nearly nine centuries after Marcus set out on his journey from Puhar, another fictional character, a young warrior by the name of Vandiyathevan made a similar journey across Chola lands to the then imperial capital of Thanjavur. The wildly popular serialized novel that describes Vandiyathevan's adventures – Kalki Krishnamurthy's *Ponniyin Selvan* – is an obvious inspiration for this book.

But I was less interested in kings and wars; I wanted to write about the people of the land and the cultures they interacted with. For me, that came alive in the Sangam literature of a few centuries earlier – in the songs of *Paṭṭiṉappālai*, *Puṟanāṉūṟu*, *Kuṟuntokai*, and of course, in *Cilappatikāram*, the operatic tale of a tragic heroine who burns the city of Madurai in a rage.

This period became doubly interesting when I realized that it intersected approximately with the period in Roman history that I have always been fascinated by (thanks primarily to Robert Graves's *I, Claudius* and John Williams's *Augustus*). In the first century CE, the 'discovery' of the sea route across the Arabian Sea resulted in the flourishing of trade between the Roman empire and southern and central India. The prosperity of the Tamil kingdoms was closely tied to this trade, and this created a thriving merchant class while the kingdoms fought over the spoils of trade. This was also a time of great social upheaval, with the twin religions of Jainism and Buddhism making great gains over Brahmanical Hinduism.

In an effort to bring this period to life, as I started writing the story of Marcus gallivanting across the Chola kingdom, what this narrative was really about changed constantly in my mind. At one point, it was a bildungsroman; at another, it was about insurgency against an oppressive monarch; then it became a story about the ordinary people of the kingdom; in one version it even became an impossible love story, though I knew I couldn't carry that one through. But through it all there was one underlying thread that remained constant: that this is a book about divergent ideas and visions and how they find accommodation in a syncretic culture such as the one that must have existed in that time and place. Perhaps this is only in my imagination but for me it is sufficient.

ACKNOWLEDGEMENTS

The Grand Anicut is all fiction and I have not hesitated to take slight liberties if reality, or what goes for reality (as this is a severely contested period in terms of history and chronology), didn't fit the narrative. Having said that, the novel draws heavily from historical sources and literature relating to the early centuries of the Christian era.

For Tamilakam, this comprises of the poems of the Sangam corpus which I read in translations by A.K. Ramanujan, George L. Hart and R. Parthasarathy. This book owes an immense debt to their works. The one notable exception which I did not read in translation is *Paṭṭiṉappālai* – I made my mother go through an annotated version in Tamil which she paraphrased over several weeks while I jotted down notes. Thanks to her patience.

There is no dearth of Greco-Roman historical sources for the period. My focus was on trade and, hence, the works I found most relevant were: *Periplus of the Erythraean Sea* (authorship unknown), and accounts of the Greek geographer Strabo and the Roman chronicler Pliny, the Elder, who died in the eruption of Vesuvius in 79 CE.

The one contemporary book I kept going back to over the course of writing *The Grand Anicut* is Raoul McLaughlin's *The Roman Empire and the Indian Ocean: The Ancient World Economy and the Kingdoms of Africa, Arabia and India*, which is a must-read for anyone interested in ancient trade routes.

Thanks are also due to:

Cibani Premkumar, editor, for her deep and insightful engagement with the story of Marcus;

Poulomi Chatterjee, publisher, for offering a home to *The Grand Anicut* and for pushing it through to the finish line;

Meena Rajasekaran, designer, for the many iterations of the cover and coming up with a stunner, and Jit Chowdhury, illustrator, for the maps;

R. Sivapriya, editor, for pointing me in the right direction when Marcus was going absolutely nowhere;

Kanishka Gupta, agent, for the swiftness and efficiency with which he does his job;

Abdullah Khan, fellow writer, for putting me in touch with Kanishka;

Rahul Santhanam and Hema Manickavasagam, friends, for the many hours they spent dreaming up titles and taglines;

Toshi aka Mallika, daughter No. 1, for keeping me straight every single time and for the genesis of this book which started out as a mealtime story when she was a wee toddler;

Misha, daughter No. 2, because she doesn't believe her mother could be a writer since all authors sign autographs and she has never seen me sign one. (I remain hopeful that seeing her acknowledged in this book would change her view.)

Dionysus and Bacchus, wine gods. I was going to go with Dionysus, but Toshi reminded me that this is, after all, a Roman story and I should go with Bacchus. Since I wish to anger neither, I'd like to thank them both for all the wine over the years.